CVF

D0996267

SPECIAL MESSAGE TO READERS

Neil Smith grew up in the United States and Canada and now lives in Montreal. His first book, the critically acclaimed story collection *Bang Crunch*, was chosen as a book of the year by *The Washington Post* and *The Globe and Mail*, and was nominated for the Hugh MacLennan Prize and the Commonwealth Writers' Prize for Best First Book (Canada). He also works as a translator from French to English.

BOO

When Oliver 'Boo' Dalrymple wakes up in heaven — a place called Town — the eighth-grade science geek thinks he died of a heart defect at his school. But soon after arriving in this hereafter reserved for dead thirteen-year-olds, Boo discovers he's a 'gommer', a kid who was murdered. What's more, his killer may also be in heaven. With help from the volatile Johnny, a classmate killed at the same school, Boo sets out to track down the enigmatic Gunboy, who cut short both their lives. Along the way they are helped by Thelma, a 'do-gooder', and Esther, a trainee do-gooder. Will the group of friends find Gunboy and kick him out of Town, like the gommers want? Or is there more to the mystery than meets the eye?

NEIL SMITH

BOO

Complete and Unabridged

CHARNWOOD
Leicester

First published in Great Britain in 2015 by
William Heinemann
London

First Charnwood Edition
published 2016
by arrangement with
Windmill Books
Penguin Random House UK
London

A catalogue record for this book is available
from the British Library.

ISBN 978–1–4448–3001–9

Published by
F. A. Thorpe (Publishing)
Anstey, Leicestershire

Set by Words & Graphics Ltd.
Anstey, Leicestershire
Printed and bound in Great Britain by
T. J. International Ltd., Padstow, Cornwall

1	1.01
H	
Hydrogen	

Do you ever wonder, dear Mother and Father, what kind of toothpaste angels use in heaven? I will tell you. We use baking soda sprinkled on our toothbrushes. It tastes salty, which comes as no surprise because baking soda is a kind of salt known as sodium bicarbonate.

You never wonder about toothpaste in heaven, do you? After all, you are agnostic. But even believers seldom ponder the nitty-gritty of their afterlife. Thinking of heaven, they imagine simply a feeling of love and a sense of peace. They do not consider whether the pineapple they eat here will be fresh or come from a can. (We actually receive both kinds, though certainly more canned than fresh.)

This book I am writing to you about my afterlife will be your nitty-gritty. One day I hope to discover a way to deliver my story to you.

As you know, I died in front of my locker at Helen Keller Junior High on September 7, 1979, which was exactly one month ago today. Before I died, I had been reciting the 106 elements from the periodic table. My locker number (No. 106) had inspired me, and my goal was to memorize all the elements in chronological order. However, when I reached No. 78, platinum (Pt), Jermaine Tucker interrupted by smacking me on the head.

'What the hell you doing, Boo?' he said.

I told you once that my classmates called me Boo on account of my ghostly pale skin and my staticky, whitish-blond hair that stands on end. Some of them considered me an albino, but of course I am not: a true albino has dark red or almost purplish eyes, whereas mine are light blue.

'Boo! How ironic,' you may say, 'because now our son *is* a ghost.' You would be mistaken, of course, because this is not true irony. Irony would be if Jermaine Tucker had said, 'Wow, Boo, I truly respect and admire you for memorizing the periodic table!' Respect and admiration are the opposite of the feelings I aroused in Jermaine and, for that matter, in most of my classmates.

Did you realize I was a pariah? If you did not, I am sorry I never made this clear, but I did not want you fretting about something you could in no way control. You already worried enough about the inoperable hole in my heart and had long warned me about straining my heart muscles.

Jermaine walked off to class, and I continued undeterred with my count as scientists Richard Dawkins and Jane Goodall watched me from the photographs I had taped to the back of my locker door. For the first time ever, I reached No. 106, seaborgium (Sg), without stealing a peek at the periodic table hung below the photos of Richard and Jane.

My feat of memorization, however, must have overexcited my heart because I immediately fainted to the floor. I could say I 'gave up the ghost,' especially in light of my nickname, but I dislike euphemism. I prefer to say the truth simply and plainly. The plain and simple truth: my heart stopped and I died.

How much time passed between my heart's final chug in the school hallway and my eyes opening in the hereafter I cannot say. After all, who knows which time zone heaven is in? But as I glanced around the room where I found myself, I certainly did not see the clichéd image of heaven. No white-robed angels with kind smiles gliding out of a bank of clouds and singing in dulcet tones. Instead, I saw a black girl snoring as she slept in a high-back swivel chair, a book at her feet.

I immediately knew I was dead. My first clue: I saw the girl perfectly even though I was not wearing my eyeglasses. I even saw the title of her book (*Brown Girl, Brownstones*). Indeed, I saw everything around me with great clarity. The girl wore blue jeans and a T-shirt with a decal of a litter of angora kittens. Colorful beads dangled from the ends of her cornrows, and they reminded me of the abacus you gave me when I was five years old.

I lay in a single bed, covered in a sheet and a thin cotton blanket. Other than the swivel chair, the bed was the only furniture in the windowless room. Overhead a ceiling fan spun. Hung on the walls were abstract paintings — squiggles, splotches, and drippings. I sat up in bed. My naked chest seemed whiter than normal, and the bluish arteries marbling my shoulders stood out.

I peeked under the blanket and saw I was not wearing pajama bottoms or even underwear. Nudity itself does not bother me, though: to me, a penis is no more embarrassing than an ear or a nose. Still, do not assume that I had found the Helen Keller gym showers, for example, a comfortable place to be. That communal shower room was a breeding ground for the human papillomavirus, which causes plantar warts. And on two occasions there, Kevin Stein decided that it would be sidesplitting to urinate on my leg.

'Excuse me! Hello!' I called out to the girl in the swivel chair, who woke with a start. She stared at me wide-eyed.

'May I assume I am dead?' I asked.

She lurched out of her chair and hurried over, accidentally kicking her novel under the bed. She grabbed my hand and squeezed. I yanked it back because, as you know, I dislike being touched.

'You ain't dead, honey,' she said. 'You passed, but you're still alive.'

'Passed?'

'We say 'passed' here instead of 'died.' Passed, like you did good on a math test.' She gave me a smile that exposed a gap between her front teeth wide enough to stick a drinking straw through. When she sat down on the side of the bed, it listed because she was heavy. I once read an article on longevity in the magazine *Science* that claimed that thin people live longer. To offset my holey heart, I tried to prolong my life by keeping a slim physique. Needless to say, my efforts came to naught.

'Let me introduce myself,' the girl said. 'My

name's Thelma Rudd, and I'm originally from Wilmington, North Carolina, where my family runs the Horseshoe Diner.' She asked what my name was and where I came from.

'Oliver Dalrymple from Hoffman Estates, Illinois,' I told her. 'My parents have a barbershop there called Clippers.'

'Do you know how you passed, Oliver Dalrymple?'

'I believe I died of a holey heart.'

'A holy heart?' She looked puzzled. 'We all have *holy* hearts up here.'

'No, I mean my heart has an actual *hole* in it.'

'Oh, how terrible,' she said, and patted my leg.

Thelma went on to explain that she belonged to a group of volunteers known as the 'do-gooders.' 'I always sign up for rebirthing duty here at the Meg Murry Infirmary,' she said. 'I like welcoming newborns like yourself.'

I asked how long a 'rebirthing' took.

'It's over in the blink of an eye.' Thelma blinked several times. 'A do-gooder's always on rebirthing duty at the Meg. We never know when we're gonna get a package.'

She patted the mattress, and I eyed the bed, its rumpled blanket, and its pillow with the indent from my head. The bed did not look mysterious or miraculous in any way. 'We just materialize here?' I asked.

Thelma nodded. She gave me a probing look, eyes so deep-set I figured she, too, once wore glasses. 'You know, hon, you're the calmest newborn I ever did meet,' she said. 'You wouldn't believe the hysterics I seen in my

5

nineteen years in Town.'

'Nineteen years!?' I said. 'But you look *my* age.'

'Oh, we're all thirteen here.'

This particular hereafter, she clarified, was reserved for Americans who passed at age thirteen. 'We call it Town,' she said. 'Us townies believe there's lots of towns of heaven. One for every age — one for people who pass at sixteen, one for people who pass at twenty-three, one for people who pass at forty-four, and so on and so forth.'

'Thirteen,' I said, mystified. 'You are all thirteen?'

'Townies never age. We stay thirteen all our afterlives. I look exactly the same as when I came here nineteen years ago.'

You will find this nonsensical, Mother and Father, but this stagnation in the hereafter saddened me more than the realization of my own death did. I would never grow up, never go to college, and never become a scientist. And, frankly, I had seen enough of thirteen-year-olds back in America — their stupidity, cruelty, and immaturity.

Thelma noticed my sudden distress. 'Oh, but we grow wiser the longer we stay here,' she said. 'Well, at least some of us do.'

'Segregating the afterlife by age seems logical,' I said to be a good sport. 'After all, if the dead were all housed in the same place, Town would be seriously overpopulated.'

I then asked, 'Will I be here for eternity?'

She shook her head. 'No, us townies only get

five decades here. After our time's up, we go to sleep one night and never wake. We vanish in the night. All we leave behind is our PJs.'

'Oh my,' I said. 'Where do we go next?'

'Some say we move to a higher level of heaven, one with better food, sturdier plumbing, and sunnier skies,' Thelma replied. 'Others wonder if we reincarnate back to America. But the truth is, nobody really knows where we go.'

Thelma got up from the bed and opened the door to a walk-in closet. She came out carrying a pair of jeans, T-shirts, boxer shorts, and socks, which she laid on the bed.

'What's your shoe size?'

'Seven,' I said.

She went back into the closet to find me some shoes.

'Do you have any penny loafers?' I asked, because they are the shoes you would always buy me, Mother.

'Town has no leather shoes,' Thelma called out. 'Leather's dead cow and heaven ain't no place for the dead.'

While she was in the closet, I slipped the boxer shorts on and then the jeans, which were covered in red, white, and blue patches from the Bicentennial three years ago. 'So only Americans come here?' I asked.

'Yep. We don't get no foreigners. Just people who lived in the U. S. of A.'

I thought of absurd science-fiction films where the characters on distant planets spoke fluent American English but never Swedish or Swahili.

'What about different religions?' I asked as I

selected a tie-dyed T-shirt from the half dozen shirts on the bed.

'Oh, we aren't divided by religion. We get all kinds here. Baptists, Catholics, Mormons, Jews, Jehovah's Witnesses. You name it, honey, we get it.'

She came out carrying a tatty pair of sneakers, which had the letters *L* and *R* inked on the toes. She handed them over. 'What religion are you?' she asked.

'Atheist.'

She let out a whoop of laughter. 'I don't always have much faith in a supreme being myself,' she said.

I sat on the bed and put on the sneakers. She sat beside me and picked lint off my T-shirt.

'I ain't religious, but I am a spiritual person,' she said. 'You spiritual, Oliver?'

'I have never had a spiritual day in my entire life.'

She gave me a gap-toothed smile. 'Well, your entire American life's over, honey,' she said. 'But your afterlife's all set to begin. Maybe you'll find yourself some spirituality here.'

What do people mean by 'spirituality' anyhow? Do they mean they feel instinctively that a higher power guides their life and controls the world around them? Or do they simply mean they feel wonder or awe in the face of beauty? The beauty, say, of a cello concerto in E minor (a favorite of yours, Mother) or of the stratified layers of siltstone, mudstone, and shale making up the Painted Desert (a favorite of yours, Father).

Remember when we witnessed the aurora borealis on a cruise ship to Alaska? We felt awestruck watching gas particles in our atmosphere collide with charged particles from the sun and create arcs of eerie green and pink light that spanned the starry backdrop of night sky. Yet we did not for a moment feel the kind of spirituality that suggested a god (a strapping, curly-headed Zeus, for instance) was crouching behind a cloud with an assortment of colored flashlights to beam across the heavens.

Religious people never think about toilets or toothpaste in heaven, but they often picture the landscape here. They imagine trickling brooks, snow-peaked mountains, thundering waterfalls, and lush forests. They imagine places where they felt awed by natural beauty, where they felt spiritual.

Well, forget the brooks, mountains, waterfalls, and forests. To get a good picture of Town, imagine instead a vast public-housing project. The three-story redbrick dormitories where we live are low-rise tenements. As for the other buildings — schools, libraries, cafeterias, community centers, warehouses — they are plain but solid structures. They are much like the buildings back in Illinois, but with one big difference.

Buildings in Town can 'fix themselves.'

Over time, a crack in a wall smooths over, crooked steps even out, and loose floorboards stabilize. If, for example, somebody accidentally kicks a soccer ball through a pane of glass, that pane, over a period of weeks, grows back within its frame. Sometimes a bored townie breaks the window in his dorm room on purpose just to watch the glass slowly reappear.

Three weeks after I arrived, I broke a pane of glass on purpose, not out of boredom but rather to conduct an experiment. I did not want to let in the outside noise since I am a light sleeper, so instead I took a hammer to a pane in the shed that sits atop my residence, the Frank and Joe Hardy Dormitory. Early every morning, I head to the roof to watch the sunrise and check the glass growing in the window frame. With a ruler, I measure the day's growth to see whether it is constant. So far, it is not: the glass grows one inch on some days and three on others. Puzzling.

With a jackknife, I cut a line down my left forearm this week. Do not fret, Mother and Father: I am conducting an experiment to time how many days my wound takes to vanish.

Apparently, we heal faster in heaven. We are also immune to serious diseases, so the children who died of, say, leukemia need not worry about suffering again. Also, blindness and deafness do not exist in Town, so imagine the amazement and bewilderment of a person like Helen Keller when she awakes in a world she can see and hear.

Does Town fill me with awe? Yes, it often does. Yet in the month I have been here, I have met few people who share my wonder for such banal things as toilets, light switches, and garbage chutes. Flush a toilet here and where does your urine go? Turn on your desk lamp and where does the electricity come from? Throw an empty pineapple can into a garbage chute and how far down does it fall?

Some townies claim that our garbage falls all the way back to America. They believe that the chutes are a kind of portal back home and that other such tunnels back to America may exist here. I need irrefutable proof before believing in such a phenomenon. To check the depth of the chutes, I recently tied a child's beach pail to the end of a hank of yarn and lowered the pail into a chute. Though I had posted notices about my experiment on all three floors of the Frank and Joe, my dorm mates ignored them and dropped down bags of trash that knocked the pail from its lead and ruined my experiment. No matter. I will try again.

The mode of transportation in Town is ten-speed bicycles. Their paint is often chipped, and their chains sometimes fall off, but they work well enough to go from point A to point B (no riding on the sidewalks, though). The bicycles belong to everybody; in other words, we may not *own* one specific bicycle that catches our fancy. Yesterday I reserved a ten-speed at the bicycle depot and rode it to the Guy Montag Library to spend the afternoon browsing the stacks. I tied the requisite red ribbon to the handlebars to show that the bicycle was in use, but when I came out of the library later, my borrowed ten-speed was gone. One would assume that angels respect rules and do not filch what is not theirs. Sadly, townies have the same foibles as the people of Hoffman Estates.

Another disappointment: our libraries have only books of fiction. How I long for a book on entomology or astronomy! But, no, I must make do with murder mysteries, comic books, literary novels (umpteen copies of *Lord of the Flies*, for example), and young-adult novels about such topics as teen pregnancy and drug addiction. True, Town has no insects, so a book on entomology seems useless, nor does it have teen pregnancy (the only kind of birth here is rebirth) or drug addiction (though there is no marijuana, a boy in my dorm claims he smokes chamomile tea leaves to get 'mellow yellow').

Town, in fact, lacks many things Americans take for granted: telephones, televisions, newspapers, high-rises, cars, traffic lights, supermarkets, mailboxes, and much more.

One thing Town has that American towns do not is gigantic concrete walls — four Great Walls called the North Wall, South Wall, East Wall, and

West Wall that surround our home and rise an estimated twenty-five stories high. Slabs of concrete the size of dinner plates sometimes fall off the walls and shatter on the ground. The lower sections are covered in murals done by artistic children. Sometimes groups of townies gather at the foot of a wall and scream or sing together in hopes that somebody on the other side will answer back. So far, no reply has ever come.

Town's lucky number is thirteen (on account of our age), and so it is divided into thirteen zones arranged in a patchwork: One, Two, Three, Four, Five, et cetera. (The Frank and Joe, by the way, is in Eleven, near the North Wall.) Some townies imagine Town as a rectangular concrete terrarium and all of us in it as lab mice. They wonder if a terrarium to the south houses thirteen-year-old Mexicans and a terrarium to the north, thirteen-year-old Canadians. They think of our god as a scientist conducting endless experiments in a gargantuan laboratory filled with angels.

How I wish our god were a scientist, like evolutionary biologist Richard Dawkins or primatologist Jane Goodall. (As I told you time and again, you two are the spitting images of Richard and Jane even if Mother insists she looks more like a blond Olive Oyl.)

In my opinion, our god is not a scientist but instead an eccentric hippie artist. I call him Zig because the name sounds hip and groovy (hereinafter, Mother and Father, whenever anyone says 'God' to refer to the god running

13

our heaven, I will change the word to 'Zig' in my story to you). I picture Zig as a skinny man with long hair and a beard, like depictions of Jesus Christ, though Zig does not wear robes but rather faded jeans and T-shirts printed with such things as daisies or the yin-yang symbol. On his feet, he dons flip-flop sandals, which are popular in Town. In my mind, he smokes marijuana (not chamomile tea), burns incense, and wears mood rings on several fingers. Zig must not be a real, honest-to-goodness god because gods are generally thought to be infallible, whereas our Zig is always messing up. For instance, the toilets here constantly get blocked and overflow. As townies say, 'Zig don't know sh*t about plumbing.' (Since you are opposed to swearing, Mother and Father, I am softening the blow with an asterisk.)

Zig never sends us chemistry sets, astronomy textbooks, protractors, or periodic tables. Instead, he sends us poster paints, pastel crayons, chalk, pencils, and markers, all in a full spectrum of colors. We even receive canisters of spray paint (which explains the graffiti everywhere).

Our father who *art* in heaven (ha-ha).

Zig also sends us instruments like ukuleles, acoustic guitars, trombones, fiddles, tambourines, and harmonicas. Kids are musical here, and I would join in if I did not have a tin ear, a weedy voice, and two left feet. Who am I kidding? I would not join in even if I had twinkle toes and the baritone voice of an opera star.

Zig sends us sports equipment as well — footballs, baseball bats, badminton rackets, basketballs, field hockey sticks. I must admit I find these items sinister: at Helen Keller, I was regularly humiliated in gym class. During murderball, for instance, I was always the most savagely murdered, and hence I was never fond of team sports.

In fact, my policy back in America was this: steer clear of others. It is a policy, Zig willing, I will also adopt in Town.

3	6.94
Li	
Lithium	

Heaven has no churches, but it has what are called houses of good. On the fifth week of my stay in Town, do-gooder Thelma Rudd takes me to the Jonathan Livingston House of Good to attend a punch party. A punch party may sound as violent as murderball but is in fact just an evening cocktail party where the drinks are fruit punch. Thelma is not a girl with a steer-clear policy. She says I, as a newborn, need to get out and meet people to forge friendships — especially since I have no roommate yet.

'But I never had any friends back in Hoffman Estates,' I reassure her, 'and I never suffered ill effects.'

She raises an eyebrow and says, 'Oh, baby, don't lie to Thelma.'

I think back to my friendless days at Helen Keller. In science class, I had no partner with whom to dissect frogs. Nobody wanted to be paired with me despite the A+ he or she would earn by riding my coattails. Before I adopted steer-clear, I tried at times, especially back in seventh grade, to engage my fellow students in conversation. I first practiced in front of my bedroom mirror because, in the past, things I had said had caused offense or irritation. To my mirror I said, 'Hello, Cynthia Orwell. How were cheerleading tryouts today? Did you perform the splits to your liking?' When I said the same thing to the real Cynthia Orwell, she scrunched her nose as though I gave off a foul smell. She said, 'Oh, Boo, don't be schizo. Get lost, okay?' I learned I was no good at small talk, perhaps because I do not know how to make talk small.

I try to think of something to say to Thelma as we walk along a sidewalk and bicycles zoom by in the street. Weather is a small topic. I glance into the gray sky with its thin, wispy clouds (cirrus). So far, every day has been warm. I estimate high seventies or low eighties with a drop of five to ten degrees at night. I wish I had a thermometer, but thermometers are another thing Town does without, perhaps because there are no extremes to measure. The weather here is always early summer.

Sadly, there are no birds in the sky. Heaven is without bird life, animal life, or even insect life, except apparently for an occasional specimen that slips in. Maybe Zig thinks Americans tortured other creatures enough back home.

Thelma and I turn down John Clayton Street. The names of streets are written in indelible ink on cardboard wrapped in cellophane. These signs are then taped or nailed to the sides of buildings (as they are in Europe). Buildings, streets, and parks bear the names of characters from novels, and every so often local residents vote to change or update a name. I am about to ask who John Clayton is when Thelma says, 'You'd make a fine do-gooder, Oliver.'

'Have you been smoking chamomile tea

leaves?' I reply. 'I'm no people person.' I pick up a rock lying next to the sidewalk. 'I'm more comfortable with rocks. I'm a rock person. This little friend of mine has iron oxide bands.'

Despite the no-bicycles-on-the-sidewalk rule, a boy zips by on a bike with a sparkly banana seat. The handlebar grazes Thelma. 'Watch out, lard butt!' he yells.

Thelma grabs my banded friend from my palm and is about to whip it at the cyclist, but she refrains. She closes her eyes and mumbles, 'Zig give me strength.'

Thelma Rudd also lives in the Frank and Joe Hardy Dormitory, but a floor below me on the second. The do-good council assigned her to be my guidance counselor. She is responsible for checking on me, so she often drops by my room to ask how I am faring. I insist all is fine (actually what I say is 'hunky-dory,' because you use that odd expression, Mother and Father, and I picture your faces whenever I say it). Thelma often eyes me with a mixture of concern and bewilderment. She must suspect me of hiding something because last time I said 'hunky-dory,' she said, 'Tell Mama the truth.'

Some of the older girls — by 'older' I mean the thirteen-year-old girls who have been here for twenty years or more — like to refer to themselves as 'Mama.' They act motherly toward a newborn. They sew patches on the seat of his jeans. They bring him a bran muffin for breakfast to ensure that his bowel movements are regular. They call him 'honey,' 'sweetie,' 'baby,' and 'pet.'

Ever since I told Thelma that you, Mother, are

a fan of jazz standards, she has been singing me bedtime lullabies from the American songbook. I may be past the lullaby age, but in Thelma's eyes, I am still a newborn. Last night she chose 'Begin the Beguine.'

On Merricat Blackwood Street, Thelma stops in front of an old warehouse where dozens of townies are pushing rattling shopping carts filled with canned goods like green beans, creamed corn, pears, and chickpeas.

Thelma says, 'We had a delivery today.'

I ask to go in because I have never seen inside a food warehouse. The space is the size of the Helen Keller gymnasium, but instead of bleachers along its periphery, the warehouse has racks of metal shelving that stand high enough that ladders are needed to reach the top. These shelves serve as rebirthing beds for the canned goods, boxes of cereal, rice, pasta, bags of potatoes, carrots, apples, and all the other simple foods we eat here. The food is vegetarian because, as Thelma would say, meat is death, and nothing truly dead can exist in Town.

'Does the food appear in the blink of an eye?' I ask Thelma. 'Just like a newborn?'

'Yep, but the food don't come till we remove every single morsel from the last delivery.'

We leave the warehouse and continue up the street to the Jonathan Livingston House of Good. It turns out to be a community center with furniture that seems to come from a rummage sale. The miniature fridge and stove in the kitchenette are dented. The wooden chairs around the room are mismatched and chipped.

The coffee table is a battered steamer trunk with leatherette handles hanging half off. The plaid couch where Thelma and I take a seat is shabby with quilts laid over spots where the stuffing fluffs through. Hung over the couch is a cuckoo clock with no hands to tell time. Every few minutes, the little shuttered window on the clock swings open and a platform with nothing on it sticks out and then darts back inside.

Most townies at the house of good wear the same purple armband Thelma has around her left biceps. The armband is a symbol of do-goodism. Other than the armband, they dress like everybody else, in jeans and T-shirts.

The boys here, like the boys at the Frank and Joe, have jagged haircuts. There are no barbers in Town, so we cut one another's hair, and consequently some of the boys have bald spots. As barbers yourselves, Father and Mother, you would be appalled. At least hair grows faster in heaven, in the same way wounds and scabs heal more quickly.

Girls' hair is less hacked because girls usually let their hair grow long. The girl who sits down with Thelma and me has long golden hair, the type seen in shampoo ads in America. Thelma introduces us; the girl's name is Esther Haglund. Esther would never be chosen to star in a shampoo ad: she is a dwarf, albeit a tall one (she is about a foot and a half shorter than I am). She has the larger cranium and bulging forehead common among dwarfs.

'Esther's a do-gooder in training,' Thelma

20

explains to me. 'That's why her armband is light purple.'

'Mauve,' Esther says. 'And I knit it myself.' She touches the band around her left biceps.

Thelma points out the pleated skirt Esther is wearing. 'Esther makes all her own clothes.'

I just stare. I have never been around a dwarf before.

'So how do you like do-goodism so far?' Thelma asks her.

'Well, I'm no complainer, but, Thelma, I swear the residents in my dorm can be pigs sometimes. I make them snacks, organize their school schedules, offer a shoulder to cry on, and even darn their damn socks, and then they leave a Zig-awful mess in our kitchenette and expect me to clean it up. One of them even said to me, 'You do-gooders live for sh*t like this.' '

Thelma shakes her head.

Esther notices my staring. 'Do you have a question, Oliver?' she asks.

'Yes, Esther. I was wondering, what type of dwarfism are you afflicted with?'

'*Afflicted* with?' Esther's eyes bulge. 'What the hell kind of talk is that?'

'I am having trouble recalling the types of dwarf — '

Thelma cuts in: 'He's a newbie, Esther.'

'I don't give a fig if he's a newbie or an old boy. That question was plain rude.' She turns to me. 'We don't say 'dwarf' — we say 'little person.' You got that, kid?'

I nod my head.

Esther reaches for her glass of punch on the

side table and then heads off into the crowd of do-gooders in her bowlegged gait.

'I guess I made a friend,' I say to Thelma. (This comment, please note, is true irony.)

She pats my leg. 'Don't mind her.'

'I wonder why Zig doesn't fix dwarfs,' I say. 'After all, he can fix cancer and blindness.'

'Being a little person ain't a disease, Oliver. It don't need no fixing.'

I mull this fact over and then ask, 'What about children with Down syndrome?'

'Well, some people claim retarded kids come here a little smarter to make their afterlives easier.'

'Zig adjusts their IQ up?'

'That's what people say, but who knows if it's really true.'

I have a frightening thought: maybe Zig adjusted my IQ *down*. Maybe my IQ was too high back in Hoffman Estates and prevented me from interacting normally with my peers. Mr. Miller, my old English teacher, once said, 'Oliver, being over-smart is a handicap.' At the time, I thought Mr. Miller was bitter because I had corrected his grammar in class. ('It is easy: 'who' is a subject and 'whom' is an object,' I told him as he eyed me with such vexation I feared he would crack his yardstick over my head.)

I do not know my actual intelligence quotient, Mother and Father, since you did not want me tested. You did not want me skipping grades. 'You stick out enough as it is,' you reasoned, Father. In hindsight, I deem your decision wise because had I never spent time with children my

22

own age, I would be completely out of my element here.

Somebody else catches my eye at the house of good. A boy over by the hors d'oeuvres table is taking quick nibbles of a carrot stick. He is a black boy with an Afro, but he has white splotches on his arms and a few on his face, including a kind of starburst patch on his forehead.

I point out the boy to Thelma.

'That's Reginald Washington,' she says. 'He's the president of our do-good council.'

'He has vitiligo,' I say. 'It's a disease that destroys the pigmentation in the skin.'

'He came to Town like that, but the spots haven't spread none since he got here. He says Zig put a stop to them. One of the reasons he became a do-gooder was to thank Zig.'

Reginald Washington claps his hands for attention. He stands at a podium set up near the hors d'oeuvres. 'Kindly lend me your ears, my friends.'

He gives a talk about do-goodism, the importance of helping others instead of floundering around aimlessly in one's own head. He holds a small bullhorn, which he uses to amplify certain phrases so they sound like the word of Zig. 'Do right by others, and they will do right by you!' he thunders as the do-gooders nod their heads — all but Esther, who rolls her eyes.

That do-right tenet is malarkey. For example, I once allowed Oscar Stanley and Larry Schultz to copy from my geometry homework, and did they do right by me? No — the next day, they tripped me as I was walking down the front stairs of Helen Keller, and I sprained my ankle.

I stop listening to Reginald. I prefer to flounder in my own head, thank you very much. I wonder again if my brainpower has fallen a notch in the afterlife. I work myself into such a lather that I feel in mourning for those lost points of IQ. I finally excuse myself and go to the boys' room, where I sit on the toilet and recite the periodic table to make myself feel better.

I will tell you right away that the next scene is a dream. I dislike stories where a dream is presented, even briefly, as reality. I do not appreciate such trickery and will never know-ingly deceive you, Mother and Father.

So here is the dream I have on the night of the punch party: I am lying in the center circle of the empty basketball court at Helen Keller. Along one wall is stretched a banner reading, GO, TROJANS, GO! The me in my dream believes he has been reborn in America because his eyeglasses are on his face and he is once again stark naked. He stands and starts heading toward the gym doors when, in the blink of an eye, the space fills with secondhand supplies — couches, stoves, bicycles, boxes of books, mattresses. So many objects are piled around that he must climb over them in an attempt to reach the gym doors. As he clambers over crates of the same mystery novel (*And Then There Were None*), he hears a pounding coming from the doors. Despite his atheism, he feels that some higher power is knocking. He stubs his toe and twists his ankle as he climbs through the debris, but he finally reaches the exit and swings the doors open. A blinding light greets him. He says to the light, 'Are you there, Zig? It is I, Oliver.'

Then a voice says, 'Are you there, Oliver?' This is where my dream ends. I wake up and realize somebody is knocking on the door to my room.

'It's me. It's Thelma.'

'Give me a moment,' I call out in a half mumble. After the punch party, Thelma had said she had an all-night shift in the rebirthing room at the Meg Murry Infirmary. What is she doing back at the Frank and Joe already?

As I slip out of bed, moonlight is streaming through my open drapes. The moon here is full every night. Again, puzzling. I switch on my desk lamp and squint from the sudden brightness. The clock on my desk says a quarter to three.

I shuffle to the door in my oversize pajamas. When I open it, I think for an instant I am still in my Helen Keller dream because standing beside Thelma Rudd in the dimly lit corridor is a member of the Trojans basketball team. He is not in uniform, but I recognize him all the same.

'Zig sent us a late package,' Thelma says, but I do not even glance at her because I am looking at the boy.

'Johnny Henzel?' I say.

The boy nods. He stares at me in the same transfixed way I stare at him. He looks thinner than he did in Hoffman Estates. His buzz cut exposes his ears, one of which is bigger than the other. His eyelashes are so dark he seems to be wearing mascara.

'Did you also have a heart defect?' I ask.

'What?' Johnny Henzel says.

'A hole in your heart,' I say. The chances of two deaths by the same cause at the same school in the same semester are infinitesimally small, I know, but I am half-asleep.

'Let's step inside,' says Thelma, but nobody moves.

Johnny runs his hands over his hair, scratching his scalp and wincing a bit. Finally, he stops scratching and says, 'We didn't die from a f*cking heart defect, Boo.' His voice is hoarse, shaky. 'We got shot by some crazy kid at school.'

A scream. Not in the corridor outside my room, but in my mind. A memory of a scream that rang out in the hallway of Helen Keller.

My voice comes out in a whisper: 'You must be mistaken.'

Johnny Henzel drops his knapsack. He moves toward me and opens his arms. He hugs me to him, his sweaty head resting on my bony shoulder. Even though I dislike being touched, even though I was never hugged by anybody but you two, I do not pull away. I pat between his shoulders gently, the way a mama does, as Johnny Henzel sobs and sobs in my arms.

5	10.81
B	
Boron	

Remember your favorite story about my inability to cry? The encyclopedia story? The incident took place when I was four and we had just moved to 222 Hill Drive in the Sandpits Apartments so you could take over the local barbershop. You had left me in the den with my plastic dinosaurs while you unpacked dishes in the kitchen. A dreadful racket soon had you scurrying back to the den, where you discovered that the bookshelves on which you had placed a set of encyclopedias earlier had proven too flimsy. Three shelves had given way, scattering volumes A to Z. There I sat among the toppled books, staring placidly into the face of my toy ankylosaur, a dinosaur with an armored body and a bony tail club.

'A whole bookshelf of encyclopedias fell on our little egghead,' you said, Mother, in wonder, 'and he still didn't crack.'

'Our son has the head of an ankylosaur!' you added, Father.

Oh, how I liked when you told that story! I miss you, Mother and Father. Given my holey heart, you must have braced yourselves for my early death, but surely you did not expect my life to be snuffed out by a boy with a gun.

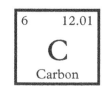

Johnny Henzel did not die immediately. After he was shot, he was taken to the Schaumburg Medical Center, where he lay in a coma and never awoke. He tells Thelma and me that despite being unconscious, he could sometimes hear what people said to him.

'The doctors even told my folks to talk to me,' Johnny says. 'They never mentioned the shootings, though. They thought if they did, I wouldn't get better.'

It was his ten-year-old sister who told him about his murder. When their parents were out of the room fetching some lunch, she leaned in close to Johnny's head, swathed in its turban of bandages, and whispered, 'Gunboy got you!'

'Brenda said my folks refused to say the killer's name out loud. They'd just call him 'the boy with the gun.' She told me not to worry 'cause Gunboy couldn't get me no more. He'd shot himself dead.'

'He is dead too?' I say, astounded.

Johnny makes one hand into a pistol and holds it to his own temple. He nods and pulls the trigger.

He and Thelma are sitting Indian-style on the opposite bed. I sit on my own bed, hugging my pillow. I think I am in shock: I did not die from the over-excitement of learning 106 elements by heart.

'Who was Gunboy?' I ask Johnny, whose eyes are still bloodshot from crying.

'I don't know for sure,' he replies. 'Brenda never mentioned him again. She just kept pleading with me to wake up. 'Open your eyes, Johnny! Please open your eyes!' '

'If Gunboy is a true boy, he must have been a student at our school,' I say. 'Oh, goodness, he may be thirteen. He may have been reborn here in Town!'

'I doubt it,' Thelma says. 'Zig may be a dope, but I can't figure he'd ever let in a killer.' She turns to Johnny. 'You didn't get a look at him?'

'No, not the day of the shooting. I just remember walking down the hall minding my own business. I saw Jermaine Tucker and Cynthia Orwell and Larry Schultz and Oscar Stanley,' he says. 'I saw you, Boo, standing at your locker. And then nothing.'

'If we die in a real horrible way, Zig erases the very last seconds of our deaths,' Thelma says. 'It's for our own good.'

'Gunboy probably shot me in the back of the head,' Johnny says. 'And got you, too, Boo. You didn't see nothing?'

'I was facing my locker,' I say. 'But I may remember the sound of a gunshot and even a scream. I am not sure, though. It is all very fuzzy.'

'Who at your school would want to shoot you boys?' Thelma asks.

Many a former classmate of mine took

pleasure in hassling me and hurting me, but would any of them actually shoot me in the back?

Johnny narrows his eyes. 'I think Gunboy was a new kid at school.'

'Why do you think that?' I ask.

'I see the b*stard's face. He comes to me in my nightmares.'

'Your nightmares?'

'All the nightmares I had at the hospital when I was in my coma. Gunboy haunts me, man. He won't leave me the f*ck alone.'

'Maybe you *did* catch a glimpse of him,' Thelma says.

'The kid in my dream has an ugly mug, evil eyes, big ears, and messy hair like a punk rocker. I think I might have even seen him around in the months before we got shot.'

I try to picture such a boy. But I died on only the fourth day of the school year, so I might not have noticed any new boys. Perhaps he was not in my classes. 'It's possible Gunboy killed other thirteen-year-olds,' I say. 'Other classmates of ours may be here too.'

'We can check the rebirthing books at the different infirmaries,' Thelma says. 'We'll see if Zig sent us any more packages from Hoffman Estates, Illinois.' She gets up from the bed and pats Johnny's shoulder. 'We'll talk more in the morning, honey. You need to get some sleep.'

'Why does he need sleep?' I say. 'He was just in a coma for five weeks.'

Thelma ignores my comment. She comes over and tries hugging me to her big, soft body, but I have had my fill of hugs tonight, so I move away and climb under the covers. She sings a few bars of 'In the Still of the Night' as she tucks in my blanket.

After Thelma leaves, I watch Johnny shuck his clothes and don the striped pajamas Thelma stuffed into his knapsack. As he slides into bed, I wonder if he is afraid to go to sleep in case he falls back into a coma or has a nightmare about Gunboy. But I do not ask. I reach over and turn off the light on my desk. We lie in the dark in silence.

Finally, Johnny says, 'I'm glad you're here.'

When I do not reply, he goes on: 'I don't mean I'm glad you're dead, or passed or whatever the hell they say. I'm just glad I'm not alone. I'm glad a friend's here with me.'

A friend. He called me a friend. Odd. We seldom spoke back in America, but then again, Johnny was shot in the head, so perhaps he does not remember things exactly as they were.

'Good night, Johnny.'

'Good night, Boo.'

But it is not a good night because not for one minute do I sleep.

You knew Johnny, Mother and Father. He delivered our *Tribune*. He seldom stopped by Clippers, though. His hair was shoulder-length, but it was probably shaved off before the surgeons treated his head wound.

I had actually predicted an early death for Johnny back in Hoffman Estates. He was a skitcher. Do you know what skitching is? It is an illegal winter activity whereby a person crouches behind an idling car, grabs its bumper, and then skates down the icy street as the car drives away.

Johnny was a speed demon, as the ribbons he had won as a sprinter on the track team proved. But I saw this perilous activity as a death wish. Furthermore, I saw a paradox because he also served as a school crossing guard. As a skitcher, he flouted the safety rules of the road and risked life and limb; as a crossing guard, he helped younger kids navigate busy roads safely.

I was once witness to his daredevilry, during the winter before our passings. As you know, I always rose early because I could easily survive on six hours of sleep a night. Around six in the morning, I went for my constitutional. Johnny was also up at that hour on account of his paper route, and I would see him around the Sandpits Apartments pulling a rusty wagon filled with copies of the *Tribune*. In winter, a sled replaced the wagon.

One day in January, I came across his sled left in front of a residence on the east end of the complex. I assumed he was inside making a delivery. It was snowing, and little drifts had collected atop the newspapers. I brushed the snow off so the papers would not get soggy.

Sometimes Johnny's dog went along with him on his route. Rover was a drooling basset hound with red, rheumy eyes. I glanced around for Rover, but he was not there. I did see a station wagon idling in the street, though. The owner had just scraped the ice from his windshield and was climbing back into the driver's seat. As he did so, a crouching figure shot out from between two parked cars and grabbed hold of the bumper.

The driver must have glimpsed Johnny in his rearview mirror because he pressed the gas pedal to the floor and his car zoomed down the street. It wove back and forth as though to loosen Johnny from its tail. Johnny finally let go. He tumbled headlong till he collided with a parked car.

I ran up the street to where Johnny lay dazed. His knitted pompom hat was askew. Snowflakes stuck to his eyelashes, snot ran from his nose to his lip, and smudges of newsprint darkened his cheeks.

'It's so gorgeous, Boo,' he said, staring at the dawning day.

I looked at the sky, which was a soggy graphite gray like the newspapers lying in his sled.

'Are you hurt?' I asked. 'Do you need medical assistance?'

'Lie down. See for yourself how beautiful it is.'

'We're on Meadow Lane, Johnny. A car may run us over.'

'You only live once.' (How wrong he was.)

I glanced around. Nobody was in the vicinity. There were no headlights from approaching cars. The station wagon was long gone.

Who knows why I lay down with Johnny Henzel? I try to avoid nonsense, and yet this act was nonsensical, not to mention risky. Still, I did it, probably because Johnny seemed so adamant.

'Do you see it?' he said to me as the snow wet the seat of my pants.

'What are we seeing, Johnny?'

'Oh, Boo, what we're seeing is peace.'

'Peace?'

He lifted a hand in the air and made the V sign with his index and middle fingers.

I looked through his V and saw the delicate outline of a waning crescent moon.

Then we heard the beeping of an automobile. We scrambled up, and Johnny took off toward his sled of newspapers, waving a mitten at me.

In the years he and I lived at Sandpits and attended the same elementary school and junior high, we had few conversations longer than that one in the middle of Meadow Lane last January.

In that fleeting moment in the street, I did feel a certain kinship. I do not know whether to call it friendship. We did share something, but what that something was I cannot say.

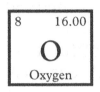

8	16.00
O	
Oxygen	

In the morning after Johnny's first night in my dorm room, I pick up his clothes off the floor and hang his jeans in the wardrobe. I ball up his socks and drop them in one of the drawers that slide out from under his bed. Yet Johnny sleeps on.

I look around the room. It is tidy and plain. I have not personalized it in any way other than to hang a drawing of a plant cell, which I did in pen and ink. Thelma has implored me to brighten up the place. With Johnny lying in the second bed, my dorm room now seems more personal (despite his dark, furrowed brow).

It is six thirty. I go to shower. I check my back in the mirror for a gunshot scar, but there is none. Afterward, I go to the roof of the Frank and Joe to measure the growth of glass in the shed's window. When I come back, just after seven, Johnny is still asleep. I write my new roommate a note: 'Dear Johnny, I went to the cafeteria to get us breakfast. Back soon. Hope you slept well.' I sign the note 'Oliver,' though I realize I will never be anybody but Boo to him.

I stick plastic containers into a paper bag to fetch us oatmeal. Townies prefer to call it gruel because they claim it is grueling to eat. I exit our dorm, and as I cut across a playing field to reach the cafeteria, I see a trio of boys laughing and kicking a soccer ball around. They can laugh and play because nobody shot them to death, I think. But then I realize I am being unfair: I do not know how they died, and perhaps their deaths were as violent as my own.

On the other side of the field, I walk through the front doors of the Sophie Wender School, which houses the local cafeteria. I immediately need to sit on a bench in the lobby because something occurs to me that makes me dizzy and weak. I wonder if Gunboy's bullet is still inside me, perhaps even embedded in my holey heart. My breathing comes in gasps. I remove the plastic containers from my paper bag and stick my nose and mouth into its opening. The bag inflates and deflates with my breathing.

'You okay, Oliver?'

I look up and see Esther Haglund.

'Are you sick?'

I plan to say I am hunky-dory, but I take the bag away from my face and say instead, 'I was murdered.'

'What?'

'I was murdered,' I repeat. 'Somebody I do not even know shot me. I assume I died on the spot. The bullet must have hit a vital organ — or maybe it even blew my brains out.'

I think of you, Father and Mother. Did you learn the news by telephone or by a police visit at Clippers? I must avoid such thoughts; otherwise I will never recover my breath.

Esther sits beside me on the bench as townies traipse through the lobby of the Sophie. Gangs of thirteen-year-olds jostle, holler, and hoot. They are as happy-go-lucky as my fellow students must have been at Helen Keller in the moments before Gunboy opened fire.

I put the bag back over my face and breathe in more carbon dioxide as Esther watches. She has widely spaced green eyes, which she blinks at me, but she says not a word. She also is terrible at small talk, despite her position as a do-gooder in training.

I put down the paper bag. 'You have nice hair,' I tell her — my attempt at small talk. 'I should know because my parents are barbers.'

She examines the ends of a lock as though checking for splits. Then she pushes her hair back and looks me in the eye. 'There's a support group here for murdered kids.'

'Support group?'

'Yeah, they call themselves 'gommers.' 'GOM' stands for 'getting over murder.' A silly name if you ask me. Gommers get together and talk about how they passed. Their anger. Their nightmares. That kind of thing.'

I must look surprised because she says, 'You aren't the only kid here who got murdered, you know. Some gommers consider their death a badge of honor. They lord it over the rest of us. They exaggerate and make their murder more gruesome than it actually was. Hope you don't do that.'

I tell her I doubt I will, especially since I did not even witness my own shooting. 'I would far prefer a heart defect as a cause of death,' I add as I place my plastic containers back in my paper bag. I wonder if a heart defect, common among dwarfs, killed Esther.

Then I stand and say good-bye. I need to fetch breakfast for Johnny and myself.

As I walk away, Esther says, 'Wait, Oliver!'

When I turn, she hesitates, but then calls out, 'Achondroplasia.' It is her form of dwarfism.

9	19.00

F

Fluorine

'Did Zig make the porridge?' Johnny Henzel asks.

'No, the three bears did,' I say. This is my attempt at light-hearted humor, but Johnny does not laugh. He shovels his gruel into his mouth and closes his eyes as though the taste is exquisite. He must not have eaten any real food during his coma.

We picnic on the throw rug between our beds. Johnny is still in his pajamas. Considering how famished he is, I forgo my own breakfast and give him the second bowl of oatmeal as well as the cashews, dried apricots, two apples, and two muffins I brought from the cafeteria. While he eats, he leans back against his bed and gives an occasional loud belch because his digestive system is not used to food yet.

I eye his scalp through his short hair. Like me, he has no scar from a bullet wound, which must mean that Zig can double as a plastic surgeon.

'I wonder if my damn picture's up in the school lobby,' he says. He reminds me that when Oscar Stanley was hit by a car last year, his school photograph was blown up and put in the glass showcase with a giant get-well-soon card. 'Your picture must be there too,' he says.

In my most recent school photograph, I wear a T-shirt printed with this Albert Einstein quote:

'Education is what remains after you forget what you learned at school.' In fact, I would be surprised if Mr. Plumb, our principal, called attention to this quote. I would be surprised if the school paid homage to me at all. I expect my classmates deemed me expendable. 'Well, if one of us had to bite the dust, better it be Boo,' they probably said. Johnny Henzel's death, however, must have caused plenty of sorrow, since he was a good athlete and a good artist.

I rise from our throw rug, go to the window, and push back the drapes. Because Johnny arrived late at night, he did not get a good glimpse of Town, and so I wave him over. He comes to stand beside me, and as he stares from our third-floor window, he says, 'This place looks a little run-down, a little like Armpits.'

Armpits, as you know, is the derogatory name some people give to the Sandpits Apartments. It is true that Town is a land of low-rises like Sandpits. 'Everything here is very plain and serviceable,' I tell Johnny.

'So it's no land of milk and honey.'

'No, it's not. In fact, we don't receive either milk or honey here. Zig seems to be a strict vegetarian.'

Johnny shakes his head in disbelief. 'Thelma told me we're stuck here for fifty f*cking years,' he says. 'And then we croak all over again.'

I tell him some townies even claim that, in the seconds before redeath, we age fifty years all at once.

His eyes go wide.

'I say poppycock till someone shows me proof.'

If only I had a movie camera to film fifty-year-olds in their sleep. There are so many experiments to conduct here.

'What if I fall out this window?' he says, looking down at the brittle shrubs and dandelions gone to seed in the Frank and Joe's front lawn.

'You'll probably survive and be carted off to the infirmary.'

I recently visited the Meg Murry Infirmary again to collect data on healing times for broken arms and legs. I explain to Johnny that because we mend quickly, some townies act irresponsibly. They ride their bicycles too fast and suffer nasty collisions.

Johnny watches people on bicycles zip by in the street below. He seems almost hypnotized by the procession. I wonder how I will adapt to his presence. I am not used to sharing my space and must already fight the urge to make his bed so it is as tidy as my own. I hope he does not leave his underwear on the floor, clutter his desk with garish knickknacks, or hang color-by-number posters on the walls.

'What happens if we kill somebody, Boo?'

I figure he is worried about getting shot again, so I say, 'I doubt there are any handguns here, Johnny.'

He turns to me at the window. He is only a foot away. I prefer to keep two feet between me and another person, so I step back.

'I wonder if he's here,' he says, looking me straight in the eye. His irises are so dark his eyes look all pupil. I know immediately whom he is referring to.

'Thelma says Zig wouldn't let him in,' I say. 'But the thought did cross my mind that maybe she is mistaken.'

'If Gunboy *is* here, he'll pay the price for turning us into frigging bones in a coffin, man.'

'What price is that?' I ask.

Johnny touches a fingertip to his eyelid and then reaches over and tries to touch one of my eyelids, but I jerk away.

'An eye for an eye,' he says.

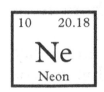

10	20.18

Ne
Neon

Johnny Henzel's body back in America is not a skeleton yet: it has not been dead long enough to have decomposed fully in its grave. In a coffin, an embalmed body takes many months to break down enough to expose bones. The decay depends on the temperature, the process speeding up in hot summer months. Johnny's eyes, being softer tissue, would rot first. Of course, if his body were mummified, decomposition would stretch over hundreds of years, and if he were buried in Alaska's frozen tundra, scientists could dig him up in three centuries, thaw him out, and then flip through our school yearbook and easily pick out which student lay before them.

Had I died of a holey heart on an Arctic fact-finding mission and been buried in the ice, I would not mind scientists digging me up centuries later and putting me in a museum showcase as an educational exhibit. To me, spending day after day in a science museum is paradise.

At Uncle Seymour's funeral, Mother and Father, you said you favored cremation, so I suppose you had my body cremated. Did you put my ashes in a ceramic urn and shelf it next to the *Encyclopedia Americana*? I hope my ashes soothe your pain. I worry about you. Mother, you are easily distracted and often forget to look both ways as you cross the highway to Clippers. And, Father, you must not start smoking Camels again. Remember Uncle Seymour's lung cancer.

I wonder if you would be happier now if you were Christian, Buddhist, Mormon, or of any other religious persuasion that puts faith in an afterlife. Would my death be easier on you if you knew that on this Halloween, I am seated in an auditorium at the Sophie and watching a variety show put on by angels?

It is Johnny's birthday today, but alas, birthdays are not celebrated in heaven because we are not getting any older. Here we celebrate only rebirthdays, the date we passed into Town.

Can you guess what costume I am wearing for Halloween?

Here is a hint: think of my nickname.

Yes, I am a ghost. I have a white sheet over my head with two large eyeholes cut out by Johnny. His own costume is simply a black domino mask like that worn by bank robbers or Zorro. He said our goal tonight was to disguise ourselves. He also had me clip his hair even shorter. I do not like touching people's skin, but I can touch their hair because hair, which consists mostly of keratin protein, as you know, is dead. Barbering must be intuitive for me, because I did a crackerjack job.

We are far from the only townies in costume tonight. However, Johnny and I are disguised not only for Halloween but also because Johnny fears we might run into Gunboy. On Halloween, townies travel far and wide.

'If he *is* here, he won't want us ratting him out,' Johnny said back at the Frank and Joe. 'If he sees us, he could attack again. We got to get *him*, before he gets *us*.'

So now in the Sophie's auditorium, Johnny twists his head around and scans the crowd for a brown-haired boy with ears that stick out — the boy he still sees in his nightmares in Town. (Since becoming my roommate two and a half weeks ago, he has screamed in his sleep several times. Needless to say, my insomnia is acting up again.)

'There are dozens of brown-haired boys with ears that stick out,' I tell him.

We are sitting in aisle seats so we can easily move closer to Gunboy if Johnny spots him. Our killer will be disguised as well, Johnny says. Maybe as a pirate with an eye patch, Frankenstein's monster with fake bolts in his neck, or the Grim Reaper with a scythe (the reaper I see is carrying a toilet plunger). As you can imagine, zombies are a popular costume since we are the living dead (ha-ha). Zombies wear white face paint with their eyes circled in dusky charcoal makeup. They rub white glue (polyvinyl acetate) into their hair so it stands on end. They wear shabby jeans with tattered legs that descend to mid-calf.

The costumes are homemade because Zig does not deliver the kind of premade Halloween costumes and rubber masks sold in American department stores. Instead, he delivers rolls of fabric and sewing machines so townies can make costumes for their theater productions and Halloween parties.

Halloween is a big holiday here, on a par with New Year's Eve. Fake blood is everywhere tonight. It is made of acrylic paint or ketchup. It drips from head wounds and runs down cheeks. It spots chests. It does not make me queasy, and even if it were real, I would not balk. Remember in sixth grade when my classmates all pricked their fingers and tested their blood type for their ABO and rhesus factor? Some students went white from queasiness. Some felt faint. I did not go white — at least not any whiter. I expected to have a rare blood type, so I was not surprised to discover I was AB+.

I spot Esther Haglund standing in the center aisle, looking for a seat before the Halloween program begins. Her hair is styled elaborately with fancy waves hanging over her big forehead. The blouse she wears is covered in sequins. She squeezes into our row and sits in the empty seat beside me.

'Hello, Esther,' I say. 'How are you doing this fine evening?'

She stares into the eyeholes in my sheet. 'Is that you, Oliver?'

'Yes, I am a ghost. What are you dressed as?'

'A newbie in my dorm gave me this ghastly hairdo,' she says. 'I'm an actress who plays an angel private eye on TV. I don't remember her name. I passed back in sixty-nine, so I don't know modern TV.'

I tell her we watched mostly PBS television at

home because my mother and father claimed that the commercial stations rotted the soul. Apparently, you two can be agnostics and still use words like 'soul' (I jest).

I introduce Johnny and Esther and ask Johnny if he knows the actress to whom Esther is referring.

'For f*ck sake, Boo, it's that stupid b*tch Farrah Fawcett. Did you live under a rock, man?'

Unlike you, Father and Mother, I am not bothered by cursing. Words like 'assh*le,' 'sh*t,' and 'c*nt' are just different rearrangements of the same twenty-six letters found in all English words. For me, 'c*cksucker' is no more offensive an expression than 'weed wacker' or 'bumper sticker.' I do tell Johnny, however, that if people must swear, they should at least be grammatical. He should say 'for f*ck's sake' with an apostrophe and an s.

'People speak appallingly in Town,' I add. 'They have no adults to serve as grammar role models.'

He looks as though he wants to shoot me in the head. 'Why you always such a d*ckhead, Boo?'

'Perhaps I possess the d*ckhead gene.'

Johnny does not laugh at my joke.

I turn to Esther. 'Thelma is one of the performers tonight, but she would not tell me what she will be doing. She wants it to be a surprise.'

'She's doing a reenactment,' Esther says, rolling her big eyes under her shaggy hairdo. 'So get ready for loads of pain and suffering.'

'What's a reenactment?' Johnny asks.

'Thelma's a gommer,' Esther says. 'She's reenacting her murder.'

Thelma Rudd is dressed as a Holstein. Her costume is a kind of padded white snowsuit spotted with black felt patches. Where in Town did she get a snowsuit? On her head is a hood with cow ears attached to the sides, one black ear and one white, but the part of the costume that draws the audience's laughter is at groin level: the udder. The four teats look to be made of pink party balloons.

She stands at the edge of the stage, twitching her tail, which is a kind of marionette because it is attached to a string that rises into the rafters.

At the back of the stage, in the semidarkness, stand four trees. I presume they are made of wiring and papier-mâché and their leaves of green construction paper or felt. A single boy steps out from behind each trunk. The four boys stand a few yards behind Thelma with their arms behind their backs. They are big boys — tall and muscular — and look older than thirteen, though of course they are not.

'Moooo! Moooo!' one of them cries out. Then another joins in, then another, till they are all mooing. Louder and louder. 'Moooo! Moooo! Moooo!'

Thelma smiles sweetly. Nervous giggles erupt from the audience.

Beside me, Esther whispers, 'I can't watch this.'

The white boys close in on Thelma. They surround her. They carry thin branches, which they use to poke her back, buttocks, and udder.

'It's supper and I'm sure hungry for a burger,' says one boy.

'This cow has enough meat on her to feed an army,' says another.

'I bet she gives *chocolate* milk,' says the third.

'String her up!' says the fourth.

Three of the boys keep prodding Thelma as the fourth boy mimes throwing something skyward. Down from the rafters comes a rope with a noose tied to its end.

One boy says, 'She's so fat she'll break the damn branch.'

The noose slowly descends to the stage as the lights dim. By the time the noose reaches Thelma, only a spotlight is left, trained on her face.

'For once in my short little life, I wasn't fat enough,' Thelma says, slipping the noose around her neck. 'The branch held.'

Then the lights go out completely. We hear footsteps as the actors move offstage.

Beside me, Esther whispers, 'Is it over? Can I open my eyes?'

But it is not over. A voice onstage starts singing. It is Thelma. She is still there.

The song she chose is one of your favorites, Mother and Father. It is a Billie Holiday song about bulging eyes, twisted mouths, and blood on leaves. It is a song about hanging from a poplar tree.

12	24.31
Mg	
Magnesium	

When all the performances are over, townies gather in the Sophie's gymnasium, where black and orange streamers hang from the ceiling and balloons bounce across the floor. In one corner, a group of townies wielding knives is all set to enter the pumpkin-carving contest. Disco music plays on a hi-fi system set up under one of the basketball hoops, and a group of green-faced Frankenstein's monsters do a spastic dance that looks like a conniption fit. Do-gooders — they wear their usual purple armbands over their costumes — pass around trays of a fruit punch called blood. The chunks floating in the drink are not tumors from a witch's heart as claimed but pieces of maraschino cherry.

Some old threadbare sofas and armchairs have been moved into the gymnasium. I sit on a love seat, and Johnny and Esther cram in on either side. I feel their body heat even through the sheet. I can be close to one person briefly without discomfort, but two people simultaneously are hard to bear unless those two people are you, Father and Mother. I wiggle in my seat, and Johnny says, 'Oh, I forgot you can't stand being touched.'

'Because you got murdered?' Esther asks.

'No,' says Johnny. 'Even back in America, he

hated it. Remember, Boo, in gym when we did wrestling? You were paired with Jermaine Tucker, and when he grabbed you, you went limp like you fainted.'

I get up and pull off my ghost sheet. My hair stands straight up from static (or maybe I saw a ghost, ha-ha). The lights are so dim in the gym that in the unlikely event Gunboy is gyrating on the dance floor to 'Disco Duck,' he will not see us.

I tell Johnny and Esther the story of Uncle Seymour's funeral to explain why I do not like touching others. As you will remember, Mother and Father, his friends and relatives stood around his open casket and talked, mostly about his bakery and how he was famous for cinnamon buns, which were served at the gathering.

Uncle Seymour had always been kind to me. He was an artistic fellow. For my eleventh birthday, he gave me a pretty cake decorated not with eleven candles but with eleven test tubes.

When I saw Uncle Seymour lying in his casket, I realized at once that my dislike of touching applied only to the living. People are ecosystems. The pumping of blood. The dividing of cells. The growing of bones. The killing of cancer cells by soldier cells. It is dizzying all that goes on simultaneously in the human body. To me, two people touching is akin to two galaxies colliding. (Okay, I exaggerate a *touch*, ha-ha.)

Maybe you will say, 'But, Oliver, a decomposing body is also an ecosystem, a kind of dying galaxy.'

Still, I felt an urge to touch Uncle Seymour.

He had such an unusual nose, a bulbous schnozzola with tributaries of purplish capillaries and a field of tiny craters.

I was trailing a fingertip along the cool bridge of Uncle Seymour's nose when Cousin Maureen slapped my hand, called me a ghoul, and shoved me away. As you will recall, I knocked into Aunt Rose and overturned a tray of scones.

'So what you're telling us,' Esther says, 'is you can touch people if they've kicked the bucket.'

'Preferably.'

'But we've *all* kicked the bucket,' Johnny says.

'Passed is not the same as dead,' I say, echoing Thelma. I scan the crowd for her. I want to commend her for her riveting reenactment.

Johnny rises, grabs hold of my shoulders, and sits me back down on the love seat. Then he plunks down in my lap and throws an arm around my shoulders.

Such proximity is horribly unpleasant.

'Get off me, Johnny.'

'Five more seconds.'

'Stop it,' Esther snaps at Johnny.

'Up yours,' he says to Esther. Then Johnny races through his countdown — 'five, four, three, two, one' — and stands up again. 'You need to get used to it. With practice, you can turn into a normal human being.'

Esther gets up from the couch and kicks Johnny in the shin. 'Maybe, doofus, we don't all want to be *normal*,' she says.

'Look, if he acts like a freak here, kids will sh*t on him just like they did back in America.'

Rest assured, Mother and Father, that Johnny

54

is speaking figuratively. Nobody actually ever defecated on me (though, as I said earlier, I *was* urinated on).

Three costumed boys standing nearby must have been watching because one of them, a clown with lipstick and a line of pompoms down his front, yells, 'Pile on!' and then they all jump on the love seat. They squirm and wiggle on top of me. Their touch is horrendous, their weight excruciating, and their body odor torture. I almost expect my lungs to deflate, my limbs to snap, and my brain to lapse into a coma.

'Get the f*ck off him!' Johnny yells.

A shoulder blade presses against my face, an elbow strikes me in my side, and a knee jabs me in the groin. I whimper.

Johnny pulls off two boys, a vampire and a scarecrow, and then yanks the white-faced clown off by the boy's curly red hair (his real hair, not a wig).

I pant as the clown yells at Johnny, 'Cool it, assh*le!'

A Halloween song, 'Monster Mash,' plays on the hi-fi. The singer sings about a graveyard smash as Johnny balls up his fist and punches the clown in his middle pompom. The clown doubles over and falls to his knees. His face distorts, his mouth gapes, and his fingers claw at the floor. He has the wind knocked out of him (medically speaking, his diaphragm has gone into spasms, thus preventing him from inhaling).

Half a dozen do-gooders rush over.

'No fighting!' they yell.

Reginald Washington carries his little bullhorn.

'Have you no shame!' he thunders into it. 'This is a time of merriment and celebration, and punks like you always ruin it for the rest of us.'

Thelma and Esther accompany us home after Johnny is expelled from the Halloween party. We walk on a street whose name, coincidentally, is Boo Radley Road. It is nine o'clock. The full moon shines and stars twinkle. Both the moon and the stars stay in the exact same place every night. I want to say to Zig, 'Change the darn backdrop, will you?' Every decade or two, he apparently does change the arrangement of stars, but we are not due for a new backdrop for several years to come. Forget, however, about trying to locate Draco, Andromeda, Canis Major, Leo, and other earthly constellations: the stars over Town follow different patterns. One of my projects is to map them and create a new system of constellations. Frankly, I am surprised no other townie has thought of doing this.

'Is the sky a trompe l'oeil?' I ask Thelma and Esther as we stroll down a sidewalk lit by streetlamps with round moonlike bulbs sitting atop their stems. Zig turns the lamps on at dusk and turns them off at our curfew of midnight, whereupon the starry sky becomes easier to see. I often scan it at night from atop the Frank and Joe.

'A trump what?' Thelma says.

'An optical illusion,' I say, but she and Esther

do not understand. 'Maybe Zig hangs a backdrop in the sky to reassure us, to make us think we live in an environment like the one we knew in America.'

'This place is big on illusion,' Thelma says.

We all stop and look into the sky. I think I spot a falling star (in other words, a meteoroid), but in half a second the blip is gone.

Esther says we have the illusion that everything stays the same here, that the buildings around us do not age. Yet the buildings do slowly change over time, she says. Twenty-five years from now, they will have gradually transformed to respect the architectural norms of the day. 'We change too,' she says. 'Townies who arrived here twenty-five years ago are different from newbies who came last month, like you and Johnny.'

'In what way?' I ask.

'You know more things,' Esther says.

'Like what?' I say.

Thelma answers: 'Well, you know about stars like Farrah Fawcett Majors and her bionic man. You know what a light saber is and a lava lamp. You know the words to 'How Deep Is Your Love?' and 'Stayin' Alive.' And you know the names of the brothers and sisters on *The Brady Bunch.*'

'I do not know any of these things,' I tell Thelma.

'Boo is an exception to the rule,' Esther says.

'Johnny probably knows,' I say. I look for him. He walks far ahead by himself, with my ghost sheet tied around his neck. For an instant, he reminds me of myself back in America because I was such a loner. I am at ease with solitude, but I do not believe Johnny is. His present solitude, therefore, is much sadder than my former.

'Is your friend okay?' Esther asks me.

I say I do not know. At least, because of his newborn status, he will not be punished for fighting. Newborns are allowed to make blunders for their first six months, whereas the clown who piled onto me will face the do-good council and be grounded in his dorm room for a day or two.

'It's Johnny's American birthday,' Thelma says. 'Birthdays are hard on newbies 'cause they don't turn fourteen. Besides, first months are always hard. My first months, I was a mess. So let's give poor Johnny time to come around.'

'What about you, Esther?' I ask. 'Were you a mess when you arrived?'

Esther tosses her big hair out of her eyes. 'Oh, I was ever so grateful.' Here she clasps her hands against her chest and switches her voice to a higher pitch. 'Thank you, dear Zig, for giving me an afterlife.' She places her palms together in prayer and adds, 'But, my all-powerful, all-knowing deity, does this prepubescent freeze mean I'll never have a real pair of knockers?'

Thelma lets out a whoop of laughter.

As you know, I do not whoop, chuckle, or giggle, but I do crack smiles. Hence, a smile is cracked.

'Hey! Hey!'

'Slow down!'

'Come back here!'

Our merriment is interrupted by shouts in the

night. It is Johnny. He runs toward us, in the all-out sprint he was famous for as a member of the Helen Keller track team. He is chasing a boy on a ten-speed. The cyclist zooms past, and I turn and watch him speed away from us and from Johnny. Under the streetlamps, I see the cyclist has brown hair. And big ears.

Johnny runs past us. With his black mask and flapping white cape, he looks like a superhero. He tries to catch up to the bicycle, but his effort is in vain. He comes to a sudden stop under a streetlamp, and the girls and I hurry toward him. Before we reach him, he turns and jogs back to us. He pants because his five-week coma has left him less physically fit.

He grabs a fistful of my T-shirt and bounces on his toes. Behind his Zorro mask, his eyes are wild.

'Holy f*ck, Boo, it was him!'

Johnny Henzel drew my portrait in sixth grade while we and our classmates at Lakeview Elementary sat under our desks waiting for the roof to be ripped off the school. A tornado had been spotted in Cook County that day. The sky outside had turned sickly green, and winds were howling. We heard the wind clearly because in weather like this the windows were kept open so they would not blow in and injure us with flying glass.

As my classmates and I took refuge under our desks on the dusty wooden floor (what a slapdash job the janitors had done), Oscar Stanley and Fred Winchester wondered aloud about deadly tornadoes that had struck the state in the past. I told them about a twister that had stormed through the county decades before, torn the roof off a town hall, and sucked away a town councillor, who was found three days later, at the bottom of a pond a mile away.

'He was wearing only his underwear,' I said. 'His other clothes had been ripped from his body.'

Mr. Proman stuck a ruler under my desk and poked me in my ribs. 'Shut your fat trap, Mr. Dalrymple,' he said, because Andrea Dolittle and Patsy Hyde were whimpering from fear. Poor

Andrea Dolittle was known to vomit unexpectedly (for instance, she upchucked during the testing of our blood types).

Johnny Henzel sat in front of me that year. It was the first year of elementary school that he and I were in the same class. We did not talk much to each other. In any case, I paid my peers little more mind than I paid other bland objects in the classroom, like a blackboard eraser or a wastepaper basket. The one thing of interest I had noticed about him was the double crown atop his head. A double crown, according to Grandmother, meant two separate spirits inhabited a person's body. Hogwash, of course. (Does Grandmother still believe her dachshund puppy is the reincarnation of Uncle Seymour because of a shared fondness for rum-and-raisin ice cream?)

Under his desk, Johnny held a sketch pad and a pencil. As the winds roared and Andrea, Patsy, and several others girls shrieked and sniveled and Mr. Proman walked the rows of desks growling, 'Silence!' Johnny Henzel whispered to me, 'Can I draw you?'

I consented. If a tornado did demolish the school and kill me, the sketch might survive and serve as a record of my final moments and a memento for you to cherish, Mother and Father. (Perhaps you have a similar memento today, such as that photograph of me aboard the *Spirit of Alaska*.) It felt odd to pose stock-still for a sketch, however. In fact, no classmate of mine had ever looked at me with such genuine interest as Johnny did that day. As his pencil scraped across the page, I felt the unease — albeit a milder version — that I feel when somebody touches me, so after a while I asked if I might close my eyes.

'I'm done with the eyes,' he replied.

I wondered if he would sketch an unflattering caricature. Maybe he would draw me as the ghostlike apparition crossing the bridge in Edvard Munch's *The Scream* (that hysterical fellow and I share a pointy chin). But after forty minutes were up and the principal came on the public address system to announce that the tornado had swept out of the county, Johnny showed me his drawing and it was no caricature. It was, in fact, a good likeness of me, a boy crouching under a desk and waiting patiently for his life either to end or to carry on. I stared at myself, at my wispy hair, my triangular face, and the dark circles under my eyes. 'You have talent, Johnny Henzel,' I said.

He shrugged and closed his sketch pad. I thought he would offer me the drawing, but he did not. I never saw it again.

Now, two years later, Johnny Henzel again sits on a floor with a sketch pad and pencils, which I picked up at his request from a nearby warehouse using the coupons we townies receive to buy supplies. This time, however, the floor is the roof of the Frank and Joe, and the sky is not tornado-green but rather the usual gray covered in a sheet of clouds. Johnny, the temperamental artist, described it earlier as a sea of fire-extinguisher foam.

As he draws, he talks about secret tunnels to

63

America, the so-called portals that supposedly lead us back home. He heard about them from portal seeker Harry O'Grady, the boy who lives across the hall from us. 'You should be out looking for portals, Boo. That's a science experiment worth doing.'

'I'm not sure it's a science, Johnny. I think it's more like wishful thinking.'

I examine the glass window in the shed atop our building. The glass has completely grown back. The entire gestation period of the window's birth was thirty-one days — about the length of an earthly month. I want to test again to see if I obtain the same result twice, so I take my hammer and strike it against the glass till the window again shatters. Johnny glances up briefly at the noise, and I go into the shed and use a whisk broom and dustpan to sweep up the shards.

When I come out, I remind Johnny of the sketch he did of me during the tornado drill and ask him whatever became of it.

He shrugs.

I tell Johnny that Mr. Plumb, our principal at Helen Keller, should have placed his sketch of me in the school lobby instead of my yearbook picture. I looked more like me in his sketch than I did in my photo. This is a compliment, but Johnny does not reply. His eyes focus on his page. His brow furrows. He licks the tip of his pencil.

My roommate has not showered in days and smells like fried onions. I mention this, and he replies, 'Don't stand too close, then.'

'Did you not realize,' I say, 'that the name Oliver is an Irish Gaelic noun meaning 'he who does not stand too close'?'

He ignores my lighthearted banter because he is concentrating on his drawing. This time, of course, he is not drawing me. In a few days, we are to have a meeting with the do-good council from Eleven, and he will bring along what he calls a 'wanted-dead-or-alive poster.'

Last night, Johnny had another nightmare about our killer. He woke up yelling at around three o'clock, a scream so earsplitting it seemed to pierce every wall, brick, and floorboard at the Frank and Joe. I scrambled out of bed, clicked on the light, and tried shaking him awake, my heart thumping so fast I expected its hole to whistle. Johnny stared up at me, eyes bulging, mouth agape, screams still coming. I had never slapped a person in my life, but I slapped Johnny — so hard I left an imprint of my palm on his face.

He did not want to talk much about his nightmare then, or this morning. I try again. 'What happened in your dream, Johnny?' I say nonchalantly as I examine my glass shards, which are all the same size, a half inch in diameter.

Johnny stops drawing. He looks up at the mackerel sky (the holy mackerel sky, ha-ha) and then back down at me. 'You really want to know?' he says.

I nod.

'Well, Gunboy was chasing me in Woodfield Mall. He was taking potshots at me but kept missing. He cornered me in that store by the food court that sells beanbag chairs. Then he gave me an ultimatum. He'd let me go if I could explain why I loved life.'

'How did you do that?'

'I told him about Rover, what I love about my dog. His bloodshot eyes and fishy breath, his big sighs and meaty paws. How he was proud to be a paper-dog delivering the *Tribune*. And how he read the comics and wanted his own strip like Marmaduke.'

'Did Gunboy let you go?' I ask.

'If he'd let me go, you think I'd be screaming my f*cking head off?'

'I suppose not.'

'No, Gunboy said my story was crap and he was doing me a favor blasting it out of my brain.'

Curious, I ask to see his dead-or-alive poster.

He hands me his sketch pad. 'Ring a bell?'

I do not recognize the face from my four days in eighth grade. If the boy had just started at Helen Keller on the Tuesday of that first week, I probably did not notice him. Maybe he was even in seventh grade. Or, more likely, the boy who Johnny sees in his nightmares is not the boy who shot us at all. This Gunboy he sees may be purely a figment of his own imagination.

In Johnny's sketch, Gunboy's face has misaligned features, as though his head were sliced down the middle and glued back together, but not quite evenly. One eye higher than the other. A crooked nose. Big ears out of kilter. Wild, tousled hair.

'He has empty eyes like David Berkowitz.'

'Who?' I ask.

'Son of Sam, Boo. You *have* heard of Son of Sam, right?'

'The madman who shot people in New York.'

'*Thirteen* people.'

You turned off the news, Mother and Father, whenever stories of violence aired. 'Our ears are too sensitive,' you often said, Mother. So I never learned much about Sam and his son. In any case, news stories were of interest to me only when they revolved around science — fresh observations about the atmosphere of Saturn's moon Titan, for example.

Johnny, however, read about David Berkowitz in the newspaper. 'The guy was a lunatic. He said a neighbor's bloodhound was possessed by a god who told him to shoot people. A f*cking nutcase, man. He should have gotten the death penalty.'

Johnny stares at his sketch. 'Gunboy's like the Grandson of Sam.'

'If Gunboy is here,' I say, 'Zig was sleeping on the job.'

Johnny scrambles to his feet. '*F*cking Zig!*' he yells at the clouds. He bounces on his toes and swings his fists at the air. '*Don't you know what the hell you're doing, you son of a b*tch?*'

I try to lighten the mood. 'Maybe our Zig was the actual god inside Mr. Berkowitz's blood-hound.'

'Huh?'

I adopt the voice of a cartoon dog with a lisp. 'Excu*the* me, *thon* of *Tham*, I'm *Thig* and I order you to a*thathi*nate the people of New York *Thity*.'

I am not normally this playful. Maybe Zig has altered my personality to better suit my surroundings.

Johnny stops shaking his fists at the clouds. He glances at me with a startled look. Then he bursts out laughing.

'What i*th tho* funny?'

He laughs so hard his eyes tear up. He wipes them with his fingers. This is the first time Johnny Henzel has laughed since his passing. I feel prouder than the time I increased the pH of my urine by consuming citrus fruits.

Consequently, a smile is cracked.

Esther Haglund decides to call our killer *Gumboy*. During the meeting with the do-good council from Eleven, she draws on her notepad a quick 'dead-or-alive' sketch in which Gumboy resembles a smaller, younger version of the clay figurine Gumby. Son of Gumby, I suppose.

She is trying to keep the mood light.

Esther does not sit on the council, but she is here for moral support while Johnny tells the council about our deaths at the hands of Gunboy, and she is also an eyewitness to his recent sighting of a boy who looks like our killer.

The council meets at the Sophie in what seems to be the principal's office. We are seated around a rickety board table with cloudy plastic glasses of water set before us. Johnny, Esther, and I are on one side, and on the other sits the council: president Reginald Washington, vice president Elizabeth 'Liz' McDougall, secretary Thelma Rudd, treasurer Arthur 'Arty' Hollingshead, and reporter Simon Pivot. On the walls are taped posters from past elections of council members. The poster for the president reads, WASHINGTON = JUSTICE FOR ALL.

By chance, Reginald is talking about justice, but today he does not have his bullhorn to stress certain words. 'In my humble opinion, our heaven is founded on justice,' he says, 'the justice of providing a child who lived only thirteen years with a normal life span.' Reginald talks with his hands, like a boy making shadow puppets on a wall. His hands are piebald — brown with white spots. I would like to ask him about his vitiligo — does he believe it to be autoimmune? — but Thelma has instructed me not to bring it up. He is sensitive, she told me. People sometimes call him 'the Dalmatian.'

'Heaven has never harbored a true murderer,' Reginald says. 'Personally, I'm not convinced the boy you saw, Mr. Henzel, is your killer. The eyes can play tricks. But if you do discover your Gunboy lives here, we'll need to take measures to ensure he doesn't harm other townies. Our Zig isn't infallible. If he's mistakenly let through somebody who should have been barred entry, well, we may need to act ourselves to seek the justice you and Mr. Dalrymple deserve.'

'Do you have jails here?' I ask.

'We have the Gene Forrester,' Thelma replies. She is taking the minutes of the meeting on yellow foolscap and now slips her pencil behind her ear. 'But few townies get locked up. You got to do something real bad to go to the Gene, like stab a kid or break somebody's leg. If townies get caught stealing bikes, well, they just do community service.'

'What kind of service?' I ask.

'Mopping floors, cleaning toilets, chopping potatoes in the cafeteria.'

'That ain't enough for Gunboy!' Johnny cries. He holds up his dead-or-alive poster for all to see. 'He's pure evil. You can't just have him cleaning the can.'

'I understand your anger,' vice president Liz McDougall says. Zig prevents dental cavities but, sadly for Liz, does not correct buckteeth. 'But our council doesn't usually deal with offenses more serious than fistfights, bullying, and theft.'

Treasurer Arty Hollingshead speaks, and as he does, I wonder about the need for a treasurer in a heaven that adopts a coupon-and-barter system instead of money. Arty says the council may have to consider a very serious jail sentence if Gunboy is discovered. 'Apart from Zig,' he says, 'there's nobody looking out for us up here, so we must look out for each other and decide what's right and what's wrong.'

As the council members talk, Johnny keeps running a hand up and down the basset hound decal on his T-shirt, which I found for him at a clothing warehouse. He strokes the decal in the same way he used to stroke the back of drooling Rover during his morning paper route.

To stop the conversation, Reginald holds up a hand as a traffic cop would. He suggests that Johnny and I go on a bicycle trip to the infirmaries located in the other zones of Town. Even though Johnny spotted the alleged Gunboy in our own zone, that person, Reginald points out, does not necessarily live nearby. 'He may reside in Three, or as far away as Six,' Reginald says. As council president, Reginald will draw up an official letter allowing us to check infirmary records to see who was reborn on or around the same date I was. Perhaps we will find Gunboy or even another eighth grader who died in Gunboy's attack. With assistance from local councils, we can interview any relevant child. Even if we do not locate an actual student from Helen Keller, we could come across a recent newbie from Illinois who might provide key information on our killer — a name perhaps, or a motive. After all, our killings must have made news headlines.

'To make things easier with the other councils and the infirmaries,' Thelma says, 'why don't I travel with you boys? As a gommer myself, I might be of service.'

'I may as well go too,' Esther says. 'Because if you find Gumboy, you gommers will need somebody with a level head — so you don't rip off *his* head.'

Reginald looks across the table at Johnny and me. He wants to know what we think of the road trip. I am game, not because I especially want to confront the mysterious Gunboy, but rather because I want to see more of heaven, to verify how things operate in the different zones.

When I answer Reginald, I look at Johnny. 'I enjoy travel,' I say.

Johnny's forehead is sweaty from nerves, but because I badgered him into showering this morning, at least he does not smell of fried onions. He nods at me. 'If we catch Gunboy,' he says to the council, 'me and Boo should be the ones deciding what punishment that pr*ck gets. Can you promise me that?'

The council members exchange glances.

'We can promise you,' Reginald says, 'that the punishment will fit the crimes.'

Zig gives us no direct guidance. He makes no official announcements. He does not appear in the holy mackerel sky and shout through a bullhorn, '*Do not swipe another townie's bike!*' or '*No food fights in the cafeteria!*' But if we townies delve into the matter of guidance further, we will realize Zig directs us by means of inclusion and omission — in other words, the things he delivers and the things he withholds.

For example, if we stop by a supply warehouse on a delivery day, we will find freshly arrived bars of soap and bottles of shampoo. Zig is telling us to wash our bodies and hair. But we will not find deodorant, mouthwash, or perfume, which he must consider unnecessary. We will find blue jeans and sweatshirts, but no dress pants or tweed jackets. We will find typewriters, but no printing presses or photocopiers.

We will find sports equipment, musical instruments, paperback novels, and vinyl records. The items may look secondhand — some baseball bats are chipped, some books dog-eared, and some albums scratched — but these items tell us something nonetheless. They tell us what Zig deems valuable. In this way, they are our guides.

Johnny, Thelma, Esther, and I are thinking of Zig on the first morning of our road trip when we stop to visit a museum set up in the Guy Montag Library. It is known as Curios (rhymes with 'Cheerios'). 'The items on display are things we think Zig let slip through by accident,' Thelma tells us as we park our bicycles and tie ribbons to their handlebars. (Esther is one of the very few townies to actually *own* a bike. Hers is a smaller model that a bike mechanic redesigned especially for a little person. It is painted pink and even has pink streamers and a pink basket.)

Our group heads up the library stairs to the exhibition space on the top floor. Thelma leads the way. As the oldest townie among us (in heaven years), she likes to chaperone. By the time we reach the third floor, she is winded. 'Doggone stairs!' She pants and dabs her forehead with a tissue.

Curios is laid out with a series of small rooms displaying objects in glass showcases, which appear to be aquariums turned upside down. The first object we see on display is a can of corned beef. The product is in an oblong tin. Attached to its side is a simple key used to open the tin. Corned beef is a curious object because Zig sends us only vegetarian food.

'Oh, wow! Far out!' Esther says. 'I'm so moved I feel faint. Somebody catch me.' (Another example of true irony.)

'Oh, hush up,' Thelma says, peering so close to the aquarium that she leaves a shiny nose print on the glass. 'I'm feeling homesick. You wouldn't believe how many corned beef sandwiches I ate in my day.'

'I *would* believe,' Esther says, but Thelma ignores her.

'It's so far from real meat it might as well be vegetarian,' Johnny points out. 'It tastes like a mix of roadkill and Jell-O.'

Thelma reads aloud the typewritten index card taped to the side of the aquarium. The card claims nobody knows where the word 'corned' comes from. 'This popular luncheon meat,' the card says, 'contains no corn.'

'The word 'corn' once referred to any coarse particles,' I say. 'In this case, the particles were the coarse salt used to cure the beef.'

'How do you know this dumb stuff?' Johnny says, unimpressed, but I know Thelma is thrilled because I can see the gap between her front teeth.

Thelma starts to unpeel the index card from the glass. 'I should introduce Oliver to Peter Peter, the curator,' she says.

'Peter Peter?' Johnny says.

'His real name's Peter *Peterman*, but people call him Peter Peter.'

'He's a square, but Thelma thinks he's a dreamboat,' Esther says. 'He's the real reason we're here, isn't it, Thelma?'

'Is he is or is he ain't my baby?' Thelma says in a singsong. She tells me to follow her, and she and I head off, leaving Johnny and Esther behind. As we walk through the halls, I glance at other items on display. I see a collection of batteries (D, C, and AA), an avocado-colored rotary telephone, a policeman's nightstick, and a radio, which must pick up only static because there are no radio stations in Town.

We come across the curator next to a small tank of sea monkeys. He is setting up a poster explaining that sea monkeys are in fact brine shrimp, which are closely related to seahorses.

'Hi there, old boy,' Thelma says. ('Old boy' is a term of endearment that townies use for boys who have lived here for forty-five years or more.)

Peter Peter does look older, since he has wispy hairs above his lip and more musculature than, say, I do, which is not a difficult feat. I assume, however, that he had lip bristles and muscles on the day he arrived here. Some say old-timers are wiser, given the number of years in heaven they have under their belts.

'I'd like you to meet Oliver Dalrymple,' Thelma says to Peter Peter. 'He's a newbie.'

We nod hello, and I say, 'I was unaware Town was home to brine shrimp.'

'We do receive occasional nonhuman life,' Peter Peter says. 'A kitten, a budgie. My personal favorite was Lars, the gerbil that came to heaven in a crate of tennis balls.'

'Oh, he was such a sweet little fella,' Thelma says. 'Remember how he used to stamp his hind legs when he got all excited?'

'Yes, that was a kind of mating dance, except the poor boy had no ladylove.'

Peter Peter stares at Thelma. 'What a tragedy,' she says.

They are possibly flirting, but I am no expert on such matters. I interrupt them with the etymology of 'corned beef.'

'Of course,' Peter Peter says, bouncing his palm off his forehead. 'The word 'corn' meant any kind of crop or grain, not only the maize of American Indians. So it makes sense the word refers to anything grainy — like salt.'

'I am almost certain about the etymology,' I tell him. 'How unfortunate that Zig sends us no encyclopedias or dictionaries to verify such things. Unless reference books are among the curious objects in your collection.'

Peter Peter shakes his head. 'No dictionaries or encyclopedias. At least not yet. But new unusual objects appear all the time, so perhaps a full-edition Webster's dictionary will slip through one day. I can only hope.'

Thelma tells Peter Peter that I have a keen interest in science. 'Maybe you could use an assistant,' she suggests.

'Science?' Peter Peter says. 'Well, do I have a treat for you!' He asks Thelma and me to wait for him while he goes to his office on the other side of the hall to fetch something. After he trots off, we notice that the visitors who were giggling around a nearby showcase have dispersed, and the object within is now revealed.

Thelma edges toward the showcase. 'Is that what I think it is?' she says.

The object is a square plastic envelope the size of a saltine cracker.

'A condom,' I tell her. 'A sheath placed on the penis during intercourse as a method of birth control to prevent sperm — '

'Oliver,' Thelma interrupts. 'You don't need to give me no eddy-mology about that thing, okay.'

'I don't know the etymology of 'condom,' only its purpose.'

Peter Peter returns from his office wearing cotton gloves. He lays a magazine atop the case holding the condom display.

My heart flutters and hiccups — not literally, excuse the artistic flourish, Mother and Father. I am excited because what the curator laid before me is the magazine *Science*. Glory be, it is a recent issue, from October 1979.

'May I touch it?'

Peter Peter removes his cotton gloves and passes them to me. 'To keep oil from the fingers off the paper,' he says. My hands tremble slightly as I slip on the gloves. I wonder if the two of you latched on to a way to forward my favorite magazine to me here. An absurd thought, I know.

'When did it arrive?' Thelma asks.

'Just last week from Four,' says Peter Peter.

'Are there other issues?' I ask as I examine the magazine, whose cover girl is the beautiful ugly mug of a brown bat. The lead article talks about echolocation.

'Not of *Science*, but other magazines sometimes come in,' Peter Peter says. 'I have a *Life* from 1956, a few *National Geographics*, even a movie magazine from the thirties with the Scarecrow, Tin Man, and Lion on the cover.'

The librarian at Guy Montag had told me the only magazines usually delivered to Town are comic books, so such finds are indeed curious.

'I wonder if Zig is telling us something by letting these things through,' Thelma says.

'Possibly,' Peter Peter says. 'Or they may simply be an oversight on his part.'

I leaf through the pages. 'Look, an article on cryogenics,' I say.

'Cyro what?' Thelma asks.

'Cryogenics. You know, the popsiclization of death!' (Ha-ha.)

'Oh, Oliver, you look like a curious object yourself,' Thelma says.

I continue turning the pages, but my giddiness is cut short by Esther, who hurries toward us. Her face is grim. 'You better come quick,' she says.

'Johnny?' Thelma asks, and Esther nods. We all follow her back through the exhibition halls, past showcases containing prescription eyeglasses, a bottle of red wine (CHÂTEAU BEL-AIR, reads the poster), and a lunar globe. I am so worried that Johnny may have gotten into a fistfight again that I do not stop to examine the globe.

I see my roommate in front of a showcase in one corner of the room. Nothing looks out of the ordinary, at least not till we gather around him and I see his eyes. They are red and puffy as though he is having an allergy attack. His breath is also wheezy.

'What's wrong, Johnny?' I ask.

Esther says, 'Look in the case.'

The curious object, lying in its showcase on a white cushion, is a small revolver. It looks like a toy gun; if it were not deadly, it would even look cute. As you will recall, Mother and Father, Uncle Seymour bought one like this to protect himself after his bakery was held up.

'Goodness,' Thelma mutters, placing a hand on Johnny's shoulder. 'Come away from there,' she says, but Johnny brushes her hand off.

'When did this gun arrive?' I ask Peter Peter.

'A week ago, from Six. It can't fire, though. It has no bullets.'

'Johnny, this can't be the one,' I say.

'How do you know?' His voice is as hoarse as on his first days in Town. 'It looks the same, Boo. I swear to Zig it does. Just like the gun I see in my nightmares.'

'Guns all look the same,' Esther says. 'They're all horrid. Let's split, Johnny.'

She tries to slip her hand in his to pull him away, but he barks, 'No!'

We leave Johnny alone. At Thelma's suggestion, we go over to the doorway to the exhibition hall to wait for him, and then Thelma tells Peter Peter about Gunboy and our mission. We are interrupted by some visitors entering the hall, whom Peter Peter asks to avoid the display in the left-hand corner because 'that chap over there is repairing the showcase and needs space to work.'

As we wait, Peter Peter asks if I would be interested in a job at Curios. 'We could indeed use some young blood around here,' he says.

Despite my eagerness, I ask if we could speak of his job offer another time. 'I need to watch over my friend right now,' I say. I take off the white gloves and hand them back to him.

'Certainly,' Peter Peter says. He tells Thelma to drop by again soon for a lunch date and then bids us all adieu with handshakes before he heads back to work on his sea monkey exhibit.

From the doorway, the girls and I continue to watch Johnny. We see him only from the back. He does not move an inch. He does not make a sound.

'You'd think he was praying at a church altar,' Esther says. 'Like I used to do when I was Mormon in Utah, back when I gave a damn about Joseph Smith.'

'Who?' I ask, and she explains that Joseph Smith was the founder of Mormonism. In his backyard, the man dug up golden tablets that contained a god's invisible writings that only Mr. Smith could read. 'A crock of sh*t, I'm sure,' she says. 'But come to think of it, no more far-fetched than this place we ended up in.'

As I listen to Esther, I keep an eye on Johnny, on the double crown on the back of his head. When a visitor draws too close to my roommate, I call out, 'Give him space to work.'

Eventually Johnny turns and walks over to us. His eyes are no longer red. His face looks curiously serene.

'You ready, sweetie?' Thelma asks.

'Yeah, I'm ready,' Johnny says. 'I'm not scared no more. I'm ready to catch that b*stard.'

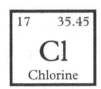

'Show some backbone,' Johnny says. 'Gunboy didn't steal your bike, Boo. He stole your *life*.'

Later in the day, as we finish our picnic lunch in Jerry Renault Park in Ten, Johnny decides I need boxing lessons to prepare for our battle with Gunboy — who, Johnny supposes, has rounded up a posse of goons we will need to defeat. My roommate and I have taken off our T-shirts. I look like the ninety-pound weakling I am, and Johnny, given his fluid diet in the hospital, is no Atlas either. He stands before me, jaw clenched, staring me meanly in the eye. 'Look fierce,' he says, and I furrow my brow.

'Boo, you look as fierce as an albino bunny,' Esther says. She is eating her cucumber sandwich on a patch of grass infested with weeds, which grow everywhere in Town. Dandelions must be heaven's official flower. Also, the grass is usually really long here because we have no mowers.

Johnny raises his fists to spar, and I think of the expression 'put up your dukes' and wonder again about etymology: how did a title of British nobility transform into a fist?

Johnny punches me in the shoulder, and I back away. He follows and punches me again. I look around for Thelma, who should return soon from the nearby cafeteria, where she went to fetch extra fruit for the road. 'Thelma wouldn't want us fighting,' I say.

'Forget your mama,' Johnny replies, 'and hit me back.'

'But I have no reason to hit you, Johnny.'

'I'm not Johnny, damn it,' he cries. 'I'm Gunboy and I want to snuff you out, you jockstrap.'

I raise my fists to humor him.

He bops around and calls me names like 'd*ckhead' and 'assw*pe.' I find the whole exercise pointless. I am about to respond, 'I'm rubber, you're glue,' to show how childish he is being, but then he cuffs me in the jaw — lightly, but still it hurts. I reason that the only way to end the silliness is to wallop him.

I ball up a fist and swing it at his jaw. *Baf!* The blow hurts my hand. Johnny staggers back. He bends over, hands on his thighs, wincing in pain. 'Sh*t,' he mutters, and then spits on the ground.

I see a red blob in the grass. 'Is that blood?'

'I bit my f*cking tongue.'

'Serves you right, Rocky,' Esther says.

Johnny's eyes water. He spits again. More blood. I ask him to open wide so I can examine the wound. He gapes his mouth.

'Incisors as sharp as a dog's. No wonder you punctured your tongue.'

He wiggles his tongue. The gouge is on one side of the tip. I must check the wound regularly so I can mark the healing time in my ledger.

Thelma arrives with a bag of oranges and bananas. 'For the love of Zig, what's going on here?' she yells, shaking her bag of fruit at us. 'Where are your shirts? Why's Johnny spitting up blood?'

Esther explains about the boxing lesson as Thelma tsk-tsks. 'For goodness' sake, I can't let y'all out of my sight for five minutes.'

'Why are you trying to change Boo into something he's not?' Esther says to Johnny. 'It won't work. We don't change here. We're stuck. Stuck for fifty years at thirteen.'

Thelma disagrees. 'We grow up in other ways, Esther.'

'I don't feel more mature than back in Utah,' Esther says. 'Except then I didn't believe in dorky Jesus, but didn't have the guts to say so.'

'That's maturity, honey,' says Thelma. 'The guts to say what you believe.'

'What about you boys?' Esther says. 'Feel any different than down in America?'

'I feel more social,' I say, 'but I fear it comes at the cost of a lower intelligence quotient.'

'Well, is it better to be dumber with friends or smarter without?' Esther asks.

'And you, Johnny?' Thelma says.

Johnny shrugs. He looks into the gray sky, perhaps checking for beauty in the cirrus clouds. 'We should hit the road,' he says. 'It's getting late.' He slips his T-shirt over his head, and I do likewise. We head back to our bicycles parked near the monkey bars, us boys walking ahead and the girls tagging behind.

'Kids at school thought you were weak, Boo,' Johnny tells me. 'But nothing could get to you. They'd tease you, punch you, steal your lunch, call you a geek and a f*ggot.'

A geek was originally a circus artist who performed morbid acts like biting heads off live chickens and swallowing frogs. I am obviously, given my vegetarian diet, no geek. As for f*ggot, I have no tendencies, homosexual or hetero-sexual, and since I am forever thirteen and dislike touching others, I may never develop any sexual interest — which, from what I hear about sex, is for the best.

Johnny went on: 'They'd trip you to the ground, and you'd lie there looking at something nobody noticed, like an anthill spilling out of a crack in the sidewalk.'

How I miss ants! What interesting creatures! Their pheromones, their metamorphosis, their caste system, their incredible strength.

'You were strong, man. Stronger than me. Stronger than any of us.'

'Thanks, Johnny,' I say. 'I try not to let the outer world wreak havoc with my inner one.'

Johnny stops me in the playing field. 'Can you do me a favor, Boo?'

'A favor?'

'When we catch Gunboy, can you be strong?' He assumes his boxer pose, dukes raised.

I nod in agreement.

'Because I'm not sure *I'm* going to be.'

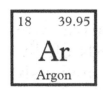

That night, we stay in the Jim Hawkins dormitory. The dormitories in Town always have a few empty rooms available to accommodate visitors. We are in Ten, a zone that looks no different from Eleven. It has the same buildings, which resemble junior highs from cities and towns across America.

Our little group dropped by the infirmaries in both zones earlier this afternoon, but their records showed no births on or around September 7, 1979, the date of my passing.

I enjoyed visiting the infirmaries because I could chat with the nurses on duty about healing times of broken and fractured limbs and collarbones. At the Mary Lennox Infirmary, we were permitted to explore the rebirthing room for a few minutes. I was struck again by how plain — and, frankly, non-magical — a rebirthing bed looked. Johnny and I pulled back the covers, peeked under the mattress, and slid underneath the bed, but we found nothing out of the ordinary.

By nine thirty, the four of us are exhausted from cycling and walking all day, and are in Esther and Thelma's guest room wearing our pajamas, which we have carried with us in our knapsacks. Thelma is applying a bandage to a blister on Esther's foot. She tells us she plans to courier a letter to the gommers to say we will attend their meeting scheduled a few days from now in Six. Meanwhile, I am writing about our adventures in my ledger at the desk, and Johnny is flipping through a map of heaven that the do-good council gave us. Because heaven has no printing presses, all maps are hand-drawn. The maps are in a spiral binder, each page devoted to one zone. They are approximate since heaven has no helicopters to fly over the terrarium to take the true lay of the land.

Thelma tells Johnny he would make a fine mapmaker because he likes to draw. She is always trying to find Johnny and me an occupation. As newbies, we are not required to work for our first six months in heaven, but after that, we need to settle on some part-time job. Cook, librarian, teacher, nurse, tailor, barber, launderer, courier, bike mechanic, and window washer are a few of the positions available. Townies tend to rotate in and out of different jobs.

'I wanna be a portal seeker,' Johnny says. 'I wanna find a tunnel back to America and go on a haunting.'

According to portal seekers, a townie can return to his hometown and 'haunt' his loved ones.

'Don't be gullible, Johnny,' Esther says. 'There's no such thing as a portal.'

'You don't know that,' Thelma replies. 'Maybe we ain't found one yet, but they could exist.'

'I hear some kids have found portals but don't want to tell the rest of us,' Johnny says. 'They want to keep their finds a secret so only they can go on hauntings.'

Esther says one idiotic portal seeker tried throwing himself down his dorm's garbage chute. He was convinced that our trash tumbled back to America.

'Garbage chutes are too narrow to climb into,' I say. 'That's an old wives' tale.'

Thelma corrects me: 'An old *girls'* tale is what we say here.'

'Last week, I saw a kid climb into a clothes dryer and inspect the lint drawer for a portal,' Esther says. 'I wanted to slam the door shut and turn the machine on, but I didn't because I'm a do-gooder in training.'

'Yes, honey, you're pure goodness,' Thelma says, patting Esther's bandaged foot.

'If I found a portal,' Johnny says, 'I'd visit Rover and take him on long walks. My sister must be taking care of him. She loves animals. We were supposed to open a pet shop together. We were going to call it Zoo. When I was in my coma, Brenda kept saying, 'Don't die, Johnny. We got to open Zoo.' '

If she went on a haunting, Thelma says she would visit her three siblings, Antoine, Ralph, and Shawna. 'They're in their twenties and thirties now. They might have kids of their own. I could babysit them. A ghost babysitter who'd tell them ghost stories. The kids would love me.'

'I'd haunt my old church,' Esther says. 'I'd fly over the pulpit and tell all those pious suckers that Osmond Family albums are the devil's work.'

As a ghost, Johnny says, he would also haunt any members of the Manson family still not in jail. He would scare them into becoming honorable citizens — crossing guards, accountants, librarians, school nurses. Thelma and Esther nod, since news of the Manson family's grisly activities has spread to Town through the mouths of newbies.

Johnny decides to draw Thelma and Esther posed as ghosts. He drapes them in bedsheets, their faces peeking out, but because the sheets have a blue trim, the girls look less like ghosts and more like Mother Teresa. The girls sit side by side on one bed, and Johnny sits on the other, drawing them on the sketch pad he brought along in his knapsack.

While he works, Thelma sings us Cole Porter songs. When she starts in on 'Miss Otis Regrets,' she stops after the first verse and says she forgot the lyrics. She switches to 'Too Darn Hot.' Thelma is telling a white lie: she did not forget the lyrics. As you know, Father and Mother, in the second verse of 'Miss Otis Regrets,' Miss Otis draws a gun and shoots her lover down. Thelma does not want Johnny to hear a macabre story about a shooting, because she is a real do-gooder and a real friend to Johnny. And to me, too, I suppose.

By the time Johnny finishes his sketch, all four of us are yawning. We go off to the bathrooms in the corridor to prepare for bed.

In the boys' room, Johnny brushes his teeth after sprinkling his toothbrush with baking soda, which is kept in a box on the edge of the sink.

This is a good sign that he is perking up; he does not always clean his teeth without my urging. While he brushes, I strip down and slip into a shower stall. I always wash thoroughly before bed, especially given the cycling we did today. It is important to wash sweat and sebum from the body: even though things like cancer are absent from heaven, acne pimples, jock itch, and offensive odors are not.

When I come out of the shower, I take my towel from my knapsack and wrap it around my waist. I do not see Johnny and assume he went back to our room, but no, he is crawling on his hands and knees under the line of sinks. He is examining the piping and maybe wondering where our water supply comes from (I often wonder that myself).

'I'm checking for portals,' he says, trying to pry loose tiles from the wall under the sink using the arm of a nail clipper.

'If there were a portal here, somebody would have found it by now.'

'You don't believe in portals, do you?'

'Believing in portals is like believing in telekinesis. Until you bend a spoon with your mind, I can't believe.'

As I put my pajamas back on, Johnny says, 'You didn't say what you'd do on a haunting, Boo. Would you go see your folks?'

I rub my towel over my hair. I feel the lump at the base of my skull, which you, Mother, call my mathematics bump. You claim it helped me learn my times tables at age five.

I tell Johnny that if I went on a haunting, I

would deliver to you the book I am writing about my afterlife. However, I would not hang around long, because that would be cruel, would it not? It might give you hope, Mother and Father, that I would come back to life for good. But I would only be a ghost, not a real boy. I would never grow up. I would never go to MIT as Father wished; I would never work for NASA as Mother wanted.

I explain all this to Johnny, but he does not reply. He stays underneath the sink picking at the tiles. I go back to our room, hang my clothes in the creaky wardrobe, and climb into bed. Through the wall, I hear Thelma's whoop of laughter.

I often cannot fall asleep when I am overtired, but not tonight. I nod off in the blink of an eye (eyes, actually) with the desk lamp still on. This is a minor miracle.

Another minor miracle occurs a moment later.

Johnny comes flying into our room, yelling, 'Boo, Boo!' He yanks the blanket off me and pulls me out of bed by my pajama top, popping a button. 'Follow me!' he cries.

'You found a portal?' I mumble.

'No, but something almost as good.'

I follow him back to the bathroom. He hurries to the last sink and points into the basin.

'Look,' he whispers. 'A curious object.'

'Zig almighty!'

Sitting beside the drain is an insect at least two inches long. It has dark amber wings folded over its body and a black splotch on its pronotum (the plate covering its head and upper thorax).

91

'Is it a kind of roach?' Johnny says, leaning in close to the basin.

I nod. 'Zig must have a weird sense of humor. You know what this kind of cockroach is called?'

Johnny shrugs.

'Death's head.' I point to its pronotum. 'That black splotch is said to look like a death mask or a vampire's scowl.'

Johnny's face lights up as it has never done before in the hereafter. He lays a hand, palm up, in the sink, and the death's head (*Blaberus craniifer*) marches over his fingers and sits on his lifeline.

Johnny names the cockroach Rover in honor of his beloved basset hound. How did Rover the roach end up in heaven? Johnny concludes that the death's head did not *pass* in the sense of die but did pass through a portal connecting life in America with life in the afterlife. The bathroom sink may be a portal, he says, nodding confidently. I am less certain. I need more evidence before drawing such a conclusion.

We are in Thelma and Esther's room, where Johnny has placed Rover in a large margarine container he found in the dorm's kitchenette. He added an apple core, pieces of orange skins, and a potato peel as food.

Thelma tells us that though a gerbil, a kitten, and a budgie have all made their way to heaven, this to her knowledge is the first insect. 'Peter Peter is gonna be knocked for a loop!' she says.

Johnny puts his ear close to the margarine container. 'I can hear him. It's like he's whispering something to me.'

'It must be its wings rubbing together,' I say, although I do not hear anything.

'Rover will bring us good luck,' Johnny tells us. 'He'll help us hunt down Gunboy.'

Esther does not like insects. She squealed when we first showed her the death's head. 'If you ask me,' she says, 'that gross sh*t fly of yours is a jinx.'

Despite her warning, luck smiles on us in the first few days after the death's head joins our group. The sun shines brightly during this time. The skin of my companions turns browner, whereas mine, lacking melanin, remains ghostly pale (sunburns, by the way, do not exist in Town).

We make good progress during these days and visit four more zones (Nine, Two, Eight, and Seven). On the third day, in the rebirthing book at the Paul Atreides Infirmary in Seven, we come across the name of a newbie from Chicago who passed the day after me. Nina Mitchell. When we visit her at her dorm, she says she recalls little from the news reports other than 'Some kids got killed at a school.' When Johnny implores her to think harder, she makes a valid point: 'I'd remember more if a double-decker bus hadn't run me over the next day.'

'Don't get discouraged, son,' Thelma tells Johnny when we are leaving Nina's dorm. 'We're making headway.' She reminds us about the gommer meeting we will attend tonight. 'We should've gotten the gommers involved from the get-go,' Thelma says. 'If anybody can help us find a murderer, it's murder survivors.'

We pedal all afternoon toward Six, but go at a leisurely pace because Esther's legs are too short to cycle fast on her bike, which Johnny calls her 'pinkmobile.' Johnny in fact prefers to go slowly because then he can easily check the faces of oncoming cyclists. Three times already on our road trip, he thought he spotted Gunboy, but when he raced after the big-eared boy, he discovered that the cyclist was simply a look-alike.

We arrive at the infirmary in Six, which is called the Deborah Blau Infirmary. The building has cracked white pillars out front, which, Johnny says, make sense because they look like broken femurs, and the infirmary is where a townie with a broken leg would go. But as she gets off her bicycle, Thelma contradicts Johnny: 'The Deborah is different. It's not for broken bones. It's for broken souls.'

'Broken souls?' I ask as I tie my ribbon to my bike.

'Mental cases,' Esther says. 'The Deborah is for kids with mental problems.'

'An asylum?' I ask.

'Not exactly,' Thelma says. 'These kids don't have multiple personalities or think they're superheroes. They're just a little sad and confused. We even call them 'sadcons.' '

'*I'm* a little sad and confused,' Esther says. 'But do you see me checking in at this place for some R and R?'

'You're not sad and confused,' Thelma says.

'Sometimes I am,' Esther insists. 'But I don't mope around in my jammies all day like a sadcon.'

'What do you do when you're sad and confused, Esther?' I ask.

'I go on road trips with you mental cases.'

Johnny is fishing his margarine tub out of his

knapsack so Rover can also visit the Deborah. Without looking at us, he says, 'I used to see a shrink.'

After a pause during which Thelma, Esther, and I throw one another surprised glances, Thelma asks, 'What kind of shrink, honey?'

Johnny scratches his double crown. 'I can't remember exactly. His name was Harold. He had hairy nostrils and ears, which were really gross, but still he was a nice guy.'

'What did you talk to him about?' Esther asks.

'I don't remember much. But I used to show him my artwork. He was really into it, especially the abstract stuff.'

'But why did your folks send you to him?' Esther asks.

Johnny gives a jerky shrug. 'I guess I was a sadcon.' He heads up the lopsided steps of the infirmary, holding the margarine tub in front of him like a casserole he is bringing to a patient. He has punctured holes in the side and top of the tub so the death's head can peer out.

You never sent me to a psychologist, Mother and Father, but I was often asked to speak to Mr. Buckley, a school counselor who was worried I did not fit in. It was on his advice that I practiced friendship speeches in front of my mirror at home ('Hello, Jermaine Tucker. Did you watch the Cubs game yesterday? Whom did they play against?'). Mr. Buckley said I was a round peg and all the holes at Helen Keller were square, and he grew exasperated when I explained how to bisect a round peg and cut a square shape from it. 'Enough with the geometry!' he yelled, and I shut up because I dislike being yelled at. I am thankful you never hollered at me, Father and Mother.

When I saw Johnny around Sandpits or at school, he did not look sad and confused. To me, he looked like all the other boys at our school — confident, peppy, dreamy-eyed. Then again, I avoided looking too closely at my classmates.

We enter the Deborah and go to the reception desk. While Thelma explains our case to the clerk, I steal glances into the common room, where sadcons in their pajamas (as Esther predicted) are chatting or reading comic books. One boy is wearing a hat made out of twisted party balloons. These sadcons do not look different from the townies gathered in the ground-floor common room of the Frank and Joe, many of whom also don crazy hats they make themselves.

We head down the hallway to check the rebirthing book in the main office.

'Are only sad and confused thirteen-year-olds born at this infirmary?' I ask Thelma.

'No, any kind of person can be born here,' she tells me. 'Townies who check into the Deborah might have had serious mental problems back in America. Maybe even schizophrenia.'

'The word 'schizophrenia' means 'split mind,''
I say.

'Some of them claim they were schizo back in America,' Esther says, 'but I bet they're exaggerating just to get out of working.'

'Gunboy was crazy,' Johnny says. 'Maybe *he* checked in here.'

We stop dead in our tracks. Esther says, 'Good point.'

Thelma gives us permission to wander the floors of the patient areas while she checks the rebirthing book. 'But promise me, Johnny, that if you think you spot Gunboy, you won't lose your cool.'

'I'll be as cool as a cucumber,' Johnny says, smiling slyly.

I do not believe him.

'Cool as a jalapeño pepper is more like it,' Esther says. To Thelma she promises, 'We'll keep an eye on him.'

Thelma reminds us that we must contact the local do-good council if we come across our killer. 'It ain't up to you to dish out punishment.'

'I'll be good,' Johnny says. 'Cross my heart and hope to redie.'

As we walk down the halls of the Deborah, we peek into rooms where sadcons are reading in bed, staring out their window, or snoozing with earplugs stuffed in their ear canals. We wander around an inner courtyard filled with rose-bushes. We walk through the cafeteria (today's special: rigatoni) and also through an arts and crafts class where a dozen people are making sock puppets. (Esther says that instead of sock puppets the sadcons just need 'a good sock in the head.' Sometimes I wonder how she managed to pass her do-gooder training courses.)

Along the way, Johnny pulls his dead-or-alive poster from his backpack to show around. 'Seen this kid anywhere?' Nobody has. One sadcon we come across crouched in a stairwell says, 'He looks like me.' Nonsense. She is a redheaded girl mottled with freckles.

Johnny also approaches the do-good staff, again with no luck. Maybe only the most caring and kind do-gooders are posted at an asylum. They probably listen carefully to a sadcon's problems and lend helpful and heartening advice. I would not be able to hold down such a job because I have no wise advice to offer other than, 'Sadness and confusion can be fleeting. Wait awhile and maybe they'll wane.'

We trail up and down the hallways of the first two floors to no avail. After we are denied entry to the third floor (because the most serious mental cases reside there), Johnny decides to take Rover to the roof for some exercise. I follow him while Esther goes off to find Thelma.

The Deborah's rooftop affords a wide view of Six, the schools, the parks, the warehouses. We slip off our knapsacks and sit on the little concrete wall surrounding the roof edge. Johnny peels off the lid of the margarine tub (which he has taken to calling the roach's 'camper'), and the death's head climbs out and scurries along the wall.

'We're getting warmer,' Johnny says.

'I estimate eighty degrees,' I reply, squinting at the yellow blur of the sun hidden behind a cloud. 'But then again, it's always about eighty degrees in the afternoon in Town. I think I'll miss seasons. Back in Hoffman Estates, the leaves will be falling from the trees now.'

'I'm not talking about seasons, Boo. I'm

talking about Gunboy.'

I stare at my roommate. His irises are the color of old Lincoln pennies. 'How do you know we're getting close?'

'I feel it in my bones.' He rubs his bony knees. 'Maybe I'm some kind of divining rod that feels things others can't. Maybe I'm different from other kids.'

Because he looks so serious, I ask if he had this sixth sense back in America.

'Possibly. That's maybe why I was sad and confused.' After a pause, he adds, 'Do you remember everything about your old life, Boo?'

'I suppose so — unless Zig erased things I don't realize he erased,' I say. 'In general, I have a photographic memory. I even recall word for word the pages from our math textbook. Page seventy-two explained the Pythagorean theorem and how to find the length of the hypotenuse.'

'My memory's a bit shot,' Johnny says with an anxious look. 'But then, I got shot in the head, so some of my brain might be missing. Some of my past as well. Like the summer before I came here. I don't remember much of that. Just snippets here and there.'

We embarked on this road trip on the basis of Johnny's memory. Perhaps that was not very wise if his memory is shaky.

Rover returns from its jaunt and climbs onto Johnny's shoulder. 'Polly wanna cracker?' he asks as if the roach were a parrot. Then a grin spreads across his face. 'He's whispering again,' Johnny says.

I stare at the roach on his shoulder to see if it

is rubbing its wings or limbs together. It seems to be doing neither. 'What do you mean it is talking?' I say.

'I can hear his little voice mumbling.'

'It is not talking, Johnny.'

'I hear something.'

'You must have the ears of Rover the basset hound.'

'My word, is that an *insect?*' a voice says.

Johnny and I turn our heads and see a girl in pajamas coming up behind us. She is the freckly sadcon from the stairwell, who believed herself to be Gunboy's spitting image. Johnny pulls Rover off his shoulder and cups the roach in his hands to show the girl. I explain that the insect is a species of cockroach known as a death's head.

'Death's head!' the girl says, her eyes round as she stares at Rover. 'Well, that's the biggest sign Zig ever sent me.'

The girl sits between us on the wall circling the roof. She has hazel irises — green, yellow, spots of brown — the deep, busy eyes that remind me of gas planets in a far-off galaxy.

'Zig sends you signs?' Johnny asks.

'He sends us *all* signs, but not everybody knows how to read them.'

'What's my roach a sign of?'

The girl gives Johnny a sly half smile. 'A portal,' she says.

'Rover came out of a portal!' Johnny's eyes light up. 'The drain of a sink that leads all the way back to America.'

'A sink's no portal!' she exclaims. 'Are you crazy?'

'So where's there a portal then?' Johnny asks, still cupping the death's head.

The girl ignores him. She strokes the insect with a fingertip. 'You got wings,' the girl says to Rover. 'So you're a *real* angel, not frauds like the rest of us suckers.'

'Despite its wings, the death's head cockroach cannot fly or even glide,' I say, 'unlike the American cockroach, *Periplaneta americana*.'

The girl blinks at me. She has an orangey stain on the front of her pajama top, perhaps pasta sauce from lunch. The cuffs of her pajama bottoms are gray with dirt.

'Are you sad and confused?' I ask the girl. Johnny shakes his head to deter me.

'Huh?'

'Sad and confused.'

She looks skyward. 'Zig above, let me grow wings. Let me soar,' she calls out, her brow knitted.

'I wonder why people suppose their gods are circling high above in the clouds,' I say. 'Couldn't they just as easily be hiding in the molecules of, say, a rock or a tree or even a roach?'

The girl's toenails, I notice, are painted purple with what looks to be pastel crayons. The death's head crawls out of Johnny's hands and onto her lap. 'What a pretty baby,' she murmurs, bowing her head to study the death-mask blotch on the roach's pronotum. A spot near her crown is almost bald. Either she has had a hack-job haircut or she has been plucking individual hairs from that spot.

The girl suddenly looks up, astonished. 'Your roach here can talk,' she says.

Johnny says, 'You hear him too.'

'I can't hear what he's saying, but he's saying something.'

'Certain roach species can make a hissing noise,' I say. 'Perhaps that is what you are hearing.'

A whistle sounds, Esther's trademark trill like the call of a red-winged blackbird. I glance down and see Esther and Thelma waiting in the parking lot beside our bicycles. Thelma waves. 'Time to go, Johnny,' I say, nodding toward the girls.

Johnny lifts Rover gently from the girl's thigh and drops it into its camper. He snaps the lid on.

'See you around,' Johnny says to the girl.

She mumbles, 'Don't count on it.'

Johnny and I head toward the stairs. As we pull open the door to the exit, the sadcon girl shouts, 'May Zig be with you!'

As we walk down the stairs, Johnny says, 'That chick looks nothing at all like Gunboy.'

When we reach the ground floor, he turns to me. 'Holy sh*t!' he shouts, his face crumbling. He races back up the stairs.

Should I follow? His running shoes slap against the steps as he climbs higher. I assume he forgot something on the roof — his sketch pad, his pencils — though why so panicky?

I cut across the lobby (a stenciled poster reads, MY SADCON PROB IS NO CON JOB) and then leave the building through a side door and cross a stretch of lawn to the parking lot. Thelma and

Esther are already astride their bicycles. I wave, but they do not see me. They are looking up. Thelma yelps and throws her ten-speed to the ground. She runs toward the Deborah.

I glance up just as the redhead girl plummets headfirst off the roof. She makes no sound as she falls. Her arms and legs do not flail. Her body does not right itself. She falls as if she is already dead. I gasp and flinch, expecting a horrible thud and the crack of her skull hitting the ground. But no thud comes. No crack either. Instead, her body passes through the solid earth as though she just dived into a calm lake.

Thelma reaches the spot where the girl disappeared. She drops to her knees. I sprint over. Thelma is panting and repeating shrilly, 'Lordy! Lordy! Lordy!' Balled-up pajamas with an orange stain lie in a flowerbed of wilting black-eyed Susans. Thelma paws at the earth as though she might dig through the dirt and bring the girl back. Esther trots toward us in her ungainly run. I look up to see Johnny leaning over the edge of the roof. I fear that he, too, will leap. Never in my life have I screamed, but I do so now: '*No!*'

20	40.08

Ca
Calcium

'Rest in peace' is a common expression in our heaven for thirteen-year-olds. It is all-purpose: it can mean 'take care' or 'see you later' or 'all the best.' A townie has supper at the cafeteria, and before she heads off for an evening at the library, she says to her tablemates, 'Rest in peace.' I do not know how long this practice has been going on, but I never use the expression. After all, we are not resting here in heaven and we are not, for the most part, more peaceful than we were in America. (Note that I do not say 'up in heaven' and 'down in America,' as many townies do. Who is to say which direction is which?)

'Rest in peace' is also an expression townies say when somebody repasses.

'Rest in peace, Willa Blake,' sadcons and do-gooders from the Deborah say as they gather around the flowerbed where the girl from the roof disappeared. They have just buried her pajamas in the flowerbed and planted a colorful pinwheel on the spot. Every so often, the pinwheel twirls, and even though there is a slight breeze today, a patient pipes up to say that Willa herself is making it move.

My companions and I stand off to the side with our bicycles. Thelma wants us to stay awhile to show our respect. Johnny tells us he had a sudden hunch that Willa would harm herself. 'I raced back to the roof, but I got there too late,' he says.

The Deborah's manager, a short boy named Albert Schmidt whose baby-fat cheeks make him look ten years old, wants to know what Willa Blake said on the rooftop. 'Not that it makes much difference,' he admits. He tells us Willa had been talking about suicide for months.

'She talked about growing angel wings,' I say. 'And finding a portal.'

The asylum manager shakes his head. 'Oh dear,' he says. 'Willa was a portal seeker. She thought the portal back to America was suicide. Angels who kill themselves in heaven, she said, fly back to America as ghosts.'

'How come you let her on the roof then?' Johnny says, irate. 'Why didn't you tie that crazy chick to her bed?'

Albert says Willa in fact did not have roof privileges, but the staff cannot keep track of patients every hour of the day.

'If I was you, honey, I'd keep Willa's portal theory hush-hush,' Thelma tells Albert. 'If word gets out, we might have other portal seekers leaping from rooftops.'

When the asylum manager leaves, Esther tells me suicide is rare in heaven. 'Yeah, we have idiots, assh*les, and freaks up here, but nutcases who dive-bomb off buildings? No, they're scarcer than a tube of toothpaste.'

It is hard to commit suicide in heaven. When a person falls from a rooftop, he usually does not die. Yes, he sustains major injuries — broken legs and ribs, concussions and the like — but he survives and eventually recovers in an infirmary. But sometimes all the king's horses and all the king's men (forgive me for being fanciful) cannot put a townie back together again. Poor Willa Blake probably died outright because she landed squarely on her head. Here in heaven, a dead person vanishes in the blink of an eye. *Poof!*

I wonder where the freckly girl is now. Is she finally dead for good? Or is she in another level of heaven with worse plumbing, uglier buildings, and lumpier gruel, cursing her bad luck because she is not back in America after all?

'I'm sorry, but Zig is supposed to cure severe sadcons before they get here,' Thelma says, looking befuddled. I have noticed that she apologizes whenever Zig does something embarrassing or uncaring, as if she is to blame for his blunders.

'If Zig *is* a Mr. Fix-It,' Johnny says, 'he makes big freaking mistakes.' He is looking skyward, as though Zig is hovering overhead and watching the fine mess he made.

'What if Zig cured Gunboy?' I say. 'What if Gunboy is no longer psycho? Maybe he's now a normal boy who volunteers at a cafeteria, plays softball on his zone's team, and hopes one day to serve as a do-gooder.'

Johnny glares at me. I stare back, and when I finally blink, he says, 'You want to let him off the hook? Is that it? If you're wimping out, just go back to the Frank and Joe, okay?'

He looks at Thelma and Esther and sees in their faces that they, too, must have asked themselves the same question. They have probably even discussed it in private.

'Screw you all,' Johnny spits. 'I'll find Gunboy myself, and I don't care if he's now an angel giving harp lessons to do-gooders, I'll pound his head in with a brick.' He is shouting now: '*You hear me?*'

Mourners around Willa Blake's gravesite throw us annoyed looks because we are being disrespectful. Two girls in plaid housecoats, who were wrapped in each other's arms, stop their weeping and stare at us, aghast.

Johnny's cheeks burn as he slips his knapsack on and mounts his bicycle. Thelma says, 'Honey, let's get some advice tonight at the meeting, okay? Let's see what the gommers think we should do.'

Johnny does not reply. He pedals away furiously without a glance back. He almost collides with more of the Deborah's sadcons who are coming to pay their respects.

I watch him speed down the street, pass a brick school, and converge with other cyclists out today, regular townies not on a quest to settle scores.

Thelma squeezes my arm and says, 'Don't worry, Oliver. Everything will be hunky-dory.'

Esther mutters, 'Don't bet your afterlife on it.'

YOU DON'T HAVE TO FORGIVE, reads a poster hung in the room where the gommers are meeting at the Ponyboy Curtis School. The lettering is done in red glitter sprinkled over glue. A second poster, also sparkly, is placed below the first. It reads, BUT YOU CAN IF YOU WANT.

I half listen to Thelma explain the Gunboy story as I sit on a shabby sofa with stuffing coming out of the arms. Beside me sits Esther. Gathered around us are twenty-two gommers, some of whom may have forgiven their murderers and some of whom may have not.

Have I forgiven Gunboy? I am not sure. To me, he is as mysterious as Zig. Both are invisible to me. Zig works behind the scenes. Gunboy also did his work behind the scenes (or at least behind my back), so I find it hard to summon hatred or harbor ill will toward my killer. If Gunboy had shot you, Mother and Father, I could be merciless. I could pick up a brick, as Johnny suggested, and strike Gunboy's head again and again till his deranged mind spilled from his skull. But for my own passing, hatred is harder to drum up because here I am in a new world that is fascinating.

And, as I said earlier, what if Zig did indeed reform Gunboy? Then my grasp on the brick would be shakier.

I wish Johnny were here to tell our story himself, but he did not turn up at the Jack Merridew Dormitory, where we are to pass the night in Six, even though he has our itinerary with him. I left him a note in the room we are supposed to share in case he shows up later. It reads, 'Dear Johnny, when we find Gunboy, I promise to put up my dukes. Please come to the gommer meeting (see the map I drew on the back). Your friend, Oliver (a.k.a. Boo). P.S. I left you an orange in case you are hungry.'

My roommate dislikes schools, so he probably will not come. For him, walking into all these schools in heaven is akin to a boy who died in an airplane crash boarding jumbo jets forevermore in his afterlife.

As usual, Thelma is wearing her purple armband this evening as a sign of her do-goodism. She gestures a lot as she speaks, making wavy hand movements like a Trojan cheerleader. 'So Oliver and Johnny are in a darn pickle,' she says. 'Their killer may be in Town. If so, we townies have to decide what to do. As a gommer myself, I think we could use your advice.'

The gommers, seated on sofas, armchairs, and throw cushions spread across the wood-slat floor, barely moved a muscle or batted an eye as Thelma told our story. They still seem spell-bound. Some have their mouths hanging open. They remind me, in their patient excitement, of Rover the basset hound as he waited outside while his master delivered the *Tribune* at Sandpits.

A skinny girl with stringy hair speaks first. 'Hunt Gunboy down,' she says matter-of-factly, 'and drown him in a lake.'

For a moment nobody speaks. Then a boy says, 'Stab him in the gut.'

A slew of different ends for Gunboy is suggested, including 'Toss him off a bridge,' 'Poison him with arsenic,' and 'Push him in front of a subway train.'

Given the lack of lakes, bridges, arsenic, and subway trains in Town, I gather that the gommers are suggesting redeath penalties in line with their own murders. I look at Thelma seated beside me, expecting her to balk, but she does not. She just rubs her palms up and down her thighs as though wiping away sweat.

I glance at the glittery forgive/don't forgive posters. I am about to respond with irony, to say, 'Hey, you can forgive if you want,' but Esther speaks first.

'What if Johnny fingers the wrong kid?'

The gommer group leader, the girl who presumably was pushed in front of a subway train, asks, 'Why would he blame some innocent boy?'

Esther clenches a sofa cushion in her lap, and I fear she will swat a gommer with it. 'He never even *saw* his killer!' she shouts. 'He sees this kid only in his frigging nightmares!'

The boy who was probably stabbed insists a gommer's nightmares are always very telling.

'They're proof as far as I'm concerned,' he says.

The bridge boy cries, 'Hear, hear!' which is echoed by other gommers.

Esther ignores them and turns to me. 'Maybe Johnny's a little crazy, Boo,' she says, 'and doesn't know what the hell he's doing.'

The subway girl jumps in: 'The murdered are always a little crazy when they first come here. You can't understand. You aren't one of us.'

Esther says with an exasperated sigh, 'Oh, get over it already.'

Now all the gommers glare at her. Their faces look creepy and almost evil, as though they have just transformed into their own killers.

Thelma says, 'Esther, don't be rude.'

Esther huffs and then announces, 'I'm going for a pee.' She gets up from the sofa and asks me, 'Don't you have to pee too?'

Thelma always encourages us to use the facilities before we hit the road, so I nod even though I have no urge to urinate. Esther and I step around the gommers, who continue to give her defiant stares. When we are in the hallway, she tells me to follow her. She heads into the boys' room (because she is a feminist and deems separate rooms for boys and girls a form of segregation), then goes into a stall and closes the door. While she urinates, I wait at the sinks and wash my hands with a cake of glycerin soap.

'I'm serious about Johnny being a bit crazy,' Esther says from the stall. 'Was he always so weird?'

Weird? How strange that Esther considers *Johnny* the weird one. If eighth graders from

Helen Keller were asked which boy, Johnny Henzel or Oliver Dalrymple, was weirder, I would win the vote by a landslide. Any students choosing Johnny would have to be odd themselves — for example, a girl like Jenny Vasquez, who keeps in her pocketbook a zoo of plastic farm animals, which she often converses with.

I tell Esther I do not recall too much overt weirdness from Johnny, but then again, he and I had little contact. I can confirm he was not prone to fistfights, rude behavior, or spitball shenanigans at school.

Esther comes out of the stall and washes her hands. She is just tall enough to see herself in the mirror hung over the sink.

'We'd better find Johnny soon before he wreaks havoc,' she says.

'He won't wreak havoc,' I assure her.

She takes a paper towel from a stack on the sink, dries her hands, and then crumples the towel and throws it at me. 'How can I trust your instincts?' she says. 'You're biased because he's your friend.'

I pick up the balled-up towel from the floor and drop it in the wastebasket. 'As a junior scientist and researcher, I promise you I always remain unbiased.'

She raises her eyebrows.

'Neutral and objective.'

'He's bloodthirsty, your friend.'

'He's just a bit nervous.'

'There's never been a murder here, Boo. If Johnny or the gommers kill Gunboy, who knows what'll happen. Who knows how Zig will react.'

'You think he'll punish us?' This thought had not occurred to me.

'I'm not saying the ground will crack open and swallow us whole, but for sure there'll be a reckoning.'

I wonder about this, because if Zig is also overseeing America, he does not seem to pencil in days of reckoning — despite the injustice, violence, and death penalties there.

'Boo, it's up to us to stop Johnny,' Esther says. 'If we don't, we'll have blood on our hands.'

22 47.87
Ti
Titanium

After the gommer meeting ends, I am sitting alone on the steps of the Ponyboy Curtis School when the boy who was stabbed in the gut sits down beside me with a beat-up skateboard in his hands. 'Howdy there,' he says in a southern drawl. One would think that in the melting pot of our heaven, townies would eventually lose their accents, but no: the accent we come here with is the accent we have for all fifty years.

The gommer introduces himself as Benny Baggarly. Though blond, he is not pale like me. In fact, he is tanned, as if he has imported sun from the American South.

He leans in close and says, 'I tracked my killer down and now I'm hauntin' that b*stard.'

'Pardon me?'

'Hauntin' him. Ever hear of a hauntin'?'

'You mean you're a portal seeker?'

'Portal seeker? Portal finder's more like it.'

He pulls a slip of paper from his pocket. 'Don't show this to nobody. This is for you and you alone.' Benny glances around, but no one is within hearing distance. The other gommers have cycled off into the night.

Thelma and Esther are arguing on the lit basketball court beside the school. I feel a tinge of sadness because it seems our little group is breaking apart.

I unfold the slip of paper Benny passed me. On it is a hand-drawn map of Six. An X is marked in the middle of Buttercup Park, which lies on the zone's northern edge, where Six meets Five.

Benny whispers, 'We're meeting in that park tomorrow night at three in the morning.'

'Who are *we*, Benny?'

'Haunters, my boy. Go on a haunting and you can do some sleuthing. Find out if your killer's down in America or up in heaven. Hell, you might even find out the kid's real name. 'Cause it sure ain't 'Gunboy.' '

I must look skeptical because Benny offers a further lure: 'You can visit your folks too. Give your pa a hug, your ma a peck on the cheek. It'll do them a world of good.'

I slip Benny's map into my pocket and thank him for the invitation. I have my doubts about the safety of this haunting business, however. I think of poor crazy Willa Blake and her eerie dive.

Benny gets up from the steps and dusts off the seat of his pants. 'If you wanna know more, come tomorrow night. Don't be late. And make sure you come alone. This is an exclusive club. We don't invite any old Tom, Dick, and Harry.'

As Benny skates off across the schoolyard, I think, *Any old Tom, Dick, and Johnny would be more like it.*

23	50.94
V	
Vanadium	

When the girls and I arrive back at the Jack Merridew Dormitory that evening, I rush to my room in case Johnny has returned. The intact orange still on the desk tells me that no, he has not been here. Disappointed, I sit down on the chenille bedspread as Thelma comes in. I wonder aloud whether Johnny has headed back to the Frank and Joe.

Thelma's guess is that he is out showing his dead-or-alive poster around to see if he can find Gunboy himself. 'Wait a day or two, honey, and he'll show up,' she says, sitting on the bed opposite.

'If Johnny finds Gunboy, will he really bash his head in with a brick?'

'Oh, Oliver, that's just bravado talking. Johnny's scared. He's as scared as any newbie gommer. Getting over murder ain't something you do overnight.'

Her comment is directed at me too. She believes I am not emotional enough about my killing. I should not have gotten over it already.

'Do you think Gunboy deserves a bashing?' I ask.

Thelma stares at the palms of her hands as though her lifelines might reveal an answer. 'Honest to Zig, I don't know, sugar.'

She stands up between the two beds as I lay my head back on my pillow. Tonight she sings 'Lullaby of Birdland.' Her voice sweeps through the room and flows out the window. I expect other townies to come knocking on my door to hear Thelma's beautiful voice better. When she sings about a weepy old willow that knows how to cry, she closes her eyes and then I close mine. After she finishes the song, Thelma bends over and plants a kiss on my forehead. Though I usually recoil from such a kiss, I do not this time, so perhaps I am changing. Just a little bit.

'Sleep tight and don't let the death's head bite,' she jokes before shuffling off to the room she shares with Esther. I hope Johnny and Rover are looking after each other.

When Thelma is gone, I glance around. The walls look bare without the pencil sketches Johnny tapes up to make our temporary lodgings feel homier. My favorite sketch so far showed Esther zooming down the street on her pinkmobile, her hair and the handlebar streamers blowing horizontally. Johnny drew her in Wonder Woman's costume. He told me we were all superheroes tracking down our archenemy, Gunboy. When I asked which superhero I was, he said, 'Brainboy.'

Lately, I have not felt all that brainy. The smarts I have — about amoebae and nebulae and formulae — are useless here. What I need is the kind of intelligence that helps me understand why a boy might walk into a school and start shooting a gun, why one victim might forgive this boy, and why another never will.

At four thirty, I jerk awake, pulse racing because I hear Johnny screaming in his dreams, but when I flick on the light, all is quiet and the second bed is still empty. The screams must have been in *my* dreams. I drag the desk chair over to the window and sit watching the full moon and the hodgepodge of stars.

When I had insomnia back in America, I would read my school textbooks till it was light enough outside to go for an early-morning constitutional. I wish I were back at Helen Keller, memorizing the map of Africa, studying glacier formation, and conjugating verbs in French (*je meurs, tu meurs, il meurt, nous mourons . . .*).

When the pinprick stars fade out and the holy mackerel clouds float in, I change out of my pajamas and into my gym clothes. I pull on my white knee socks with red and blue stripes at the top (perhaps more Bicentennial leftovers) and then lace up my running shoes.

Outside, the day is still. No cyclists are around, and I wonder what it would be like to come to a heaven not just divided by age and nationality, but so segregated that I would be the only one inhabiting it. In other words, spending my afterlife truly alone. I shudder. I can make do with what heaven lacks: animals, cars, telephones, books of science, et al. But no people would be unbearable — even for a loner like me.

I recall a chat I had with Johnny during a morning jog almost a year ago. Though I am usually a light jogger, I was sprinting that day across a grassy backyard stretched between the buildings of Sandpits. At first, I did not notice Johnny and his sidekick, Rover, sitting on the grass and reading the *Tribune*. (Okay, the dog was not actually reading, but it *was* looking at the paper with interest.)

'You should join the track team, Boo,' Johnny called out. 'We could use you.'

I slowed down and walked back, pushing my eyeglasses up my nose. I told Johnny I would not enjoy running with others. I did not want to hear their breathing and footsteps. The sound of my panting breath and my thumping feet was calming; the sound of theirs would be annoying and distracting.

Johnny said he could understand. 'I like my alone time as well,' he told me. 'That's why I deliver the paper at five thirty in the morning.'

Then he added something I did not understand. 'Besides, I hate people too,' he said.

I was taken aback. 'Oh, but I don't *hate* people,' I replied. 'Sometimes they're a burden, especially when they interfere with my experiments and cut into my reading time, but I don't claim actual hatred.'

'Yes, you do. It's okay to say so.'

I did not wish to argue, so I said nothing. Johnny changed the topic. He asked, 'Does anybody at school know you run?'

I shook my head as Rover yawned over the sports section.

'Do your folks know?'

Another shake of the head. Mother and Father, you assumed I went for long walks in the morning. I did not want you to know I *jogged* because you would fret about my fragile heart. Already you had sent my gym teacher a note requesting that he not put undue strain on me.

Johnny looked intrigued. 'Not a soul knows?'

'You know,' I said.

Johnny smiled and stretched out an ink-stained hand. 'It's our secret, then,' he said.

I shook his hand quickly, hoping the newsprint would not transfer to my skin.

Now, as I jog down the streets of Six, I keep an eye out for the troubled soul that is Johnny. Maybe he, too, is out early. Perhaps he slept poorly and is already up.

Few townies have risen, besides some early birds gathered with shopping carts at a warehouse, doors thrown open to reveal shelves packed with a jumble of supplies. Let us hope the delivery includes a valuable curious object — like a telescope.

I jog on till I reach Buttercup Park. Despite the portal it may contain, the park looks as ordinary as the rebirthing beds. It consists of a grassy field for sports, a scattering of trees, picnic tables, and a slightly rusty jungle gym. I have a soft spot for jungle gyms. They were invented by the son of a mathematician as a way to help children grasp three-dimensional space. This one is a 3-D grid five cubes long, five cubes wide, and five cubes tall.

I inspect the park but find nothing out of the ordinary, apart from a cracked blue vinyl Elvis Presley album probably used as a Frisbee. I do not know what I expected to find. What would a portal look like? The porthole door to a washing machine? A sewer grate? A manhole cover?

If I did find a portal, would I have the gumption to climb into it? I think of fearless brothers Frank and Joe Hardy, flashlights in hand, as they slink down a dark, mysterious passageway, as on the cover of *The Secret of the Lost Tunnel*. Maybe if Johnny were here, I would climb through a portal. I would get to the bottom of *The Mystery of the Lost Gunboy*.

24   52.00

Cr

Chromium

The next infirmary the girls and I visit, the Sal Paradise Infirmary in Five, is not a mental hospital. This comes as a relief because broken bones and concussions are easier for a researcher to study than sadness and confusion. My research assistant, Esther, and I check healing times with the do-good nurses. In one bed lies a comatose girl who fell off a roof in a skateboard accident. Unlike Willa Blake, she did not disappear in a bed of black-eyed Susans.

'Revoke everybody's rooftop privileges,' says Esther. 'We klutzy angels shouldn't be trusted up there.'

Afterward, we go to the main office, where we find Thelma at a desk thumbing through a rebirthing book bound in red leatherette.

'Bingo,' Thelma says. She has come across the name of a girl who passed in Illinois not so long after Johnny's own passing. 'Is Schaumburg close to Hoffman Estates?' she asks.

'They're practically twin cities,' I reply.

I glance over Thelma's shoulder at the ledger. Typed on the page are the names of newbies, along with their place of origin, date of passing, cause of passing, and zip code in Town. Thelma points to the name Sandy Goldberg. In the Cause of Passing column is written the word 'peanut.'

'She was done in by a nut, Boo,' Esther says. 'You have that in common.'

'Peanuts are no joking matter,' I tell Esther. 'If you're allergic, even a lick of peanut butter can trigger anaphylactic shock. Your throat swells shut and you suffocate.' I hold my hands to my throat.

'Rest in peace, poor sweet girl,' Thelma says as she jots down Sandy's particulars on a slip of paper.

'How do you know she's sweet?' Esther says. 'She might be a b*tch. Maybe Sandy ate a peanut on purpose just to get attention.'

Thelma huffs and says, 'Why do you always think the worst of people?'

'Because people *are* the worst,' Esther says.

Thelma looks up. 'Zig give me strength,' she says as though he is twirling overhead on a blade of the ceiling fan.

'Do you think Zig listens to you?' I ask.

'I hope so,' Thelma says, closing the book. 'But he probably has bigger fish to fry.'

'He isn't our daddy to go running to when the going gets tough,' Esther says. 'He wants us to figure things out ourselves.' She picks up a snow globe paperweight from the desktop and shakes it. Inside are a tiny boy and girl sitting side by side in a sleigh and wearing matching earmuffs.

'We expect certain things from him,' Esther goes on. 'A place to live, food to eat, clothes to wear. And he expects certain things from us.'

'What kind of things?' I ask.

124

'That we make do with what we have. That we show one another a little respect. That we don't let loose the worst in us.'

While Thelma is returning the rebirthing book to a filing cabinet, Esther gives me a wink and slips the snow globe into Thelma's knapsack.

After we leave the infirmary, I suggest lunching in Buttercup Park, which is close by. We order takeout from a local cafeteria and then wander into the park. Thelma and Esther sit on either end of a seesaw. Given the difference in their weights, Thelma's end remains grounded and Esther's end stays lifted in the air. We eat peanut butter sandwiches, which we chose in honor of Sandy Goldberg.

Despite their argument the other day, Esther and Thelma seem good friends again. They are joking and laughing together, and Thelma is even touched when she discovers the snow globe. 'North Carolina never got much snow, and Town never gets none, so this snow is all I'm ever gonna get.' Still, she thinks we should return the stolen globe to the infirmary, but Esther insists it will never be missed.

I am unfamiliar with the art of friendship: the teasing, quarreling, and reconciling. How many days should a person remain upset, for example, when a friend utters an insensitive comment or shows disloyalty? These are figures I should jot in my ledger.

How many days will Johnny remain cross with me?

After I eat my sandwich, dried apricots, and wheat crackers, I make a display of picking up litter in the park and dropping it in a trash bin. In reality, I am looking for a portal. I even move the bin aside to see if a portal is hidden beneath. I find nothing.

The afternoon is spent on a wild-goose chase in search of Sandy Goldberg. Using her zip code, we track her down to her assigned dorm, where her roommate tells us she is taking a still-life painting class at the Charlie Gordon School, but at the school, the teacher tells us she dropped the class in favor of a badminton workshop at the Marcy Lewis Gymnasium. At the Marcy, a gym teacher tells us Sandy excels at the vertical jump smash and was sent on tour with the local badminton team. She will be back later in the week.

During all these travels, my bicycle chain falls off twice. Now I really miss Johnny, because he is an expert with bicycles, whereas I end up with grease smeared over my hands and T-shirt.

That night in my room at the dorm, I try to do a drawing of my friend, a wanted *alive* poster, to show to the portal seekers attending tonight's haunting. I am no portraitist, so my sketches in my notebook look amateurish. They look like any brown-haired boy. They could even be Gunboy.

It is frustrating that the image I see in my head is not recreated on the page. I crumple up drawing after drawing and then go into the hallway to pitch them all down the garbage chute.

It is now a quarter after midnight. In two hours, I leave for the haunting, and I will not sleep tonight. No matter. I have done without sleep countless times in my life, and I will make do this time as well. Yet when I lie on my bed and look up at the twirling ceiling fan, I feel a kick of anxiety in my stomach. Though I do not believe that Zig is watching over me, I find myself repeating Thelma's words: 'Zig give me strength.'

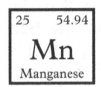

25 54.94

Mn

Manganese

In heaven, we need to look for magic in the little things. Flashlights, for instance. Townies might not be awestruck when they click on a flashlight and a light beam appears before them, but when they unscrew the end of the magical metal tube and discover it contains no batteries, awestruck is how they might react.

Yes, believe it or not, our flashlights work fine without an apparent energy source. But the light comes from somewhere, does it not? What is the energy source? Maybe invisible particles float in the air to power our flashlights, desk lamps, and streetlights. One day I will turn my attention to such conundrums.

In the meantime, I have a confession: just as Esther pinched a snow globe, I stole the flashlight I hold in my hands. It comes from a do-good station at the dorm. I hope you are not disappointed in me, Mother and Father, but these are desperate times. I could have signed out a flashlight with help from Thelma, but I did not want to alert her to my antics this evening. She would have disapproved. After all, non-do-gooders are prohibited from wandering around after midnight unless there is an emergency.

I am venturing out after curfew, when the streetlamps are dark and Town seems ominous and sinister in the shadows of the night. Not that the night is itself ominous and sinister. I will not run into ghosts (or I will run *only* into ghosts, depending on how you view us townies, ha-ha). I have never been afraid of the dark. As you know, even as a youngster, I did not need a night-light in my room. I never lay in bed petrified by a saber-toothed tiger ready to spring from my closet. I never woke in the night screaming my head off.

While I stroll down the streets with my flashlight, I wonder if Johnny will show up for this rendezvous of portal seekers. I have good news for him: our discovery of Sandy Goldberg from Schaumburg (whom Esther has taken to calling 'the nutter'). Once we track down Sandy, she might be able to provide clues about Gunboy and his real identity.

If I spot another flashlight in the distance, I will click off my own light in case the person is a night monitor checking the passes that townies out after curfew are required to carry. I see no other flashlights around, however. Nighttime here is pitch-black, especially when thick clouds cloak the moon. It is also dead quiet (ha-ha). There are no screeching ambulances, passing trains, or beeping cars. Sadly, there are no chirping crickets either. The only sound comes from rustling leaves whenever a breeze picks up.

When I draw near Buttercup Park, I check my glow-in-the-dark Casper the Friendly Ghost wristwatch (a gift from Esther). It is ten to three. A light clicks on and off in the playground, so I turn off my flashlight and make a beeline toward the light. As I cross the soccer field, I see that the light comes from atop the cubic jungle gym. Somebody is perched up there and acting as a beacon. It appears to be a boy, though not Benny. Benny is short, and this boy seems to be tall. His arm with the flashlight is stretched overhead as though he is imitating the Statue of Liberty.

I stop a few yards away. 'Hello there,' I call.

'Zip it!' the boy barks.

I lower my voice. 'Is Benny Baggarly around? He invited me to a haunting.'

'Just get in your f*cking cage, dog.'

A second figure climbs out from the jungle gym and moves toward me. As the beacon turns on, I see this second boy is Benny. 'Come sit with me,' he whispers, patting my shoulder. 'But no talking.' He holds a finger to his lips.

I follow Benny through the bars of the jungle gym, an awkward crawl in the flickering light. Once I am within the structure, I glance around. There are others here. I can hear them breathe and see them fleetingly when the beacon turns on. They sit in a cluster on the bottom bars. Everyone is too close for comfort. I want to ask the others if they have seen Johnny, but talking is forbidden. Minutes go by in silence. To kill time, I scan the park, but no other flashlights are approaching.

The boy standing over our heads — he must be the group leader, the head honcho of haunting — finally climbs down through the bars and perches in the very middle of the cube.

'Roll call,' the boy announces. 'Remember we

use pseudonyms here. No real names.' He passes around his flashlight, which slaps from hand to hand. Each haunter states his alias and then holds the flashlight beneath his chin, clicking it on for a second to show his face.

'Ace.'

'Doug.'

'Shelly.'

'Funk.'

'Jack Sprat.'

'Crystal.'

Benny says, 'Ratface,' and a few people giggle. The group leader hisses, 'Silence!'

Lit from underneath, we all look ghostly, and so when it is my turn, I give my real alias: 'Boo.'

I hand the flashlight up to the leader. He says his pseudonym, 'Czar,' and then he also clicks the light on and shines it toward himself. In the split second before the light turns off, I glimpse a sour-faced boy with crooked features, big ears, and messy brown hair.

The dead-or-alive poster come to life.

Gunboy! Gunboy in the flesh! A pain pierces my chest. Gunboy so close I could reach over and touch him.

I recall my promise to Johnny to be strong, but I am as petrified as a child with a saber-toothed tiger growling in his closet.

In the pitch-blackness, I hear Benny Baggarly whisper, 'May I go first, Czar?'

'I told you assh*les to shut the f*ck up. You don't speak unless spoken to. Understood?'

Nobody speaks.

'*Understood?*'

'Yes, Czar,' half a dozen voices whisper back.

I do not answer. I am speechless. My heart is thumping its irregular beat, but at least the sharp pain is abating. In my head, I chant, *Hydrogen, helium, lithium, beryllium, boron, carbon, nitrogen, oxygen, fluorine.*

Did Gunboy recognize me when I shone the light in my face? Maybe I was not visible long enough. Or maybe he did not get a good look at me back at Helen Keller.

'Most of you know the drill,' Gunboy says. His voice is raspy, as though he, like Johnny, yells in his sleep. 'I'll take you onto the baseball diamond one at a time and portal you back home. While you wait your turn, I don't want to hear one peep out of you. If I do, I'm canceling this haunting, you f*ckers *capisce*?'

'Yes, Czar.'

Neon, sodium, magnesium, aluminum, silicon.

There is a shuffling movement in our little circle as Gunboy pushes through the haunters and climbs through the bars of the jungle gym. Now he is standing outside, and the rest of us remain in our cage. 'Jack Sprat, you're up first,' he says. He turns on his flashlight and aims it at the ground as a boy near me wiggles out of the jungle gym. Gunboy and Jack Sprat head onto the baseball diamond, and I follow the light with my eyes, expecting any moment to hear Jack Sprat's bloodcurdling scream.

To Benny, I say, 'What's going on? What will he do to Jack Sprat?'

Benny's hand clamps over my mouth. 'Shush!

Czar will have a conniption!'

I push his hand off. 'I need to know. It's life or death!'

Somebody else whacks me in the head.

'Shut up, spaz,' whispers the girl nicknamed Crystal.

I crawl through the bars of the jungle gym as someone pulls on the tail of my T-shirt, but I kick back and the person lets go. I must get away. I do not have Gunboy's real name, but perhaps with the little information I do have, Thelma can track the boy down. I am ready to hurry back to our dorm to wake the girls when I see a beam of light flitting across the baseball diamond. Gunboy is coming back! Damnation! For a moment I am frozen in place, but I shake off my fear and put up my dukes. If he shines his light on me and launches an attack, I will fight him off. The light beam draws ever closer. My nerves steel. My heart booms. My blood races.

Just before the light falls on me, a voice calls out, 'Are portal seekers meeting here tonight? I'm a little late.'

That voice is instantly familiar.

'Johnny Henzel?'

The cone of light sweeps across me. I put down my dukes.

'What the hell you doing here, Boo?'

Behind me, the portal seekers hiss, 'Shush!'

I have not seen my roommate in a day and a half, but it seems longer. 'Looking for you, Johnny,' I reply. 'I was out looking for you.'

'Zip your mouths,' Crystal calls out.

'What's her frigging problem?' Johnny says.

From out in the field comes a roar of frustration. Then this: 'Can't you follow one simple order, you c*cksucking, motherf*cking retards?!'

In the baseball diamond, a circle of light is growing larger and more menacing. Our killer is racing toward us.

'Dang it all to hell!' says Benny Baggarly.

'I'll never get to Tampa now,' Crystal whines.

Our killer screams, 'Imbeciles! Morons!'

Johnny says, 'What the f*ck's going on?'

'Gunboy,' I sputter.

'Huh?' Johnny says, shining his light in my eyes.

Two galaxies colliding. That is what I expect as Johnny swings his cone of light from me to the boy rushing toward us across the playground.

For a moment, nobody speaks. The portal seekers must be trembling in their cage. In the dim light, Johnny appears stunned. His mouth drops open. He takes a step back.

Gunboy comes to a stop a few feet from Johnny. The boy looks feral, furious. His eyes glow red. His hair stands on end. 'I'll murder you f*ckers,' he snarls.

'Have mercy on me, Czar,' Crystal from Tampa says. 'I'm an innocent bystander.'

'Did I tell you to speak?' Gunboy says. In the instant it takes for our killer to turn toward Crystal in the jungle gym, Johnny steps forward and raises his magical flashlight high. Then he smashes it against the boy's head.

A sharp, sickening *crack*.

Gunboy goes down in a heap. His own

flashlight rolls across the sand and comes to a stop at my feet, partly lighting the scene of Johnny taking his revenge, screaming like a madman as he bashes his truncheon against the body of an unconscious boy.

In the darkness, the blood looks black.

26 55.85
Fe
Iron

We race through the night, Johnny and I, the beams of our flashlights crisscrossing, the panting of our breath overlapping, the thumping of our feet synchronizing.

We are speed demons, frantic, scared, and trying to outrun a terrible act I fear may cost us our afterlives.

27	58.93

Co
Cobalt

28	58.69

Ni
Nickel

29	63.55

Cu
Copper

Czar's real name is Charles Lindblom. Does the name not sound innocent? Like the name of an upright bank manager or a gallant aviation hero making a transatlantic flight. When I shared this thought with Johnny, he said that to him the name Charles Lindblom sounded no more innocent than the name Charles Manson.

I am visiting Czar at the Sal Paradise Infirmary. I come in disguise, if a baseball cap can be considered a disguise. Johnny and I found it in our hideout. We have been holed up in an unused janitor's office in the basement of the Marcy Lewis Gymnasium next to the West Wall in Five. All day long, we hear the bouncing of basketballs overhead. The sound would drive us crazy, Johnny half-joked, were we not already so.

Another item found in our hideout is a Hardy Boys novel, in fact *The Flickering Torch Mystery*. I am pretending to read the book during my visit. The title is oddly fitting. After all, a kind of torch — a flashlight — led to Czar's stay at the Sal.

The patients here are all recovering in the same room, a long hall with cubicles separated by curtains that can be drawn for privacy. From what I have overheard, seven patients were injured in bicycle accidents and one patient, a cafeteria worker, suffered burns from an overturned pot of linguini.

Though I am telling you I am visiting Czar, Mother and Father, I am actually seated beside the bed of a girl named Nilaya Singh. I am pretending to be a friend. When a real friend of hers dropped by yesterday and asked who I was, I lied that I was one of Nilaya's skating pals. Nilaya is the girl who was skating on a rooftop, lost control of her board, and sailed off the roof. She is in a coma and not expected to wake for another week.

This is my third visit to Nilaya's bedside. Each time, I stay for about twenty minutes. Today I brought her a bouquet of wildflowers I picked outside our gymnasium hideout. Her face is puffy and bruised, and her dark hair is bound atop her head. Her arms are covered in scratches from the branches of the bushes she fell into. I sit watching her and jotting down her healing times on the bookmark inside my Hardy Boys mystery. I wish I were in fact her skating pal and had no ulterior motive. Instead, my ulterior motive lies in the next bed: Charles Lindblom. He is also in a coma, as Johnny was back in Illinois. 'An eye for an eye,' Johnny said about that.

Two security guards sit on either side of Czar's bed to protect him in case the person or persons who beat the patient to a pulp return to finish the job (say, smother him with a pillow).

The boy lying there is no longer recognizable from Johnny's dead-or-alive poster. His face is so battered he looks more dead than alive. His skull is fractured, his cheekbones are shattered, and his eyes are bandit-ringed with the infinity symbol. His swollen lips puff out grotesquely.

Do you wonder how a simple flashlight did such harm — especially one without batteries? Rocks. Johnny filled the empty body of his flashlight with rocks. He had a hunch he would need a weapon on the night of the haunting.

Johnny insists I visit the infirmary daily to check if Czar has passed. But despite his severe injuries, he will not. The boy is slowly healing. I do not tell Johnny this, however. 'Odds are Gunboy will die and disappear,' I lie. That is the outcome Johnny hopes for. Yet each day, the bruising fades and the swelling goes down a little more. Each day, Czar comes closer to waking up.

A nurse named Miss Heidi arrives to wash Czar and change his bandages. She tells the guards to take a break and then tugs the curtains partway around the bed, but I can still steal peeks through a gap. The nurse cleans Czar's wounds with cotton pads dunked in a basin of warm water that is slowly turning pink. She is a big girl, heavier even than Thelma. She is also a chatterbox. She must suppose that the comatose hear and understand voices around them (just as Johnny heard his sister and parents during his coma).

'I know what you were doing, Chucky boy,' she says, running a washcloth over his limbs. 'You were hypnotizing townies and messing with their heads. You convinced them a pitcher's mound was a portal they could travel through back to America. Well, I'd lay off those hauntings of yours. No good can come of them, as you learned the hard way.'

One rumor going around is that Czar failed to hypnotize a townie, who grew enraged and clobbered him. A second rumor is that a demented killer is roaming Town. Yesterday I overheard other nurses at the infirmary mention both possibilities.

'Never pretend to be as magical as Zig,' Miss Heidi advises. 'His magic ain't perfect, and if you pretend you're him, you're bound to make a heap load of mistakes.'

Miss Heidi balls up her washcloth and scrubs Czar's armpit. 'Don't you fret,' she says. 'You'll be up and at 'em in no time, old boy.'

Old boy? Why would she call Czar that?

As soon as Miss Heidi leaves with her basin of water, I slip between the curtains and hurry to the end of Czar's bed. Hung there is a clipboard with a sheet of paper that lists the patient's particulars. I grab the sheet and scan down it.

Holy moly! Charles Lindlom died on July 11, 1933!

30	65.38

Zn

Zinc

Before heading back to our hideout, I stop by a local school to pick up take-out supper from the cafeteria. I ask the server to fill plastic containers with sweet potato stew and a salad of corn and black beans.

'Portions for two, please,' I say.

I am wearing my baseball cap as well as sunglasses. The server says, 'Nice glasses, honey. The style suits you.'

This is true irony. The sunglasses are pink and have rhinestones embedded in their frames. Johnny found the glasses in the janitor's office, and he insists I wear them outside our hideout so nobody recognizes me. I do not wear them at the infirmary, however, because I fear looking suspicious.

While I am preparing to leave, a do-gooder in a purple armband stands at the cafeteria podium, a bullhorn in one hand and a written announcement in the other. 'Your attention, please,' he calls out. 'Given recent events, many of you have voiced concerns about being outside after dark.'

Diners seated at the long tables in the cafeteria stop their chatting and lend the do-gooder their ears, a rare sight because diners usually pay no heed to special announcements (just like the students at Helen Keller).

'The do-good council assures you that the cowardly attack on a local townie a few days ago was not random. It targeted one specific boy. Some of you fear that a crazed murderer is on the loose. Our information tells us otherwise.'

A redheaded boy waves his knife and fork and shouts, 'I confess! I did it! I'm the murderer!' He pretends to knife the girl sitting beside him. Many diners erupt in laughter. As I scan the tables, though, I see a boy who is not laughing. It is Benny Baggarly. He is staring into his bowl of stew.

'So feel free to circulate after dark,' the do-gooder goes on. 'But remember that anyone caught out after midnight will face detention. Thank you.'

I push my sunglasses up the bridge of my nose, grab some napkins, and hurry out of the cafeteria to bike back to our hideout.

I must tell Johnny about our mistake. Charles Lindblom is an old boy; he is not Gunboy.

I accept a share of the responsibility for what happened because I warned Johnny that Gunboy was approaching when Czar emerged fuming from the shadows. Had I kept quiet, Johnny might not have mistaken Czar for Gunboy. Yet Johnny is convinced that Czar *is* Gunboy. My roommate claims he is now sleeping 'like a damn baby log,' but he is lying: I hear him moaning in his sleep. We take turns sleeping on a lumpy old couch in the janitor's office; every other night, one of us sleeps on the floor atop throw pillows.

My own insomnia is worse than ever. Last

night I even went out after curfew. A flashlight in hand, I returned to the scene of the crime. I climbed back into the jungle gym and sat in that makeshift jail for more than an hour. I had brought along a box cutter from our hideout and used it to make nicks up and down my arms and legs. While I did this, I thought about you, Mother and Father. How I missed your simple chats about banal things like the most effective blue shampoo to treat dandruff. How I wished I could portal back to America to see you, if only for a moment. Yet I knew from the beginning that Czar and the haunters were frauds. I knew they would not help me travel back to 222 Hill Drive.

I felt very alone in that jungle gym. I did not cry, but I did sigh deeply.

'Don't cry.' That was what Johnny whispered to me in seventh grade after I was singled out in the hallway and battered by the fists of Kevin Stein, Fred Winchester, and Jermaine Tucker. As I lay on the floor stinging from the attack, Johnny Henzel kneeled by my side and told me not to cry. 'It only makes it worse,' he said.

I repeated these lines to Johnny on our first night in the janitor's office. He was crouched naked in the large, rust-stained sink set up at the back of the room. He was crying because he had Czar's blood all over his face and hair. 'Get it off me! Boo, get it off!' We did not have shampoo, only a cake of soap, so I used it to lather his hair and clean his face. I believe we were both in shock. As a result, I was able to touch another person without the repulsion I usually felt. All the while, he wept soundlessly.

As I scrubbed my nails into his scalp, he shivered even though the water was hot. I filled a pail with water and poured it over his head to rinse off the soap.

'I had no choice. I had to do it,' he said. Soap had gone into his eyes, and he rubbed them fiercely. 'The same as when you have to shoot a horse when it breaks a leg.'

'A horse?'

'What Gunboy has is worse than a broken leg.' He tapped his fingers against his temple. 'He has a broken brain.'

Johnny's bloody clothes lay beside the sink. I thought about scrubbing them, but instead I shoved them in a garbage bin. As for the rock-filled flashlight, I emptied it and wiped the canister with paper napkins.

A beach towel decorated with cartoon lobsters hung on a hook on the wall. I wrapped the towel around Johnny and helped him climb out of the sink. He slipped on a puddle of water and almost fell, but I caught him. I held him up, and he gave me a glance that said, *You're stronger than you look.*

But I did not feel strong. I felt as though my brain were also broken.

The janitor's office is furnished sparsely, with the ratty couch and five wobbly school chairs fitted with desktops the size of a painter's palette. In one corner stands a stack of cardboard boxes filled with a hodgepodge of forgotten supplies. In these Johnny and I found the baseball cap, sunglasses, box cutter, and Hardy Boys novel. I was in fact looking for clothing because I no longer had a change of clothes with me and Johnny did not have many clothes with him either. On my second night here, after the Marcy closed, I went upstairs to the boys' locker room and looked for clothing left behind in the lockers. The pickings were slim for a boy as slim as I (ha-ha). I am swimming in the cutoff shorts and shirt I found. No matter. I will make do.

Few people ever come down to the basement of the Marcy. When they do, they usually just use the restroom at the foot of the stairs, and they do not wander into the other rooms farther down the hall. There is little reason to, since the rooms are stocked with castoffs.

On the evening when Johnny first abandoned us, he discovered the janitor's office while exploring the center after it closed. He broke into the Marcy by shimmying through an unlocked basement window. His aim, he said, was to find a place where nobody could attack him in his sleep. By 'nobody,' he meant Gunboy.

When I return from the cafeteria with our supper, I slip through the same window and drop to the floor. I go down the hall to the janitor's office, where Johnny is in the gym clothes I found for him in the locker room. He is doing military push-ups on the concrete floor. He claps his hands between push-ups. His T-shirt is sweaty, and his onion smell stinks up the room.

I tell him his efforts are for naught. 'Our bodies do not change. The muscle and fat we come here with are the muscle and fat we have forevermore.'

'That's not fair,' he says, winded.

'Afterlife ain't fair,' I reply. This is something Esther always says.

I set out our supper on the floor, using paper towels as place mats. I even arrange a place setting for Rover because Johnny likes to drop a spoonful of food on a coaster for his pet roach to nibble on.

'His voice is growing stronger,' he tells me as he feeds Rover. 'I hear words every now and again. Today I heard the word 'suicide.' '

'Suicide?'

'It sounded like a girl's voice. I bet it's Willa talking about leaping off the Deborah.'

I have never heard a peep from that creature.

I worry about Johnny's mental state.

He notices the scabs on my arms and legs. 'Did you get in a fight with a pocketknife?'

'A box cutter,' I say. 'It is a scab-healing experiment.'

He shakes his head; now it is he who is worried about my mental state. Then he asks for an update on Gunboy. I tell him Czar is stable and little has changed since yesterday. Johnny guesses that Gunboy will live for another month before succumbing to his injuries. 'After all,' he says, 'I passed after five weeks in a coma.'

'You two are treading the same path?'

Johnny runs a finger along the wings of his death's head as the roach feeds. 'We have lots in common, Gunboy and me,' he says.

'What exactly?'

'Hot tempers. We're both angry b*stards.'

I think back to Helen Keller and Sandpits. I do not remember Johnny being hot-tempered. I picture him seated peacefully in a corner of the library as he drew in his sketch pad. I recall him running serenely on the outdoor track that circled the football field. Everybody liked Johnny. From what I recall, our classmates did not seem to mock or bully him or try to pummel him to death in murderball as they did with me.

After Johnny and I finish supper, I rinse our plastic containers and utensils in the sink and wipe them dry with the lobster towel. Then I turn to Johnny, who is playing jacks on the floor with an old set he found in a box of junk.

I do not say, 'I have something important to tell you' (he will realize it is important). I do not say, 'You had better sit down' (he is already sitting) or 'Hold on to your hat' (he has on a baseball cap). I just say, 'Czar is forty-six years old.'

Johnny misses the ball while trying to grab five jacks at once. He glances up. 'What do you mean, forty-six?'

'He is an old boy. He came here decades ago.'

He frowns and spits out, 'Don't f*ck with me.'

'Why would I f*ck with you? I make it a lifelong habit never to f*ck with anybody at any time.'

I sit with him and his jacks. I explain about a group of visitors who came to see Czar just before I left the infirmary today. They talked about his skills as a magician and the shows he had put on. He would saw his assistant in half, free himself from tricky knots, and hypnotize audience members so they would crow like roosters and hop like bunnies. The shows these people talked about took place years before.

From my pocket, I pull out the patient information sheet I stole from the infirmary. I hand it to Johnny, and he reads aloud Czar's date of passing: 'July eleventh, nineteen thirty-three.' Then he glances up. 'It says here he was trampled by a horse in Nevada.'

He closes his eyes, puts down the clipboard, and rubs his temples as though his brain is also breaking.

I say nothing more. I wait. I think of injured horses put out of their misery with a bullet to the brain. Minutes click by. From out of the corner of my eye, I see Rover beetling across the far wall.

'Johnny,' I finally say, 'are you hunky-dory?'

His eyes blink open. 'I know what must have happened, Boo,' he says, his voice more gravelly than usual. 'In September, this Czar kid traveled to Hoffman Estates on a haunting. He broke into somebody's house, stole a gun, and then went hunting for thirteen-year-olds.'

Oh, Zig in heaven help us all.

'You do not really believe that, do you?' I ask.

He looks vexed. 'It's totally possible!' he insists. 'Maybe he even killed other kids during other hauntings. Maybe we aren't the only ones! We should contact the gommers, get them involved in an investigation. We might find other victims.'

I sigh and say, 'Czar is the victim, Johnny.'

He holds up a hand and barks, 'Don't!' Then he leaps up and throws open the door to our hideout. Usually he creeps down the hall to avoid making noise and attracting attention, but this time he runs. I go after him. He passes the restroom and takes the stairs two at a time to the lobby. When I reach it myself, he is already hurrying down a hall to the basketball court. The Marcy is still open, and townies are milling around. I head to the court, and when I arrive, Johnny is climbing an inner staircase to the indoor track built along the circumference of the space. Up on the track, he starts running, not simply jogging, but sprinting at top speed. Around and around he goes. Nobody else is up there. A few boys are practicing shots on the court. I leave him alone. I sit on a bench and wait for the speed demon to come down.

As I watch Johnny, I toy with the idea of

leaving him here and biking home to Eleven. Maybe Thelma is back at the Frank and Joe; she will know what to do. I no longer care who killed me or why, and honestly I do not think I ever really did. I prefer investigating something less grisly — for instance, how flashlights work without batteries. That is the only kind of mystery I want to solve.

A half hour later, a do-gooder comes onto the basketball court with a bullhorn. 'Closing in ten minutes,' he calls out. 'Wrap it up, folks.'

The boys on the court head to the locker room to shower and change. They punch one another on the shoulder. They call one another 'Scrotum.' They laugh affably. They are part of a world Johnny used to live in. He needs to go back to that world. When he finally stops jogging and comes down from the suspended track, I have a suggestion. I almost plead with him: 'Let's forget all about Gunboy, Johnny. Tomorrow morning, we can bike back to the Frank and Joe and start over again. We can get jobs. I can work for Curios, and you can teach life-drawing classes. Let's pretend we died of different causes. Me from a heart defect and you from — I don't know — a nut allergy.'

My own suggestion surprises me: I do not often pretend. You will recall, Mother and Father, that as a young child I pretended briefly to be evolutionary biologist Richard Dawkins, but then I decided playacting was dishonest.

Johnny's face is drawn. Around his head he is wearing a terry-cloth sweatband he must have found discarded on the track. 'A nut allergy,' he says, winded. He looks at me as though *I* am a nut.

I clarify: 'Anaphylactic shock.'

He stares at me a moment. 'Oh, okay,' he finally mumbles. Then he leaves the basketball court and heads to a drinking fountain in the lobby.

I am taken aback: I was ready for him to scold me for giving up. 'Well, good, then,' I call out. 'Very good.' I catch up to him. I put up my dukes and punch him lightly on the shoulder when he straightens up from the fountain.

Instead of going down to the basement, he heads out the front door of the Marcy. I follow him around the side of the building. He lies in the grass and stares at the darkening sky.

I remind Johnny of the day of his skitching accident back in Hoffman Estates, when he looked at the clouds awestruck. He scrunches his forehead. 'Oh, yeah, I sort of remember that.'

'You said you saw something beautiful, Johnny. What was it?'

'Beats me.'

I lie beside him and look skyward. Pinpricks of stars dot the sky. Soon I must begin mapping them.

'Maybe I was talking about heaven,' Johnny says. 'The beauty awaiting us here.'

I turn toward him in the grass. 'Really?'

He turns toward me. A single tear drips from his eye and across the bridge of his nose. 'No,' he says. Then he barks a laugh and I emit several ha-ha's. Zig knows what we are laughing about.

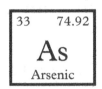

33   74.92

As

Arsenic

After the Marcy closes, we slip through the basement window and head back to the janitor's office. For our last night here, Johnny wants to play board games. 'Like normal kids do,' he says. The other day, he found a box filled with games like Don't Spill the Beans, Monopoly, Operation, and The Partridge Family Game. Clue is also among the stash, but we will not play it because, as you might imagine, Mother and Father, we are in no mood for Professor Plum bludgeoning Mr. Boddy in the billiard room with a candlestick.

Johnny reads the rules for Operation. Using tweezers, the players must act as surgeons and remove comical body parts — Adam's apple, funny bone, charley horse, spare ribs, broken heart — from a chap named Cavity Sam. In Sam's brain is a plastic ice-cream cone, alluding to brain freeze, the pain that people feel when they eat ice cream too fast.

'There is no such thing as brain damage in heaven, so Czar's brain is sure to heal fully,' I tell Johnny. 'Did you know certain townies have lost fingers and toes and their digits have completely grown back? Like the limbs of salamanders.'

Johnny looks up from the instructions. 'Don't you hack off one of your baby toes to see how

154

long it takes to grow back,' he warns.

I must admit the idea has crossed my mind.

'Czar will recover and we will accept our punishment,' I continue. 'Thelma will help us so we are treated fairly. We may have to clean toilets for months on end, but so be it.' Maybe, as a result, I will learn more about the true nature of Town's plumbing system.

'We should apologize to Czar,' I say. 'It was a case of mistaken identity, like in the Hardy Boys novel *The Missing Chums*' (another book found in our hideout).

'Please, Boo, let's not talk about that guy tonight,' Johnny mutters without looking up from the instructions. 'What an idiotic game,' he then says, throwing the instructions aside.

Instead of Operation, we play Monopoly. Johnny is the terrier; I am the wheelbarrow. Rover scampers across the board like a third game piece. At one point, Johnny holds up a Get Out of Jail Free card. Drawn on it is a cartoon fellow dressed in prison stripes. 'I should hang on to this,' Johnny says with a smirk.

He talks very little. He looks sad and confused even when he buys Boardwalk. We are both tired, too bushed to focus on buying railroads, hotels, and utilities, so we do not finish the game. We decide to go to bed.

Johnny puts Rover in its camper, but without the lid on so the roach can roam around at night if it wishes.

Before bed, I bathe in the big sink: I soap my hair and pour a pail of water over my head. I dry off on the lobster towel. It is my turn to sleep on the couch, but I offer it to Johnny, claiming I prefer the throw pillows on the floor. I fear that his nightmares may revisit him tonight. He might sleep more restfully on the couch.

After we turn off the lights, Johnny says, 'Know any lullabies, Boo?'

I do not have Thelma's voice, but I take a shot at the Cole Porter standard 'Friendship,' a song that states that, in the closest friendships, people combine their individual qualities and strengths to form a 'blendship.' I recall that you sometimes sang this song as a duo, Mother and Father, to entertain patrons at Clippers. I sing a slower, more melancholy version than you did. In the dark, my voice sounds more tuneful and, dare I say, more angelic than I remember it from before my passing. Perhaps to offset a lower intelligence quotient, Zig tweaked my singing voice.

When I finish singing, Johnny says sleepily, 'Blendship?'

'It's a portmanteau,' I say.

'A poor man's toe?'

'No, a portmanteau. It means a word that combines two different words. In this case, the two are 'blend' and 'friendship.' In French, portmanteau actually means a coatrack, but in English, it also refers to a kind of suitcase with two — '

'Boo.'

'Yes, Johnny?'

'Please shut up.'

'It's only a nightmare!' I call out in my sleep because I hear Johnny scream. One quick, panicked shout. I blink my eyes open in the dark. Circles of light dart across the walls and floor. The ceiling light turns on. My pupils constrict. My eyes squint. There are people in the room. Half a dozen people. In my daze, I think nonsensically that the janitors are here to take their office back. Then they are on top of me. Three janitors. They throw off my sheet, grab my arms and legs, and roll me on my side. Their faces look both grim and thrilled. My face squashes against a pillow. I spot Rover scrabbling along a baseboard. Across the room, janitors attack Johnny too. He screams bloody murder. One janitor atop him pulls out a curious object — handcuffs. As my arms are wrenched behind my back, I feel pressure on my wrists and hear a click. Janitors have handcuffed me. I go limp, the same as when the boys piled atop me on Halloween. So much for staying strong. Johnny does not go limp. He scissors his legs up and down. With bare feet, he kicks a janitor in the head. Another janitor smacks Johnny hard in the face with the back of his hand. Johnny stops screaming when a janitor snips off a length of duct tape from a roll and sticks it over his mouth.

157

These janitors, I finally realize, are wearing purple armbands.

Tonight Zig is playing jacks with thousands of twinkling stars across the heavens. I can even see the Milky Way, or at least the whitewash Zig uses to paint the night sky. I focus on the beauty above to distract myself from my ordeal.

I am tied with skipping ropes to an infirmary stretcher, which the do-gooders are now dragging across a grassy field in the manner of a sled. Before I was tied down, I was wrapped in a blanket, and so I feel like an American Indian baby bound in a papoose, except a baby would not have its hands cuffed and its mouth taped shut no matter how strict its parents might be. If my mouth were not taped, I would call out to the second stretcher being hauled across the field. I would tell Johnny not to panic. The do-gooders are kind and charitable, after all, so other than a little rope burn, we should come to no harm.

Two do-gooders are pulling a rope that is attached to my stretcher as a leash. They have flashlights to lead the way. A third do-gooder follows behind to ensure that I do not fall off. Again, if my mouth were not taped, I would tell these boys that this dramatic capture is pointless because Johnny and I planned to turn ourselves in at the crack of dawn.

Every previous night in the janitor's office,

Johnny and I had placed desks in front of the door because there was no lock to keep intruders out. Tonight, however, we had not bothered. I imagine Johnny is cursing himself for that. I turn my head to catch sight of my roommate's stretcher and his own trio of escorts.

I see the other group's flashlights glimmering at the opposite end of the field. They seem to be going in a different direction. Zig almighty, the do-gooders are splitting Johnny and me up!

Where are they taking him? Maybe Czar has woken, and they will take Johnny to the infirmary so his victim can pick him out in a kind of police lineup. Or perhaps he is going straight to jail (Do not pass Go). But why would I not go with him? I am guilty too. I played a key role in this fiasco.

After my group leaves the field, my escorts drag my stretcher down an empty street. The night is silent except for the scraping sound of board against pavement, which reminds me of snowplows in Hoffman Estates. Since I am at curb level, the dark buildings we pass seem larger and more foreboding than usual. They loom over me as though passing judgment. If they had heads, they would shake them; if they had fingers, they would wag them.

My three escorts have not uttered a word yet, so I am surprised when one says, 'Oh, bugger, we took a wrong turn. We should be on Phoebe Caulfield Road.' They turn my sled around, and we head back and then up a different street.

I am thankful it is nighttime. If it were daytime and passersby were eyeing me, I would feel ashamed. So thank you, do-gooders, for your forethought.

We stop in front of what looks like a dorm. Two of the boys lift the stretcher to waist level and carry me down a cobblestone pathway past a hedge made up of skyrocket spruce. RHODA PENMARK DORMITORY is written on the sign above the front door. The dorm's doorgirl meets our group out front. She takes one look at me, the giant papoose, and says, 'This ain't right.'

A do-gooder says, 'Just hold the door, Inez.'

Inez holds the door as the do-gooders and I pass through. I am carried across the empty lobby and down the hall to a door marked 106, like my old locker at Helen Keller. Inez fiddles with a set of keys and finally inserts the right one and turns the lock. 'You had to gag him?' she says as she steps into the room and flicks on the light. 'He's a newbie. You could've taken pity.'

'Shut up, Inez, or we'll gag *you*.'

Dear Inez huffs and leaves the room.

The do-gooders set the stretcher on the bed. I look up at the twirling ceiling fan. For some reason, I think of Czar hypnotizing the haunters. I picture him twirling a pinwheel in front of their faces and saying, 'You're feeling *sleeeeeepy*. Real *sleeeeeepy*.' I am not sleepy, however. I am wide-awake even though it must be four in the morning.

The do-gooders untie the ropes. They roll me on my side and unlock the handcuffs. My wrists are scrawny, so they do not hurt from the cuffs, which I notice are plastic. Toy handcuffs! Johnny will be mortified.

161

I sit up, and one of the do-gooders, a boy with a big nose, says he will remove the duct tape. He has a bit of a British accent. He tugs on the corner of the tape over my mouth. 'This might hurt a bit,' he says. 'I'll go slow.'

He peels the tape, uprooting the tiny blond hairs growing above my lip. I wince and say, 'Where's Johnny Henzel?'

'We aren't permitted to say,' the British boy replies.

'It was an unfortunate accident,' I tell him. 'We mistook Charles Lindblom for somebody else — for our murderer, in fact.'

The two do-gooders exchange glances.

I try to play on their sympathy: 'We are gommers, but we haven't gotten over our murders yet.'

My second captor, who has an American accent, says, 'I need to get the stretcher back.' So I stand up, dressed only in my boxer shorts, the blanket over my shoulders, and let the boy drag the stretcher off the bed. He carries it from the room without a word.

'You'll sleep here tonight,' the Brit says. 'In the morning, the do-good president from your zone will come talk to you.'

Reginald Washington is coming to save me.

'I'll be sitting outside your door, mate, in case you need anything. My name's Ringo.'

'As in the Beatles.'

'It's not my real name,' the big-nosed boy says. 'It's just what people call me. I'm from England, you see, but my family moved to Detroit a year before I passed.'

'Are you my jailer, Ringo?'

'As a matter of fact, yes. I work at the Gene Forrester in Nine.'

'Is that where Johnny is?'

'I am not at liberty to say.'

'Look, you have to take me to Johnny Henzel right now. He is a very sensitive soul.'

Ringo shakes his head.

'He is a little unstable,' I say.

Ringo gives me a deadpan look. 'Yes, so I heard.' Then he leaves the room, shutting the door behind him.

I go to the window and draw back the dusty curtains. I try pushing up the sash, but it will not budge. In any case, even if I escaped from this room, where would I go? I cannot trot around in my underwear in search of Johnny in the dark.

Beside the window is a desk. I sit. I cannot sleep now. I will just wait for the sky to lighten and for Reginald to come. I try studying the stars in the sky, but my concentration is poor. I feel unstable myself. Zig in heaven, if I had a carving knife, I might amputate a baby toe.

36	83.80
Kr	
Krypton	

'Hey, Oliver,' a voice says. 'Time to wake up. Rise and shine. Rise and shine.'

A hand pats my head.

For a moment, I think the voice and the hand belong to you, Mother. I can practically smell the citrusy hair tonic that seeps into all your clothes on account of the hours you spend at Clippers.

I am not dead, I think. *I am not dead after all.*

But when I blink open my eyes, the face I see is not pink and skinny like Mother's. It is brown and chubby. 'Thelma,' I say, lifting my head. 'Oh, it's so nice to see you, even though you don't smell of hair tonic.'

She looks confused but then says, 'It's nice to see you, too, honey.' She smiles to reveal the gap in her teeth.

I have a crick in my neck because I fell asleep seated at the desk.

Thelma looks at the desk blotter. 'What's that you drew?'

I look at the blotter. 'A horse.' Last night, to kill time, I mapped stars and created a new constellation, not a winged horse like Pegasus but a regular horse. Yet my horse has only three legs because there were no bright stars to form a fourth. For those who believe in omens, a three-legged horse is most likely a bad sign.

Luckily, I do not believe in omens.

'I brought you some fresh clothes, shoes, and even a toothbrush.' Thelma points to the items she has laid on the bed.

'Where is Johnny? Where was he taken?'

Thelma looks away. 'Why don't you get dressed, honey? Then we'll have ourselves a little talk. I need to tell you a few things.'

There is something different about Thelma. It takes me a moment to pinpoint what. 'You are not wearing your armband,' I say.

She glances at her upper arm as though wondering where the heck the purple band went. Then she sits on the bed and hands me jeans with faint grass stains on the knees. 'Well, Oliver, I'm not a do-gooder no more.'

'Did you retire?' I ask, pulling on the pants.

'No, I was kicked out.'

'You got fired?'

'They're calling it a 'leave of absence.' The council wasn't too happy about our escapades.'

She means Johnny's escapades and mine. Our attack on Charles Lindblom lost her a job.

'Oh, Thelma, I am so sorry.'

What a horrible mess I made! You would be ashamed of me, Father and Mother! Fractured skulls, lost jobs, sad and confused friends. Not to mention that poor Rover the roach was left behind at the Marcy. Johnny will be devastated if we lose his pet!

I accidentally put my T-shirt on inside out, a sign of how stupid I have become.

'I will accept any punishment the council sees fit,' I tell Thelma, and she pats the bedsheets beside her so I will come and sit down.

Her eyes are anxious and red. 'You won't be punished, honey. The council decided you did nothing wrong.'

'But it was my fault, Thelma. I am what is called an *instigator*. I told Johnny that Charles Lindblom was Gunboy. He looked like the boy in the dead-or-alive poster.'

Thelma moves her hand in the air as though erasing words on a chalkboard.

'Listen, Oliver. I need you to meet somebody.'

She glances at the door. Then she gets up, goes to it, and edges it open. She nods to whoever is in the hallway.

The door pushes open and in come a boy and a girl. I stand up. The boy I recognize. It is Reginald Washington with his splotchy arms, face, and even kneecaps (he is wearing shorts, and one knee is pink and the other brown). He smiles and says, 'Hello there, young fellow.' As for the girl, I have never seen her before. She is very skinny, scrawnier than even I am. Two braids protrude straight out from either side of her head. Reginald nudges her toward me. She has an astonished look, as though she has seen a ghost.

To break the ice, I almost say, 'Boo!'

She takes a few more steps forward, looking at me in an odd way, as though taking stock of each individual feature — my nose, my lips, my forehead.

'It's him,' she says.

A sharp intake of breath from Thelma.

'Are you sure?' Reginald says.

The girl nods.

'On a scale of one to ten,' Reginald says, 'one being least certain and ten being most certain, how certain are you?'

A spectrum of certainty. How strange.

The girl says, 'Nine and a half.'

'May I ask what is going on?' I say.

'Honey, I'd like to introduce you to Sandy.'

'Hi, Sandy. Nice to meet you. My name is Oliver.'

'Yeah, so they told me,' Sandy says, still staring.

Reginald gives Thelma a nod. Then he says, 'Well, now, Sandy, we should get going. We have a long day ahead.'

Sandy finally tears her attention away from my face, but just before leaving the room, she turns and gives me one last look. 'Poor thing,' she says.

I do not reply. I do not know why she pities me.

Once they leave, Thelma mops her forehead and cheeks with the palms of her hands.

It finally comes to me who the braided girl must be. How stupid I have been! 'That was the girl from Schaumburg, Illinois,' I say, and Thelma nods.

'She passed after Johnny and me. She knows who killed us, doesn't she? She knows who Gunboy is.' I feel a shot of excitement. Not to mention a little ping of pain in my holey heart.

The whites of Thelma's eyes are pinker than I have ever seen them. Her face scrunches up.

'There ain't no Gunboy, Oliver.'

'What? You mean we were not shot after all?'

'No, baby, there *was* a boy with a gun.'

I am confused. 'There was no Gunboy. There was a Gunboy. How can both be true? You are making no sense, Thelma.'

Thelma takes me by the shoulders and looks me straight in the eye. Her voice comes in a raspy whisper: 'Listen to me, Oliver. The boy who shot you was Johnny.'

She is pulling my leg. I draw away, emitting a ha-ha to show that I like her joke, though I in fact find it distasteful.

Thelma Rudd is crying now, tears as big and fat as the wooden beads she wears in her hair. 'There was only two boys, not three,' she sobs. 'The killer was a mental case, Oliver! A sadcon, just like Johnny said he used to be.'

37   85.47
Rb
Rubidium

Hydrogen, helium, lithium, beryllium, boron, carbon, nitrogen, oxygen, fluorine, neon, sodium, magnesium, aluminum, silicon, phosphorus, sulfur, chlorine, argon, potassium, calcium, scandium, titanium, vanadium, chromium, manganese, iron, cobalt, nickel, copper, zinc, gallium, germanium, arsenic, selenium, bromine, krypton, rubidium, strontium, yttrium, zirconium, niobium, molybdenum, technetium, ruthenium, rhodium, palladium, silver, cadmium, indium, tin, antimony, tellurium, iodine, xenon, cesium, barium, lanthanum, cerium, praseodymium, neodymium, promethium, samarium, europium, gadolinium, terbium, dysprosium, holmium, erbium, thulium, ytterbium, lutetium, hafnium, tantalum, tungsten, rhenium, osmium, iridium, platinum, gold, mercury, thallium, lead, bismuth, polonium, astatine, radon, francium, radium, actinium, thorium, protactinium, uranium, neptunium, plutonium, americium, curium, berkelium, californium, einsteinium, fermium, mendelevium, nobelium, lawrencium, rutherfordium, dubnium, seaborgium.

38	87.62
Sr	
Strontium	

Father, you gave Johnny his last real haircut, his last before the head shave he must have had at the Schaumburg Medical Center during his stay there. The haircut occurred a few days before school started. As usual, Clippers was busy at that time of the year. Already Jermaine Tucker, Kevin Stein, Fred Winchester, and Henry Axworthy had come in, each asking for feathered bangs. You kept cracking the same lame joke about feathers: Were they Indians all of a sudden? Were Iron Eyes Cody and Sitting Bull all the rage among thirteen-year-old boys?

You like lame jokes, Father. Hence, the poster on the wall of a bald man with the caption HAIR TODAY, GONE TOMORROW. Or the sign that reads, NO, I DON'T PULL TEETH because in the Middle Ages barbers did minor surgery like tooth extraction. As you told everybody, the red stripe in the helix of the barber's pole originally stood for blood and the white stood for bandages.

In the summer and on weekends, I liked helping out at Clippers. I would sweep the floors, dust the bottles of shampoo and hair tonic kept in the shop window, and bring patrons glasses of lemonade, which, Mother, you claimed was homemade (though it came from frozen

170

concentrate). You would both send me to fetch lunches at fast-food restaurants. You wanted fried chicken, pizzas, and hamburgers: meals I disapproved of because they cut lives short. I would bring myself back a salad and a baked potato and explain to you how cholesterol built up in arteries till plaque dammed up the blood flow to the heart or brain.

I was describing arteriolosclerosis on the Saturday afternoon in late August when Johnny Henzel stopped in, hair wild and down to his shoulders. I had not seen him all summer. Henry Axworthy, who lived in our building, had taken over Johnny's paper route. I would sometimes see Johnny's sister, Brenda, walking Rover the basset hound. She looked a lot like Johnny: same double crown, same dimple in one cheek. One time I had asked where her brother had gone, and Brenda had frowned. Why did so many people frown when I attempted small talk? She had replied with a terse 'He's at camp' and then hurried off.

Johnny did not ask for feathered bangs. He asked for an eighth of an inch off (I figured his parents had sent him for a haircut he did not want). 'An eighth of an inch?' Father said. 'I never made it to high school, my boy. I can't even measure that small.'

Johnny and Father came to a compromise: a half inch. Johnny did not talk during the haircut, or even look at himself in the mirror. He simply stared at his lap. He was wearing terry-cloth sweatbands around his wrists, like those worn by tennis players, and I thought he had probably been playing tennis at camp.

When I offered him some lemonade, it seemed he barely recognized me, as though I had changed over the summer instead of him.

Father, you trimmed the half inch and then whisked away the barber's apron. (I always admired how you did this with a flourish and without leaving any hair clippings on your patron's lap.)

After Johnny paid Mother his five dollars at the cash register, I went up to him and again attempted small talk: 'So, Johnny, did you enjoy your experience at camp?'

'Camp?' he said.

'Yes, Brenda told me you were away at summer camp.'

He looked at me with steely eyes. After a pause, he said, 'Yeah, I was away at Camp Squeaky Fromme.'

'Did you have a pleasant stay?'

He finally smiled, or at least the corners of his mouth lifted. 'It was a laugh a minute, Boo, a f*cking laugh a minute.'

Then he pushed through the front door of Clippers, and the bell jingled behind him.

Mother, you asked me what was wrong with Johnny. He seemed a little off that day, you said. I told you I did not know if anything was wrong. 'He was away all summer at Camp Squeaky Fromme,' I said.

Mother said, 'Squeaky Fromme?'

'Strange name for a camp,' I said. 'It sounds like the name of a cartoon mouse.'

'Oliver, Squeaky Fromme is the crazy lady out

in California who tried to assassinate President Ford.'

'That is illogical. Why would a camp be named after that lady?'

Mother gave me a smirk. 'That boy's pulling your leg.'

I thought, *Why would Johnny Henzel pull my leg?* Jermaine Tucker, Kevin Stein, Fred Winchester, and Henry Axworthy might do so. Johnny Henzel, however, would not. He was different. He saw the beauty in slate-gray skies. He saw the appeal of early-morning solitude.

And, unlike my other classmates, he saw something good and worthy in me.

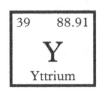

39	88.91
Y	
Yttrium	

Johnny is being held at the Gene Forrester Jail at the foot of the East Wall in Nine. Reginald Washington and Sandy Goldberg are on their way there now with the intent of identifying Johnny. Sandy claims to have the facts from back in America, but the fact is that I distrust the facts in this land I now live in. The facts of America do not apply here. The fact is that an unplugged lamp should not turn on. The fact is that thirteen-year-olds should not stay thirteen for decades on end. The fact is that people should not vanish into thin air when they die. So I will need more proof of Johnny's guilt than so-called facts from a newly passed girl from Schaumburg.

'Listen to reason,' Thelma says when I suggest the nut girl's memories might be faulty.

'But there is no rhyme or reason here,' I reply. 'If there were, heaven would not exist.'

'Oh, Oliver, if you think hard about what she says,' Thelma insists, 'you'll see it all makes sense.'

I always think hard. I am thinking hard, and nothing at all in this Zigforsaken place makes sense.

According to Thelma, Sandy Goldberg got her facts from kids at her own school in Schaumburg. Sandy swears that the shooting at Helen

Keller involved only two boys, not three. She does not remember names, but she does remember faces, and she had seen ours in the newspaper. One kid was 'a freak' and one kid was 'a mental case,' Sandy said. The mental case was suicidal and had spent the summer in a 'psycho ward.' As for the shooting, she could not remember a motive, or even any other details beyond the fact that 'One kid was weird and the other was nuts.'

Thelma tells me there was an all-points bulletin out on Johnny here in heaven. Benny Baggarly, friend of the comatose hypnotist, spotted Johnny and me at the gymnasium and reported us. It was Reginald Washington's idea to arrest Johnny in the middle of the night.

'Reginald wanted the two of you separated,' Thelma tells me. 'Being friends with Johnny, he said, would harm *your* mental health.'

'That is bullsh*t!' I shout, and Thelma looks surprised because I usually do not shout and I usually do not swear.

'My mental health is hunky-dory,' I lie.

'But, Oliver, your friend Johnny, he's . . . ' She pauses, trying to find the right word, but there is no right word, so she simply says, 'He killed you.'

'The jury is still out on that.'

Thelma and I are sitting on the bed in my temporary room. She is hugging a pillow tightly. The pillow is a stand-in for me.

'Reginald and the do-gooders are planning a trial.'

'A trial?'

'They're all fired up because heaven never had

a murderer before. They think Zig goofed. They want to fix his terrible mistake.'

'Do you think Zig made a terrible mistake, Thelma?'

My face has probably gone even whiter, even more ghostly, because she looks at me with a mix of pity and concern, just as Sandy Goldberg did. Thelma passes me the pillow to hug. I hold it limply in my lap.

'Oliver, you know how Zig changes some townies? Like retarded kids come here a bit smarter, right? And blind kids can see. Well, maybe Zig made Johnny less crazy so he could live peaceful here in Town. Is that a terrible mistake? Maybe it is, maybe it ain't.'

She is saying that just as Zig may have lowered my intelligence quotient a notch or two, he may have raised Johnny's level of sanity enough to let him function here.

'Maybe Zig changed Johnny's memories of the events,' Thelma suggests. 'Or maybe Johnny erased them when he shot himself in the head. Or maybe his sister lied to him when he was in his hospital bed.' Thelma puts a hand over her heart. 'Jiminy Crickets, I don't know what to believe, Oliver. But I don't believe what Reginald and some of them do-gooders do. They think Johnny's faking his amnesia and remembers what he did.'

I push the pillow aside and stand. My legs feel wobbly, as though I have been bicycling all day. 'I have to see Johnny,' I say.

Thelma does not want me going to the Gene. 'You're dead tired and in shock,' she says.

'Besides, Reginald and the do-gooders won't let you see Johnny. They won't even let *me*. Esther took off for the Gene, but she won't get permission either.'

'I will not be deterred,' I say.

She acquiesces, but only after forcing me to eat a bran muffin, a banana, and a handful of almonds. She then gives me her map of the zones, wishes me luck, and tells me to meet her back at the Frank and Joe tomorrow.

I hurry out of the Rhoda Penmark Dormitory, jump on a ten-speed, and pedal like mad, wishing I had thirty speeds so I could reach the jail before Reginald and Sandy do.

First, I make a quick detour to the Marcy to look for *Blaberus craniifer*. I spend fifteen minutes combing the janitor's office, even checking the Monopoly game box, but to no avail. Rover has disappeared. I hope the roach was not trampled to death in the melee last night.

I rush back outside and hop on my bike. The trip ahead will be a long jaunt requiring me to wind through a labyrinth of streets and to cross four zones (Five, One, Two, Nine). I tell myself to focus on the road. I must not become careless and smash into a streetlamp or another cyclist. I do not want to end up in an infirmary with a concussion, which, according to my notes, takes from four to six days to heal.

Still, my mind does wander. I keep picturing the hallway of Helen Keller in the first seconds after the gun went off and everybody in the hall — except the boy who pulled the trigger and the boy who was struck by the bullet — turned toward the bang. What did my classmates and teachers see?

My mind's eye imagines everyone and everything frozen in the moment. Henry Axworthy bends over the drinking fountain, an arc of water suspended before him. Jermaine Tucker drops his math book, but it does not hit the floor. Patsy Hyde's lips peel back in a scream, exposing the braces she usually keeps hidden. Cynthia Orwell dribbles a basketball that hovers a foot from her hand. The art teacher, Mr. Huston, holds a still-life drawing he is set to tape to the wall outside his classroom. Helen Keller, as always, sits posed with a mortarboard on her head in her portrait hung across from locker No. 106.

Their eyes are all turned in the same direction.

There seems to be a blind spot in my imagination, because though I see everything else perfectly, even my crumpled body at the foot of my locker, there is one thing my mind's eye cannot make out in the hallway: the face of the boy holding the gun.

40	91.22

Zr

Zirconium

The Gene Forrester Jail is the ugliest building in town. Its concrete facade is covered in black soot as though a fire once engulfed the Gene, but there was no fire because fires do not break out here. We do not even have matches. In my first month in heaven, I often tried lighting a leaf on fire using a magnifying glass and a sunray, but the experiments proved fruitless. Only a thin wisp of smoke ever emerged.

The windows at the Gene are barred, so it is lucky that buildings do not catch on fire. Another unusual thing about this four-story building is its shape: a perfect cube. Most buildings I have seen are rectangular. Also, the Gene has no exterior architectural features. No awnings or cornices, for example.

I wonder who the inmates are. They must be townies who have committed offenses like serious acts of vandalism, disturbances of the peace, and violence causing injury. Such offenses are rare here, though. Perhaps Zig subdues certain townies in order to make the most wicked of dead American thirteen-year-olds a bit kinder and to avoid bloody clashes in Town.

I get off my bicycle and tie a red ribbon around the handlebars. The day is sunny and the sky the azure color that you, Father, call wild blue yonder. It is the kind of day when you, Mother, would remind me to wear a sun hat.

As I have mentioned, our skin never burns in heaven. Yet I do feel sunburned after my two-hour bicycle ride. Maybe I am suffering from heatstroke and should look for a water fountain. I stumble up the steps of the building into the Gene's lobby, where a long wooden desk is manned by identical twin boys whose name stickers read, TIM LU and TOM LU. They are both wearing T-shirts with a yin-yang decal. I surmise they died in an accident like a house fire or a car crash. Their passing at the same time is lucky in an odd way; after all, losing a twin must be like losing a part of yourself.

The Lu twins are reading twin copies of *The Swiss Family Robinson*. 'Greetings. My name is Oliver Dalrymple. I am here to visit an inmate,' I tell them. 'A boy named Johnny Henzel.'

'Did he say Johnny Henzel?' Tim says to Tom.

'Yes, oh my, he did,' Tom says. 'He *did* say Johnny Henzel.'

I nod.

'The boy who came in last night,' Tim says to Tom as they both put down their books.

'The Grade F.'

'We *never* have Grade F's. When was the last one, Tom?'

'Before our time, I'm sure. Decades ago.'

'What does 'Grade F' mean?' I ask.

'Oliver Dalrymple doesn't know what 'Grade F' means.'

'Of course he doesn't. He's an outsider. 'Grade F' is an insider term. It means Johnny

180

Henzel did something really, really bad.'

'Heinous, you might say.'

'Yes, heinous or even egregious.'

The twins do not look at me while they talk. They look at and speak to each other.

'I wonder what he could have done,' Tom says.

'Maybe he kidnapped somebody,' Tim replies. 'We haven't had a kidnapper in ages, have we, Tom?'

'No, I can't recall the last one.'

'But kidnappers are usually classified as Grade D.'

'Maybe it was a series of kidnappings.'

'Oh my, a serial kidnapper,' Tim says. 'How despicable.'

I cut in: 'Johnny Henzel is not a serial kidnapper. He hit a boy over the head with a flashlight.'

'A flashlight?' Tim says to Tom. 'That isn't Grade F. That is Grade B, or at most C, depending on the injuries.'

'Also, it is alleged he shot somebody to death back in America.'

'*Murder!!!!*' Tom shouts.

'Keep it down, Tom! You're not being very professional.'

'Murder is definitely Grade F.'

'Could I see Johnny Henzel?' I say.

'Oliver Dalrymple wants to visit a Grade F!'

'Even Grade D's can't have visitors. Even Grade D's are in solitary confinement on the fourth floor. So imagine Grade F's!'

'But I am the boy who Johnny allegedly shot.'

'Oliver Dalrymple's the victim! Oh my! Oh

goodness! A shooting victim!'

'Well, this is highly unusual, don't you think, Tim?'

' 'Unprecedented' is the word that leaps to mind.'

Tim and Tom Lu converse back and forth like this before deciding that one of them will check with authorities to see if Johnny can receive a visit from the boy he shot.

'*Allegedly* shot,' I say as Tim pushes back his chair and heads off.

While Tim is gone, I sit on a bench in a far corner and stare at the colored floor tiles, which form a kind of circular mandala like those that Buddhist monks create out of sand. Mandalas are supposed to favor peace, but my state of mind is hardly peaceful.

People who believe in a god often think, during trying periods in their lives, that their god is testing them. Is Zig conducting some kind of experiment here in Town despite his usual hands-off policy?

After ten minutes, Tim Lu is still not back. Meanwhile, the front doors to the Gene open, and in come Reginald Washington and Sandy Goldberg. They walk with purpose, their running shoes squeaking across the mandala. Reginald takes out his official do-good council president badge. They speak to Tom Lu, who says, 'Boy, is our Grade F a popular boy today. There's a lineup to see him.' Tom nods toward the bench where I sit. I stand as Reginald and Sandy turn toward me.

Reginald narrows his eyes. He looks peeved.

'Heaven help us,' he says, loudly enough for me to hear. He crosses the floor to speak to me.

'Hello, Oliver,' he says, a forced smile on his face. 'What a surprise to see you here.'

'I want to see Johnny,' I say.

His smile disappears. 'Did Thelma send you? What was that girl thinking?'

'I want to be the one giving Johnny the news.'

Reginald slowly shakes his head. 'No can do, brother. No can do.'

'Why not? I am his friend. One of his few friends here.'

Reginald pats my shoulder. 'You've had a shock,' he says. 'You need to rest in peace. In fact, I've asked Thelma to book you into the Deborah.'

'The asylum?!' I picture Willa Blake's sickening plunge from the roof. 'That is the last place I need to be!'

Reginald tells me I can wait in the lobby till he and Sandy finish their business upstairs with Johnny and the authorities. 'Afterward, I'd like to talk to you about acting as a witness in a trial,' he says.

He returns to speak with the Lu twins. I feel exhausted. I press the palms of my hands into my eyes, just as I used to do in America when my eyes were red from reading mathematics books for hours on end. When I remove them, Sandy stands before me.

'Hello again, Oliver. You sure made good time. Reginald and me stopped along the way for blueberry pancakes. There was no butter, though. I totally miss butter, and I wish Zig would send us some, but at least we got syrup, right? Imagine if Zig decided, 'No sweets for my children.' ' She does Zig's voice low and gruff. ' 'Their teeth will rot out of their head!' That would be a tragedy and a half, don't you think? Having no sweets, I mean. Not rotten teeth. Are you a butter person?'

I have the unkind thought that her brain is the size of the peanut that did her in. 'May I ask you a question?' I say.

'Sure, ask away. I'm an open book.'

'Did Johnny Henzel target me back at Helen Keller Junior High? When he shot his gun, did he plan to hit *me*?'

I cannot stop myself from asking, even though my question implies that I believe Johnny is guilty.

Sandy shrugs. 'I hardly remember a thing, just that the other kid was in a psycho ward. I remember that 'cause I almost got sent to a psycho ward once. My mom thought I was anorexic — can you believe it? — but the reason I didn't eat much was 'cause I was just always afraid of swallowing an allergen. I was allergic to loads of things — nuts, strawberries, buckwheat, tomatoes. But nuts were totally the worst. I couldn't even — '

'You hardly remember a thing?!' I say, my voice rising and going squeaky. 'One must be absolutely certain with accusations such as yours, Ms. Goldberg!'

She shrugs again, and I finally understand the phrase 'shooting the messenger' because I want to slap her silly face.

Reginald comes back. 'We have to go now, Sandy,' he says.

'Tell Johnny I'm here,' I plead with them. 'Give him a message from me. Tell him . . . '

What to tell him? *Do not lose hope. Do not lose your mind.*

'Tell him, 'If you're ever in a jam, here I am.' ''

It is a line from the song 'Friendship.'

Tim Lu has returned and says loudly to his brother, 'Until further notice, Mr. Dalrymple is denied the right to visit the Grade F.'

Because of his council president badge, however, Reginald is not denied visiting rights. Tom Lu escorts him and Sandy to the staircase leading to the upper floors.

When they are gone, I tell myself I must be as hardy as Joe and Frank: I must concoct a plan to rescue Johnny from this place. I sit back down. I am so dog-tired that my body, seemingly without my brain's consent, lies across the bench. Thelma had given me a hooded sweatshirt to wear over my T-shirt, and I take it off to use as a pillow under my head. Tim and Tom throw me scolding looks from behind their novels, but I do not, as Johnny would say, give a flying f*ck (an expression whose etymology I cannot even guess).

Nobody else comes in or goes out. The jail seems to be the most underused building in heaven. It is so quiet that I wonder if I might hear Johnny's reaction when he learns of the charges against him.

It is unfathomable to me that Johnny Henzel was Gunboy on the fourth day of eighth grade at

Helen Keller Junior High. It simply cannot be. But even if it were true, I tell myself, it should not matter. What should matter is whether Johnny is Gunboy now, here in our heaven reserved for American thirteen-year-olds.

The front door of the jail opens. In walks Esther, wearing a pink beret. I sit up. She spots me right away and waves. I am heartened to see her. I wave back.

41	92.91
Nb	
Niobium	

42	95.95
Mo	
Molybdenum	

43	[97.91]
Tc	
Technetium	

It is New Year's Eve day, the last day of the seventies. It has been three weeks since I last saw Johnny. When I pass by the Gene's backyard, I gaze up at the windows on the fourth floor, but they are tiny — barely larger than the cover of a comic book. I cannot see whether anyone is looking out. I am not even sure which room Johnny is held in.

It can be upsetting to come here because a posse of demonstrators often gathers in the yard. I do not know why the jailers allow this. Maybe they see the demonstrations as a form of just punishment. The demonstrators, mostly gommers, from what I gather, carry placards scrawled with hurtful messages, such as JOHNNY HENZEL YOUR AN ERROR.

The worst placard I have seen, however, was wielded by Benny Baggarly, the gommer who turned Johnny and me in to the do-good authorities. His placard contained two words in big letters: REDEATH PENALTY!

Since today is a holiday, the demonstrators are not here when Esther and I show up at the Gene. I bring along a placard made from a broom handle and a piece of poster board. Esther suggested I communicate with Johnny this way. I did not know what to say. On my placard, I finally wrote, IN THE PURSUIT OF TRUTH WE ARE PERMITTED TO REMAIN CHILDREN ALL OUR LIVES. It is a quote from Albert Einstein. I hope it is not too obscure. I simply mean to say I will keep an open mind and get to the bottom of the mystery surrounding us.

Esther has come with me, but she has gone into the lobby to speak to Tim and Tom Lu. They give her whispered updates on the boy they still refer to only as 'the Grade F.' They refuse to give updates to me. They are wary of me. They call me the victim. 'Oh, the victim's back again,' Tim might say. And Tom might reply, 'When will that boy learn he isn't welcome here?'

As I wait for Esther, I stand in the yard behind the jail, my placard raised. The windows on the lower floors are normal size. In one window, I notice a jailbird with an orange baseball cap. He waves to me, and I wave my sign back.

Holy mackerel clouds are rolling across the sky this afternoon. They are Johnny's favorite, so perhaps he is peeking out his tiny window right now.

I am so absorbed in the thought that I do not at first notice that Esther has returned. She is furrowing her brow.

'What?' I say.

She bites her top lip and shakes her head grimly. Then she says, 'That stupid b*stard hasn't touched his food in a week now.'

'Johnny is not eating?'

'He's on a hunger strike.'

I glance back at the Gene.

'He'll start eating again on one condition,' she says. 'If he's allowed a visit from you.'

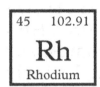

45	102.91

Rh

Rhodium

Townies can stop eating all they want, but they will never grow thinner. Thelma went on a drastic diet early in her stay in Town, but she says she simply grew so weak she started hallucinating (toucans flocking in the trees and dolphins swimming through the clouds). Whether we can die from abstaining from food nobody seems to know, because nobody — not even a sadcon at the Deborah — has stopped eating long enough.

The hypnotist Charles 'Czar' Lindblom is no longer in a coma, and once he started coming around, he was fed the types of food a baby eats: mashed potatoes, applesauce, gruel. He is now strong enough to serve as a witness at Johnny's trial, which gets under way in a week's time.

It feels lonely having my room to myself. I am glad Johnny left many of his drawings behind to adorn the walls. He did a series called *Wish Come True*. For example, there is one drawing of Thelma dressed in pearls and a sparkly gown like the dress a jazz singer might wear onstage.

He asked me to choose a subject for my own portrait. I told him to give me time to decide on a suitable wish. Were he here now, I would ask him to draw the two of us lying in the snow in Hoffman Estates and gazing at the wispy moon.

In that moment, we were truly resting in peace.

Around seven o'clock, Thelma and Esther knock on my door because we are supposed to go to a play together. Plenty of plays, concerts, magic shows, choreographies, and acrobatics will be staged tonight. You see, on New Year's Eve, townies present the most beautiful art they created in the past year. All across Town, painters exhibit their finest paintings, and sculptors their best sculptures. Guitarists play the compositions that make them proudest. Harpists strum their most angelic pieces. Singers sing their most heartrending songs. Poets stand on soapboxes and recite their most elegant poems, and storywriters read aloud their most inspired work. Townies claim they do all these things to thank Zig, but I believe they are also trying to prove they are bearing up well despite the box (i.e., the terrarium) that their god has confined them to.

Just after we leave the Frank and Joe, Esther turns to Thelma and me in the street. She is wearing a fake mink stole, what she calls her 'fun fur.' 'Let's make a pact,' she says. 'That tonight we won't talk about it.'

Thelma nods in agreement. 'We need a break, at least for a few hours.'

'Okay,' I say, even though I feel like a traitor.

The play we will see is called *The Effect of Gamma Rays on Man-in-the-Moon Marigolds*. Thelma says it is about a girl awestruck by science and mistreated by her crazy mother. It is right up our alley because I am fond of science and Esther had an overbearing mother (who nicknamed her daughter Li'l, a name Esther loathed).

We head down the street, which is teeming with bicycles and pedestrians. Everybody seems to be out this evening. Townies sing aloud and do dance steps on the sidewalk. A boy does a triple cartwheel across the lawn of his dorm and then a somersault in the air. Do-gooders climb trees in a park to hang balloons and streamers from the branches.

Exhibition tables are set up along the sidewalks. At one table sits a boy who creates origami creatures (tiger, grasshopper, giraffe, pterodactyl) and silver necklaces like those that children in America make out of gum wrappers (Town has no gum, so he uses aluminum foil). Beside him is a girl who makes shoebox dioramas of scenes from novels (for example, a jungle scene from Tarzan of the Apes). Beside her is a boy who makes papier-mâché masks, one of which has a schnozzola like Uncle Seymour's.

A girl with hair that looks cut with a Weedwacker comes up to me in the street. 'You're Boo, right?' she says. 'The murdered kid?' People recognize me lately, though there are no newspapers or television reports here to display my photograph.

'Just want to say,' she says with a shy smile, 'that I'm rooting for you.' She places a hand on my shoulder, but Esther brushes it off for me.

'Rooting for me,' I say. 'What do you mean?'

'Well, the kid who shot you, I think he really should get — '

Thelma cuts in: 'We're late for a play.'

The girl goes on: 'His just deserts.'

I do not know how to reply, so I concentrate on etymology. 'The expression 'just deserts' doesn't mean the cake or cookie we eat after a meal,' I tell the girl. 'It means what a person justly deserves.'

The girl blinks at me. 'Yeah, I know. And your killer deserves to be hung.' She does a pantomime of tightening a noose around her own neck.

Thelma pats her heart.

'The correct past participle is 'hanged,' ' I say.

'We're not talking about it tonight!' Esther yells at the girl, her arms gesturing wildly. 'So shut your big fat ignorant mouth!'

The girl backs away as though Esther is a snarling dog.

This brief encounter seems to ruin any pretense of a festive mood. On the rest of our walk to the theater, the three of us speak little. Luckily, however, the play turns out to be excellent. In it, a girl named Tillie Hunsdorfer exposes marigolds to radioactivity. Some of the flowers wither and die, while others mutate into odd but splendid creatures.

Thelma has warned us she often cries at the theater, and she does in fact weep during the final scene where Tillie's mother murders Tillie's pet rabbit. Esther hands Thelma tissues from her purse, which is decorated with felt sunflowers.

I, of course, do not weep. I am not used to attending plays. In America, as you know, Mother and Father, I did not go to the theater. I did not watch situation comedies or police dramas on television. I did not read novels. I did not do any of the things requiring a leap into a fictional world. I did not understand the need for fiction when real-life events — the true dramas occurring at the cellular level in our bodies and at the astrophysical level in our universe — were so fantastic and fascinating.

Only in the real world of heaven have I discovered a use for make-believe. One benefit of fiction: it puts your mind off your reality when your reality is off-putting. I wish I had made this discovery back in America. Maybe *Lord of the Flies* would have helped me survive junior high.

When the play is over and we are discussing the merits of its fictional world in the lobby of the school, we are brought back to reality by a poster thumbtacked to a cork bulletin board. The title of the poster reads, THE SON OF THE SON OF SAM.

It is about Johnny. His crimes. His upcoming trial. The local gommer group is urging townies to demonstrate outside the Gene throughout the trial. I read aloud: ' 'A bloodthirsty killer is in our midst and may strike again if we do not — ' '

Esther rips down the poster and crumples it before I can read to the end. 'Damn gommers,' she says, narrowing her eyes at Thelma. Thelma has in fact been kicked out of the local gommer group because she wavers on the need to punish crimes committed before a townie passed into heaven. The word around Town is that if Johnny is found guilty, the gommers are pushing for a public stoning.

'I wish we could get away from heaven,'

Thelma says. 'I wish we could go on a haunting to my grandma's house in Louisiana. We could pick peaches and make a pie. We could save a slice for Johnny to end his hunger strike.'

Esther rolls her eyes at the idea. 'Oh, for f*ck sake,' she says, adopting Johnny's expression.

Thelma looks dejected, and I probably look sad and confused.

'You two deadbeats need to cheer the hell up,' Esther says. 'It's New Year's Eve!'

'I'm scared what'll happen,' Thelma whispers. 'Gommers gunning for a stoning. Johnny not eating.'

'Our pact!' Esther cries, hands on hips.

We go sit under a weeping willow in a park. Around us, revelers play flutes, harmonicas, and Jew's harps. People sing show tunes, disco songs, and jazz standards. I ask the girls about their plans for the New Year.

Thelma will put together a musical on the life of Miss Otis from the Cole Porter song. She will write, direct, and star. Because Miss Otis was crazy, Thelma will call the musical *Out to Lunch*.

Esther will design clothes for other fashionable townies using the sewing machine in her room. Her tastes run to high fashion, so she will make items like pleated skirts and ruffled blouses. She will knit sweater vests out of acrylic yarn. She also has 'a hippie, groovy side' and will draw dozens of peace symbols with a Magic Marker on a canvas belt and bouquets of daisies on a vinyl purse.

I tell the girls I plan to write a guide to

grammar and punctuation titled *Who Is Whom?* I may also take some literature classes. Students learn about the history of the American South by reading *Huckleberry Finn* and *Tom Sawyer.* They learn about the Roaring Twenties by reading *The Great Gatsby* and *The Sun Also Rises.* They learn about justice by reading *To Kill a Mockingbird.* They learn some French by reading *Tintin.*

I will also start work part-time at Curios right after the holiday. Peter Peter wants me to help him with a new exhibition spotlighting curious townies, late thirteen-year-olds who made a name for themselves in odd ways in their afterlife.

For example, the late Frederick Koenig was a big-calved boy who, for nine years in a row, won the Tour de Paradis, a bicycle race along the streets bordering the four Great Walls.

The late Diego Alvarez, a baker's son, became Town's most celebrated chef. He whipped up mouthwatering recipes that most townies had never tasted before, like stuffed charred peppers, maple butternut soup, and portobello mushroom risotto. He left behind a cookbook titled *Diego's Diner.*

The late Lesley Gapper was a postmistress who came up with the zip codes assigned to the different blocks in the thirteen zones. Each code is a three-letter pronounceable word, like HAM, ROW, TIP, and GUT. As a result, people living on the different blocks sometimes call themselves hammers, rowers, tippers, and gutters.

On the subject of neologisms, the late Monica

Schneider created a glossary of heavenisms, words coined here or used differently here than in America. She typed dozens and dozens of copies of her glossary to distribute. The words include 'townie,' 'gommer,' 'do-gooder,' 'sadcon,' 'old boy,' and another I have learned recently, 'countdowner.'

A countdowner is somebody who stands on a rooftop on New Year's Eve and counts down minutes and seconds while townies gather around to shout 'Thank Zig!' simultaneously when the clock strikes midnight.

In fact, I will be the countdowner at the Frank and Joe tonight, so the girls and I walk back to my dorm. We head to the roof, where a dozen townies are wandering about with flashlights or penlights in their hands. Gym mats are spread everywhere so we can lie and gaze at Zig's sky as we await the spiritual moment when we will all thank our god and the lucky stars he gave us.

Over the next half hour, more and more townies appear on the roof of the Frank and Joe — not only residents but also guests from other dorms. All around me people choose a gym mat and lie down. Esther and Thelma do likewise on either side of me. As tonight's countdowner, I am the only person allowed to stay standing. I am also the only person permitted to speak before the time comes to give thanks. I stand between Esther and Thelma, a hand grasping a bullhorn and my eyes on my glow-in-the-dark ghost. When Casper's little hand points north and his big hand hits ten, I shout into the bullhorn: '*Ten minutes!*' An echo sweeps over us because countdowners all across Town are yelling the same thing, our wristwatches synchronized.

I stare skyward and picture you, Mother, with your smile that exposes your gums, and you, Father, with your eyelids that droop when you are tired.

I get lost in my thoughts and miss my Casper cue. *'Five minutes!'* comes the call from surrounding buildings. Shoot! I make my announcement, but a few seconds late.

I look up at my three-legged horse hovering in the stars. While I stare at my constellation, the stars forming its tail start to move. I blink several times, but they keep moving back and forth as though the horse is wagging its tail like a dog. Goose bumps rise on my arms. Is this a spiritual moment?

'Zig?' I whisper in the night.

I glance down at Esther and Thelma. By now all flashlights are off, so I cannot make out their expressions. Do they see the wagging stars? Does anyone else? Nobody around me seems startled or alarmed. Everyone gazes heavenward. There is barely a sound, other than an occasional cough or sneeze and the skin of people's limbs unsticking now and then from the vinyl mats.

I check Casper just in time. *'One minute!'* I shout together with countdowners atop all the surrounding dorms.

I glance back at the horse, but its tail has come to a rest, fixed again in the heavens. My eyes must be playing tricks on me tonight.

Throughout Town, hundreds and hundreds of

reborn thirteen-year-olds prepare to thank Zig for their life after death. In fact, we townies form a kind of Milky Way, each of us a star in a galaxy of Zig's making. Esther Haglund, Thelma Rudd, Peter Peterman, Reginald Washington, Tim and Tom Lu, Charles Lindblom, Sandy Goldberg, and of course Johnny Henzel.

The final countdown begins. Into my bullhorn, I shout: '*Ten Mississippi! Nine Mississippi! Eight Mississippi! Seven Mississippi! Six Mississippi! Five Mississippi! Four Mississippi! Three Mississippi! Two Mississippi! One Mississippi!*'

Off go all the streetlamps as a roar rises into the night skies. A flare erupting from the mouth of every boy and every girl across the land. A cry that is meant to be gratitude but that sounds strangely like anger.

'*THANK ZIG!*'

46   106.42
Pd
Palladium

Two days after New Year's, I am in my new office on the third floor of the Guy Montag Library when there comes a knock at my door. I expect it is the curator, Peter Peter.

Peter Peter has gone through puberty, can grow some facial hair, and speaks with a deep voice; he may look like the kind of strapping boy who used to taunt me back at Helen Keller, but he is in fact kind and patient. Sometimes I lunch with the old boy and quiz him about the forty-six years he has spent in heaven. Peter Peter is a true anthropologist, an expert on the evolution of Town and the objects sent here. He calls me son. He is older than you, Father.

On New Year's Day, he invited Thelma to a harpsichord concert in the Northeast Corner (where the North and East Walls meet). Thelma now says they are going steady, even though Esther says one date does not sound steady to her.

I put down the object I am studying — a silver cigarette lighter with a rattlesnake engraved on its side — and go open my office door. It is not Peter Peter after all. To my surprise, it is Tim and Tom Lu. Over their T-shirts, they wear contrasting neckties: Tim's is blue with red polka dots, and Tom's is red with blue polka dots.

'Tom, you have a message to deliver to the victim, don't you?'

'I certainly do, Tim. A private, sealed letter from Lydia Finkle, the jail warden.'

'I wonder what the letter says,' Tim replies.

'I asked Ms. Finkle myself, but she pretended not to hear me,' Tom says.

'Maybe the victim will open his letter and read it aloud so we'll know what Ms. Finkle wants with him.'

As usual, they do not look directly at me while they speak. Tim hands a manila envelope to Tom, who hands it back to Tim. They pass the envelope back and forth till finally I reach over and pluck it away.

'I wonder if it hurts to get shot in the back.'

'If your friend is the shooter, I imagine it hurts very much.'

'The word 'agonizing' might apply.'

'I'd go so far as to say 'excruciating.' '

I walk over to my desk and use my fake-tortoiseshell letter opener on the envelope. I pull out the letter, unfold it, and read it aloud to satisfy the twins.

Dear Oliver Dalrymple,

In my capacity as warden of the Gene Forrester Jail, I am writing to request your presence at our facility this Wednesday at ten in the morning.

I have been informed you wish to visit one of our prisoners, John Henzel, who would not be permitted a visitor under normal circumstances, given the seriousness of the accusations weighing against him. However, as I am sure you are well aware, the circumstances in this particular case are far from normal.

Mr. Henzel has foolishly embarked upon a hunger strike as his trial draws near. He has informed us that he will resume eating if allowed a visit from you. After much reflection, the board here at the jail, together with the do-good council from your own zone, has agreed to consent to Mr. Henzel's request. Please note, however, that your visit will be supervised by your council president, Mr. Reginald Washington, and limited to ten minutes.

I feel we must all work together to ensure Mr. Henzel remains fit and lucid enough to attend his trial. Can I count on your presence then this coming Wednesday? Please send me an immediate reply through my couriers.

Yours sincerely,
Lydia Finkle
Warden, Gene Forrester Jail

I go to the typewriter on my desk and remove the description of butane (C_4H_{10}) that I was writing. I crank in a blank sheet of paper and reply to Lydia Finkle.

Dear Lydia Finkle,

Thank you for your invitation to visit Johnny

Henzel. You can certainly count on my presence on Wednesday.

Before meeting you in person, however, I wish to inform you of certain facts, not about the accusations weighing against Johnny (I am sure you are familiar with those), but rather regarding my own reaction to the possibility he ended my life back in America.

The friends I have made here in heaven (and even strangers who have heard my story) all wish to know how I feel now about Johnny.

Ms. Finkle, I can assure you I do not feel vengeful or spiteful. People ask if I can forgive Johnny, but 'forgive' and 'forgiveness' are not words I would use in this case because I have never felt anger toward him.

What I feel is mercy. I feel merciful toward him because if he did commit the crime in question, he did so during a psychotic rage that bears no relation to the boy who now sits in your jail cell.

Most gommers expect me to share their desire for an eye for an eye and a tooth for a tooth. They believe if I do not feel vengeful for my own death, I should at least feel vengeful for theirs (many of their murders were indeed horrific). In other words, they want to borrow my eye and my tooth so they can then feel free to pluck out Johnny's. I do not deem such a response fair to anyone.

Death changes a child. We townies are not necessarily the same children we left behind in our previous lives. I myself am slightly less intelligent and slightly more social than the boy I left crumpled on the floor of a school hallway in Hoffman Estates, Illinois. Owing to this change in character, I can feel for another human being, something I admit I had trouble doing back in America.

I can feel friendship and I can feel mercy.

Ms. Finkle, you also must be different today from the person you once were. Maybe in America you were a vain and haughty girl devoted to collecting cashmere sweaters and Girl Scouts badges. (This is just a guess on my part based on girls I knew in Illinois.)

In any event, I expect you are wiser than the thirteen-year-old girl you left behind. I imagine that, to serve as warden, you must have great wisdom. Can I count on your wisdom to treat Johnny Henzel with mercy?

Kind regards,
Oliver 'Boo' Dalrymple

By the time I finish typing, Tim and Tom Lu are sitting on the floor of my office and playing Go Fish with a deck of cards adorned with images of bare-breasted ladies (a curious object that came in from Two yesterday). I hand over my typed letter and tell them to read it if they wish. They do so, shoulder to shoulder, their lips moving silently in tandem.

When they finish, Tim says to Tom, 'Would you show mercy to me if I murdered you?'

Tom replies, 'Are you crazy? Not on your life!'

Prisoners must dress in orange T-shirts, orange gym shorts, and orange sneakers so they are easier to recognize should they escape. Townies tend not to dress in all-orange clothing to avoid looking like a prisoner, but Esther brought me a similar orange getup to wear in solidarity during my visit to the Gene. When Tim Lu sees my outfit, he says, 'Oh, how adorable, the victim identifies with the Grade F.' Tom Lu unlocks the door leading inside the jail and takes me down a series of hallways. I carry a peach pie, which Thelma made for Johnny to entice him to start eating again.

The building's interior looks as though an earthquake of at least six on the Richter scale has struck. Usually buildings can repair themselves, but the Gene certainly seems less efficient in this regard. Doorways are so crooked that doors are beveled to close properly, deep cracks run across walls, patches of plaster are missing from ceilings, floorboards are loose and squeaky, and nail heads jut out of them to trip us up. 'Watch your step,' Tom says, pointing out a nail head or two. He leads me past the offices of the prison guards, who wear their purple armbands. At the end of another hall is a door marked WARDEN.

Tom knocks and calls out, 'Ms. Finkle, Mr.

Merciful is here.' He leads me into the office but does not leave till the warden shoos him away. Lydia Finkle is a doe-faced, straw-haired girl. She wears a sweatshirt inside out so the fluffy cashmere-like side is exposed. Pinned to her sweater is a badge illustrating a campfire. I do not know how to interpret these direct references to my letter. Is she being flippant or supportive? She sits in a swivel chair cranked to its highest height, and consequently her feet do not touch the floor. She is swinging them, and I wish she would stop.

Reginald Washington is also here. I tell myself not to stare at his splotchy skin, but it is difficult because I find his vitiligo beautiful. It reminds me of a jigsaw puzzle or an island nation such as Malaysia. The council president is wearing a striped necktie over an $E=mc^2$ T-shirt. He also has a lime-colored pick wedged into his Afro.

He is perched on one end of a threadbare couch and motions for me to sit too. I take a seat on the opposite end and hold the pie in my lap. The pie contains a nail file because Esther insisted Johnny could use a little levity. Esther and Thelma are waiting in the lobby and have suggested certain things to tell Johnny. He should stay hopeful, for instance, because we will do our utmost to free him. He should stick to the truth at his trial. The jury, we are sure, will realize he is no longer the boy he might have been in America.

Reginald says to me, 'I want you to know I am personally opposed to this meeting. It sets a dangerous precedent.'

The warden sighs and stops swinging her feet. 'Oh, Reginald,' she says. 'Let's not go down that road again.'

'It's a form of blackmail,' he says, wagging a finger at her.

I turn to my council president. 'How did you feel when you first came to Town?' I ask. 'Did you come here different from the boy you used to be? Did Zig change you in any way? Did he make you more confident? More adjusted? I imagine a boy with your condition must have attracted his share of cruelty back in America.'

Reginald exhales dramatically. 'What is your point, Oliver?' he says. 'That Zig adjusts all of us for the better? That he did the same for John Henzel? Well, that's your opinion, one that other people — like a certain Charles Lindblom — may not share.'

The warden cuts in: 'Reginald, we shouldn't say what other witnesses may or may not think.'

Reginald gives her a pouty look.

'We should proceed with the visit,' the warden says. 'The Grade F is waiting.'

So we rise, and the warden extends her hand to me. I shake it quickly. Her palm is dry, as though she rubs chalk dust over it. 'I was a fan of cashmere,' she says, looking me in the eye. 'But that was another lifetime ago when I was a very different kind of girl.'

Reginald guides me through the hallways of the ground floor to a staircase leading to the upper floors. When we reach the fourth floor, I get a sinking feeling because I notice that heavy furniture has been placed in front of certain doors. The doors are not barred like in a jail in America. They are the same kind of solid wooden doors found in any dorm in heaven.

As we walk down the hall, one prisoner shouts from his room, 'Hey, you guys, I need clean sheets. I wet the bed again.'

Three jailers in armbands slide a dresser away from Johnny's door. One jailer is Ringo, the British fellow who dragged me out of the gymnasium. He nods at me and says, 'You watch yourself in there. That chap is unpredictable. He threw his breakfast tray at me this morning. I brought him another one.'

Once the dresser is out of the way, Reginald taps on the door. 'Hello there, John. It's President Washington. I'm here with your visitor.'

Reginald unlocks the simple push-button doorknob, swings the door open, and strides inside.

Johnny Henzel is sitting on a mattress placed directly on the concrete floor near the far wall. I feel both glad and glum — glad because here he is, alive and kicking, and glum because he looks paler than I.

'I'll be your countdowner,' Reginald says. 'I'll wait here in the doorway and time your visit.'

Johnny motions me over and pats the mattress. I kick off my running shoes and join him there. He is wearing the standard orange shorts and T-shirt, and orange-ringed socks. His eyes are dark and sunken, his lips dry and cracked. He runs a hand through his bristly hair.

'Hey, Boo,' he says, his voice hoarser than on

the night he arrived in Town. 'What's new?'

'Hello, Johnny.'

I set the peach pie on the floor beside a plastic tray containing a bowl of Raisin Bran, a glass of carrot juice, an apple, and a few figs on a paper plate. Maybe this will be the meal he will eat at the end of our visit. Beside the tray is a sketch pad, along with a wooden cigar box.

I wonder if I should hug Johnny. I am usually allergic to hugs, but ought I make an exception? Johnny gives me a guarded look, as though he is a little afraid of me, or shy.

The room is the same size as our dorm room at the Frank and Joe, but other than a small chair-desk, there is no furniture. A few orange T-shirts are stacked in a corner with balled-up socks piled atop them. The walls are crisscrossed with cracks. The tiny window is too high to look out of, and I suppose it does not slide open. Off the main room is a closet-size space containing a toilet and a pedestal sink.

'Listen, Boo,' Johnny whispers, leaning close. He does not smell oniony, so the jailers must prod him into showering. 'Take a peek inside my pencil case. There's something I want you to see, but I don't want the jailers to know about it. Understand?'

I glance at the cigar box. Various dog breeds are printed on it: poodles, Great Danes, boxers.

'Yeah, they let me draw in the slammer,' he says a little louder so Reginald can hear. 'I'd go nuts if I couldn't draw.'

I pick up the box. I lift the lid.

Heavens! Inside, sitting on a raft of colored

pencils, is *Blaberus craniifer*.

I shut the box. Johnny takes it from me.

My eyebrows raise. 'How?' I say.

'He came out of my sink,' Johnny whispers, nodding toward his bathroom. 'He followed me here like a lost dog tracking down his master. The jailers don't know. They can't know or they'll take him away.'

'Seven minutes!' Reginald calls out from his post in the doorway. He is like a zoologist observing the behavior of two monkeys placed in the same cage.

'Rover has helped me find a portal.'

'A portal?' I whisper back.

'I'm getting out of here,' he says in an urgent whisper. 'I'm going back home.'

'But how?' I glance around the room. 'Where is this portal? The sink? You cannot fit down a sink, Johnny.'

'I can't explain. There's no time. But you gotta promise me something.' He grips my hands and stares me in the eyes. How dark his irises are. 'Promise me that no matter what I say at the trial, you'll go along with it.'

My stomach clenches. 'What do you plan to say?'

'Just promise me. You have to. Don't wreck this for me. Please! I'm begging you, man.' Johnny's eyes tear up, the whites reddening. His upper lip trembles. His nose starts to run. 'Please, Boo.'

'But, Johnny, who is Gunboy?' I keep my voice down. 'The boy in your nightmares, who *is* he?'

He wipes his nose with the back of his hand.

'You wanna know?' he whispers, even hoarser now. 'Gunboy is madness. My madness, your madness, everybody's madness in this f*cking nightmare of a heaven.'

'*Our* madness?'

He cradles his pencil box in his lap. He speaks to it, or perhaps to his roach, when he says, 'I was sick in the head. Gunboy was the mad me, the crazy me. He's been hunting me for a long time. Even back in America, he was after me.'

'But you are not Gunboy anymore, are you?'

'Maybe I am. Maybe I'll always be a little bit mental.' He looks at me again, eyes still glistening.

Reginald calls out, 'Two minutes!'

'I'll explain everything later, okay? Just promise to back me up at the trial. Don't contradict what I say. And don't tell nobody you're doing this. Not even Thelma and Esther.'

I simply stare at him. I do not know what to say.

'Promise me, Boo!' he says louder. 'You owe me.'

What do I owe this boy, this Gunboy? I do not know, but I nod nonetheless. 'I promise,' I say.

'Time's up!' Reginald shouts. He strides into the cell and grabs me by the arm. 'Come, come,' he says, digging his fingernails into my biceps. I do not move, so he wrenches me up, and I cry out in pain.

In a flash, Johnny grabs Thelma's peach pie. He rises and smashes it into the side of Reginald's head. Peach preserves smear across the president's cheek. Piecrust sticks to

211

his $E = mc^2$. A nail file and an aluminum plate fall to his feet.

Reginald lets go of my arm. He backs toward the door, barking, 'Guards! Guards!'

'Look, Boo!' Johnny says. 'A piebald covered in pie.'

'Get out, Oliver!' Reginald orders, wiping his face furiously with his hands. 'Wait outside.' He points into the hall.

I stay put.

Ringo dashes into the cell and says, 'Oh, what'd you do now, Johnny boy?'

'I'm sick to death of this lunacy,' Reginald says, picking peach slices off his clothes and flicking them in Johnny's direction. 'It has no place in our sweet hereafter.'

A second guard appears. Burly. A black crew cut. He walks toward Johnny, puts up his dukes, and punches him square in the nose. Johnny stumbles back and falls to the floor. I try to go to him, but Ringo grabs my arm.

The burly guard jiggles his fist and says, 'Ow, that hurt.'

Johnny lies motionless on his side, blood dripping from one nostril. Then he reaches out, plucks up a peach slice lying nearby, and plops it into his mouth. 'Happy now, j*ckoffs?' he mumbles. 'I'm eating.'

'We told the jailers not to allow the grade F that pie,' Tim Lu says, 'but did they listen to us? No, as usual, they did not.'

'And they suffered the consequences,' Tom Lu adds.

'Oh, what a brouhaha!'

'A real hullabaloo!'

The twins are watching us from their reception desk. I am back in the Gene's lobby, sitting between Esther and Thelma on a bench. The girls are trying to calm me down. I became wheezy while recounting what had happened, so Esther passed me the paper bag she keeps in her sunflower purse to treat my attacks. Now I am breathing in and out to restore my levels of carbon dioxide.

I take the bag away. 'Rover has helped him find a portal,' I whisper. 'He is going home. Or so he claims.'

'I don't trust Rover,' Esther says. 'When we had the chance, we should have flushed that turd down the toilet.'

'Johnny hasn't ate in over a week,' Thelma says. 'He might just be hallucinating a portal. The boy ain't himself.'

'Well, who the hell is the real *himself*? That's what I wanna know,' Esther replies.

I do not mention my vow to agree with whatever Johnny says at his trial, which starts in three days. I am unsure about what my promise may mean. What foolish claims is he planning to make?

The girls and I shuffle out of the Gene, our faces woebegone, our thoughts dark. We climb on our bikes. Esther and Thelma plan to go back to their dorms in Eleven, but I want to head to Curios to do some work. When I arrive there more than an hour later, a cardboard box awaits me in my office. In it are new curious objects freshly delivered from Two for me to appraise. I am glad for the distraction: it gives me a break from thinking about the madness of the past weeks and the madness that lies ahead.

I open the box and spread the items across my desk. I pick up a spray bottle of a perfume called Tigress. The stopper is designed in fake tiger fur. The bottle is half full, and I spritz some of the amber-colored perfume into the air. It smells like cinnamon.

A windup music box is another of the items. When I open it, instead of a ballerina, there appears an ugly little gnome astride a broken witch's broom. The figurine sits on a spring and wobbles while the music to the children's song 'The Wobblin' Goblin' plays. This song is close to my heart because when I was a child, you would sing it to me, Mother. I let the music box play as I examine the other new objects.

There is a paperback book titled *A Glossary of Accounting Terms*, one of the closest things to a dictionary that has been seen in heaven. I flip through the pages but find the book of little interest. After all, townies need not understand the concept of 'cash flow statements' and 'merit salary adjustments.'

There is a half-finished tube of anti-acne cream. I screw off the cap and press out a dab of the stuff. It is flesh-colored and smells of sulfur (No. 16, abbreviated as S).

I am examining a meat tenderizer resembling a small hammer when there is a knock on my open door. I look up to see my boss, Peter Peter.

'Anything of note in the new batch?'

I hold up a box of Lucky Charms cereal. Usually Zig sends us wholesome cereal like bran flakes and shredded wheat. Though Peter Peter came to heaven long ago, he has kept up with developments in America, thanks to newbies, whom he regularly interviews. Hence he knows about anti-acne creams and cereals containing miniature marshmallows in assorted colors.

'I'm surprised a warehouse worker didn't wolf those down,' Peter Peter says. Often the edibles do not arrive at our offices intact.

'It is fortified with eight essential vitamins,' I say.

'Is that so?' Peter Peter replies.

I study the ingredients list for a moment, and when I look up, Peter Peter is still there, smiling sadly.

'Oliver, may I have a word in private?'

I nod. I wonder what he means by 'in private.' Nobody else is around. Still, when Peter Peter steps into my office, he shuts the door behind him. He drags a chair in front of my desk and

215

fiddles with his necktie, which he wears in a thick Windsor knot over his T-shirt. 'I have something to propose to you,' he says, 'something I've touched on in our past discussions. You recall our talk on last-minute edits?'

I nod. Like many other townies, Peter Peter speculates that a person who died a vile death does not recall all the details. He may recall the basics. He knows, for example, that he leaped out a fifth-story window during a fire that engulfed his family's apartment, but he does not remember the searing pain as his clothes caught fire, the horrific panic, the sickening plunge, or the brutal impact with the sidewalk. I use this example because it is the one Peter Peter used with me. He died in this manner in the thirties on the Upper East Side of Manhattan.

'You mentioned I may not remember the nitty-gritty of the shooting at my school,' I say. 'That certain images, sounds, and feelings might be forever buried in my brain.'

'I never said 'forever.' '

I throw him a questioning look.

'There's a way to recover some of our lost memories, son. I know because I recovered some of mine long ago.'

I point the meat tenderizer at him. 'So you do remember the sickening plunge and the brutal impact?'

'Regrettably, yes,' he says. 'Zig does us a favor with last-minute edits. If you die a death like mine, you shouldn't know all the details. That's why I don't often talk about the method for retrieving memories. But, in your case, knowing all the facts might help.'

I lean across my desk toward Peter Peter and ask how he recovered his memories.

'I had the help of a specialist decades ago. Somebody who's now an old boy like me.'

'Will you introduce me to him?'

Peter Peter swallows, and his Adam's apple seems to get caught in his Windsor-knotted tie. He looks almost pained when he says, 'You already know him.'

'I do?'

'He's a hypnotist.'

<table>
<tr><td>49</td><td>114.82</td></tr>
<tr><td colspan="2">In</td></tr>
<tr><td colspan="2">Indium</td></tr>
</table>

The last time I saw Czar, at the Sal Paradise Infirmary, his face was so swollen and battered I could not tell what he really looked like, but when I meet him on the evening before Johnny's trial, I realize he looks only slightly like the dead-or-alive poster Johnny drew. True, both boys have big, sharp incisors and ears that stick out, but the Gunboy in the drawing had a broad nose and Czar's nose is slender and crooked. Gunboy's eyebrows were thick and black; Czar's eyebrows are fine and fair.

The day before Johnny's trial commences, Czar and I meet at Curios on the settee beside the display of American coinage, featuring ten Susan B. Anthony dollars, which I have taken out to clean. As he approaches the settee, Czar says, 'I hope you don't have a f*cking flashlight on you.'

He is making a droll reference to the attack, but fortunately his injuries have healed completely. Not even a remnant of a bruise is visible.

'You're looking well, Czar,' I say.

'No thanks to you,' he replies as he sits down beside me.

'I am so sorry for the dreadful error that resulted in your infirmary stay,' I tell him. 'Though I did not wield the flashlight, I am as much to blame as Johnny Henzel. I wish to make amends. Is there anything I can do for you?'

'Well, Petey says you're a smart whippersnapper. So what you can do is find me a real portal.'

I think of Johnny and his claim to have found one.

'Time's running out. Find me one before my expiry date.'

Czar is also forty-six heaven years old, and hence he will repass in four years' time.

'Well, I can try. Once the trial is over, perhaps I will have more time to devote to new projects.'

Czar says he will testify tomorrow. He does not recall the beating — 'Your sicko friend knocked me out cold with his first blow' — so he will talk about his injuries, his recovery, his anger.

'I'm mad as hell about the weeks you two goofballs stole from me.' He taps his index finger against my sternum. 'I'm no spring chicken. I don't have much time left, so I can't afford to be in a coma for almost two f*cking months.'

He taps his finger harder and harder to underline the seriousness of his ordeal. In fact, he looks so peeved I begin to fear for my safety. Peter Peter is around the corner in his office, and he said that if Czar becomes too brutish, I should call out. The two old boys, despite their different characters, have been friends since the year of their original passing, when they shared a room in Four. I wonder if Peter Peter appealed to Czar's sense of duty by evoking the parallels between their friendship and mine with Johnny.

'His brutality is mostly an act,' Peter Peter

assured me. 'Charles behaves like a czar because he thinks he gets more respect if he appears intimidating.'

Czar hypnotizes in private. He needs absolute silence and no distractions, and that is why Peter Peter is waiting in his office. The hypnotist wears a T-shirt with a sketch of a magician pulling a rabbit out of a top hat. 'Let's get this show on the road,' he announces. He gets up from the settee and tells me to lie down. He goes over to the light switches and dims the overhead lamps. Then he walks around the room and switches off the individual lamps we shine on our different displays. 'For a hypnosis, I like it nice and dark,' he says.

I am prepared for some form of ruse. For the so-called hauntings of his, Czar first drew information from his subjects about their former lives so he could invent stories to feed to them while they were hypnotized. But Czar has a very real power, Peter Peter told me. He can help townies recall the final moments of their deaths — in details they do not remember in their afterlife. 'Not every detail,' Peter Peter warned. 'There may still be blank spots, like missing frames in a film reel, but you'll certainly have a fuller picture of your death.'

Peter Peter said that Czar keeps this power of his mostly under wraps because it has had tragic consequences. Years ago, a gommer attempted suicide after learning the full details of her rape and death at her uncle's hands. As a result, I promised I would not speak to others about my hypnosis whatever the outcome might be.

'Don't move a muscle, okay?' Czar tells me.

The settee, though worn, is still very padded, so I feel comfortable. I cross my arms and rest them on my chest, but Czar says, 'You look like a frigging corpse in a coffin,' so I move my arms to my side.

'I want you to recount to me the details of your death,' Czar says. 'Then once you're under my spell, I'll feed these details back to you gradually like a cook adding oats to boiling water. I need to stimulate the brain slowly so it releases both the remembered memories and the lost memories. If I go too quickly, the scene will play back too fast and there'll be too many holes for you to follow what's going on.'

I am unsure whether to believe in this exercise, but out of my desperation to understand the madness that struck Johnny and me, I will give it a try. I describe my final moments in America: the hallway, Jermaine Tucker, Richard Dawkins and Jane Goodall, the periodic table, the countdown to seaborgium.

When I have finished my story, Czar kneels beside the settee. 'Breathe deeply through your nose,' he tells me. From his pants pocket, he takes out a fake gold chain with a blue bauble attached to its end. The thing looks like the gaudy jewelry sold in gumball machines in America. He tells me it is blue topaz. He swings it above my face, and I follow the bauble with my eyes.

50	118.71
Sn	
Tin	

In her graduation gown and mortarboard, Helen Keller looks down at me from her portrait on the wall. I am standing in front of my locker, No. 106, and turning the dial of my lock — to 7 and then to 25 and then to 34. Around me, I hear the laughter and cries of my fellow students. Their voices say or shout or sing such things as 'Can I borrow your lip gloss?' and 'Up your nose with a rubber hose!' and 'Shake your body down to the ground!' and 'Go, Trojans, go!' and 'Miss Stephens got herself a Dorothy Hamill do!'

I swing open my locker. Taped to the inside of its door are two magazine pictures, one of evolutionary biologist Richard Dawkins and one of primatologist Jane Goodall. My classmates have mocked me for putting up pictures of my 'parents' in my locker.

Also on the inside of my locker door is a copy of the periodic table. I have concocted a game whereby I must try to recite the elements in chronological order whenever I open my locker. I am trying to memorize all 106 of them.

I mumble the elements under my breath. Beside me, Jermaine Tucker fishes a textbook out of the holy mess that is his own locker. I am at No. 78, platinum (Pt), when he cuffs me hard on the back of the head. He is an athletic boy several inches taller than I, so his cuff hurts, but I remind myself I have a high threshold for pain.

'What the hell you doing, Boo?' he says. I ignore his question and continue with my mumbling. I find it best not to make eye contact when a classmate begins harassing me because sometimes a lack of response causes the person to lose interest. My tactic works, and Jermaine Tucker wanders off.

The noises around me, the shouts and guffaws, fade away as I fall back into the world of elements. For the first time, I *do* reach No. 106, seaborgium (Sg), without needing to steal a peek at the periodic table. My second parents, Richard and Jane, are thoroughly pleased and smile from their photographs as though to congratulate me on my feat. I smile back at them.

'Good-bye,' I whisper to them, just as I always do before heading off to class. Then I reach for something inside my locker.

Blackness. Silence.

I am now as blind and deaf as Helen Keller herself. I suppose there is nothing more to see or hear in this world. I suppose I am dead. I wait to be reborn.

But these few moments are simply missing frames in my film reel, because an instant later light seeps in, sounds erupt, and I can see again.

What I see is horrific. I am on the floor and a boy is lying within arm's reach. His eyelids flutter, his eyes look without seeing, his face contorts, and his blood seeps from the side of his head and drenches his long brown hair.

Then the darkness swallows me again. But not the silence. A scream fills my head. A scream so bloodcurdling, so nightmarish, it wakes me from my trance.

When I come to, Thelma is beating up Czar. She has pushed him to the floor and is straddling him. She slaps him in the face with her big, meaty hands. Once, twice, thrice. 'What'd you do to him?' she cries. 'Tell me, you son of a b*tch!'

Czar flails his arms. 'Ouch! Stop! Ouch!' he hollers.

I sit up, groggy, on the settee as Peter Peter runs in, his tie flapping. He hurries over to pull Thelma off Czar.

'You people are all f*cking nuts!' Czar yells as he struggles to get up. His T-shirt is torn at the neck and his hair disheveled. 'Why do I try helping you when all I get is bruises and concussions?'

Peter Peter looks dismayed. He brushes the dust off his friend's back as Thelma straightens her kitten T-shirt, which has ridden up her belly.

'I'm a professional hypnotist!' Czar cries. 'I deserve respect, but all I get is f*cking abuse!' He swats at the display of ten Susan B. Anthonys, and the dollar coins go flying and then bounce across the floor in a jingle-jangle. How upset I will be if we lose one!

Thelma comes to sit with me on the settee. 'Are you okay, Oliver?' She places her fingertips on my elbow as a gesture of concern.

'I feel very curious,' I say.

'What the hell were you doing to him?' Thelma says, scowling at Czar. 'You some kind of maniac?'

'I ain't the maniac!' Czar snaps, his voice now high-pitched. 'You people are the maniacs!'

Peter Peter steps forward. 'I'm afraid this is entirely my fault.'

Czar says, 'I should have known not to get mixed up in this filthy business.' He turns on his heel and storms off.

'Charles, wait,' Peter Peter calls out. At the corned beef display, Czar turns around and gives Peter Peter the finger.

'No need to be uncivilized,' Peter Peter calls out.

'F*ck off and redie!' Czar yells. Then he stomps out of the exhibition hall.

Once Czar is gone, I tell Thelma we were conducting an experiment. I am still dazed, still partly immersed in my horrible lost memory.

'I was worried, honey. You didn't come home this evening, so I biked here to see if you was okay and I found that kook standing over you. I thought he was killing you, 'cause all a sudden you started hollerin'.'

'Was I screaming?' It is true my voice sounds hoarse.

'To high heaven,' Thelma says.

Peter Peter explains what Czar was doing. He must trust his new girlfriend, because he discloses everything, even his own fiery plunge from his penthouse apartment. Thelma keeps patting her own cheeks as though to revive her circulation. When Peter Peter is finished, she says, 'This is dangerous information.'

Peter Peter replies, 'So dangerous I urge you to keep it secret.'

Thelma nods slowly. Then she turns to me. With a mix of dread and excitement, she says, 'Tell me what you saw, Oliver.'

I tell them I did not see who shot me. 'But I must not have died immediately from my wound,' I say, almost breathless. 'I must have passed out and then come to next to Johnny.'

Thelma and Peter Peter give me looks of sympathy. In a way, these two thirteen-year-olds are my foster parents, not Richard and Jane.

'You saw him?' Peter Peter prods. 'You saw Johnny?'

'The last thing I saw,' I say, 'was the bloody bullet hole in his head.'

'Zig in heaven,' Thelma whispers, and then she glowers at Peter Peter for having arranged this experiment. 'Who was screaming?' she asks me. 'Was it you? Or was it Johnny?'

I blink a few times, as if the light in the dim room is still too bright. 'I believe it was I,' I say. 'But I do not believe I was screaming aloud. I believe I was screaming in my head.'

Mother. I want my real mother. I want you. And, Father, where are you? I want you too. I think I may break my rule of never crying. But I do not. I sit silently on the settee and stare at a dollar coin that rolled under our display of dead telephones that will never ring.

I tell Thelma I will work into the wee hours because my insomnia will surely keep me up tonight. I do not tell her I have not slept in days. Still, she is not pleased. 'You need your rest,' she scolds, waving her hands about. 'The trial starts tomorrow. You need to be fresh.' I lie that I will sleep on the couch in my office, and she finally caves in. Before she leaves, she wraps her arms around herself and squeezes. This is our code: when she hugs herself this way, she means she is hugging me. Peter Peter tells me not to work too hard. 'Don't kill yourself, son,' he says, and then looks away embarrassed because his wording is ill-chosen.

'Rest in peace,' they both tell me as they are leaving.

I decide to spend the night here because I need to talk to Zig. I feel closer to him at Curios, probably because I am surrounded by the unusual objects he sends our way. The shelves lining my office walls are filled with these objects. A bottle of white wine from the Napa Valley, a cash register, a jumbo box of diapers, a biography of American crooner Barry Manilow, a slender electric razor used to trim nostril hairs. And on and on and on.

Some objects are obvious mistakes, things Zig

sent us accidentally. Falling into this category are diapers (newborns here are already toilet-trained, ha-ha) and nostril-hair trimmers (boys here have little facial hair, certainly no protruding nostril hairs).

But other items may not be mistakes. Two weeks ago, for instance, our heaven received its first photocopier, a clunky, stove-size machine now shoved into a corner of my office near the door. Like all electrical devices, it works without being plugged in. I suppose — and Peter Peter tends to agree — that the photocopier is a test. Zig wishes to see how we will make use of this new contraption, just as, a year ago, he sent us our first microwave oven and, decades ago, he sent us our first washing machine.

Will we use the photocopier wisely? Will we, say, copy the books, stories, and plays we write? Will we distribute these works of fiction throughout Town for others to enjoy? If so, Zig may send us other photocopiers. Or will we use the device recklessly, maybe to copy dead-or-alive posters of a Gunboy we wish to put to death?

In other words, we may be his guinea pigs. My guinea-pig theory is what I wish to discuss with him tonight. I sit at my desk and turn the crank on my music box. The little figurine wiggles on his broom as the box tinkles out its playful tune about the pitiful goblin who trades in his broken broom for an airplane.

I identify with this goblin tonight. Boo, too, is wobbly. My hand trembles as I turn the crank. My voice is shaky as I speak aloud. 'You are watching, aren't you?' I say, looking at my beat-up couch as though our old god is lounging there like an old dog. I must say I feel silly — I have never spoken to Zig like this. 'You sent us a photocopier to see what we would do with it,' I say. 'And you sent us a Gunboy to see what we would do with him.'

I am admitting aloud to Zig that Johnny may have killed someone (killed *me*, I should say). Maybe I am the last person involved to come to this conclusion. I came to it slowly because, as a junior scientist, I do not jump to conclusions.

'Johnny Henzel is a curious object, but he is no mistake,' I go on. 'You fixed him as best you could. You tinkered with his faulty parts and erased his painful memories so he can cope in his afterlife. And now you want to see how townies react to this boy you dropped into their world.'

The god sprawled on the couch stays invisible.

'Is my theory right?'

No answer.

'Speak up!'

My music box winds down. The goblin stops wobbling.

'Johnny is a test case. If we all pass your test, if we all show mercy and compassion to this boy you fixed, maybe one day you will send us more boys like him.'

I pick up my music box and turn the crank again.

'Townies all say heaven is a second chance. Why shouldn't we give Johnny his?'

No more music comes out of the music box. I

keep cranking but for naught. Darn it. Is the goblin already broken? When I shake the box, I hear something rolling around beneath the platform that the goblin wobbles on. Batteries? No, that makes no sense: music boxes run on cranks, and batteries are not needed in heaven. I take my fake-tortoiseshell letter opener and wedge it under the edge of the platform. With a little elbow grease on my part, the platform springs up.

I peek inside the box.

What the dickens?!

I drop the music box on my desk and push back my chair so fast it almost overturns. I stand there flabbergasted for a second or two before throwing an angry eye at the couch.

'What foul tricks are you playing, you old dog?'

Inside the goblin's music box, lying side by side, are two bullets.

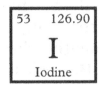

53	126.90
I	
Iodine	

At seven o'clock in the morning, Thelma and Esther arrive at Curios so we can bike to the Gene together to attend Johnny's trial. When they knock on my office door, I do not immediately respond. They push open the door and find me lying on the floor in my boxers and an undershirt. I am in an insomniac stupor. My fifth straight night without sleep. I lift a hand weakly to wave to the girls.

I am not strong. Why did Johnny ever think differently?

The girls are dressed spiffily in argyle kilts sewn by Esther. Esther has her hair in a tight bun; Thelma has on her usual beads. When they see the state I am in — unshowered, blurry-eyed, hair on end — they are fretful.

'Oh, honey, you ain't hunky-dory!' Thelma pulls me up and brings me to the couch to sit.

'You look like death warmed over,' Esther tells me as she pinches my cheeks to add some color. 'We can't have the jurors pitying you. They'll hand Johnny his butt on a platter.'

'What's this?!' Thelma yells because she notices cuts on my forearms. During the night, in my despair, I struck myself again and again with the meat tenderizer.

'A scab-healing experiment,' I lie.

'Damn it, Boo!' Esther cries. 'Pull yourself together, man.'

Peter Peter arrives in my office to wish me luck at the trial. When my boss hears Esther complaining that I look ghostly, he takes the anti-acne cream from my desk and tells her to dab some on. 'It's flesh-colored,' he says.

Thelma says, 'It ain't my flesh color, honey.'

It is not mine either. It is orangey beige. Still, Esther spreads a thin layer across my cheeks and forehead. It smells of sulfur, which, long ago, was known as brimstone. Brimstone does not bode well for the trial, but I do not tell the others this because they seem pleased now with the color of my complexion.

Peter Peter fetches a long-sleeved T-shirt from his office. It is too big for me, but at least it is not wrinkled. As I slide my scabby arms into it, he loosens his necktie and then slips it around my neck. Thelma drags a comb through my flyaway hair.

Esther rummages in her purse and pulls out an apple as well as a peanut-butter-and-jam sandwich wrapped in plastic. 'Eat,' she tells me. The apple is crisp and tart and gives me a boost. When I finish my breakfast, the girls and I prepare to leave for the jail. Peter Peter says he will close Curios today and come along with us, but I try to dissuade him. I have grown fond of our museum: it gives me a purpose in heaven other than helping Johnny. It should not be shut down, but Peter Peter cannot be deterred, and so we all head downstairs. Esther stuffs her sunflower purse into the basket of her bicycle.

Thelma suggests biking slowly so I do not sweat my makeup off.

'I assure you I rarely expire,' I say.

I mean, of course, 'perspire.' A Freudian slip due to my fatigue and general malaise.

We ride our bicycles into the street. Traffic is heavy today despite the early hour. The sky is blanketed with Johnny's holy mackerel clouds. Did Zig whip up these clouds as a good omen? Do I even believe in signs from our goddamn god?

Were the two bullets an offering from him? Well, I do not need such an offering. I hid the bullets at the back of my desk drawer in an empty eyeglasses case. I refuse to check if the bullets fit in the little revolver displayed in Curios. Go to hell, Zig! I do not need your little games!

We cycle for a good hour and a half. When we approach the Gene, we are surprised to see the number of townies the trial is attracting. Hundreds of people are crowded on the prison's front lawn. Dozens of protesters wield picket signs. Gommers, I guess. I try to avoid reading their placards, but I glimpse one that reads, PUT HIM OUT OF OUR MISERY.

While parking my bicycle, I notice a makeshift stage with a spray-painted banner that reads, LOTTERY TICKETS. Tim and Tom Lu climb onto the stage. One of them is carrying a bass drum, which he sets down. They both pick up bullhorns that had been lying on the stage floor.

'Wow, Tim,' Tom says into his bullhorn, 'the

Grade F is more popular than Jesus Christ.'

'Right you are, Tom. That's why we're holding a raffle to assign the two hundred seats available in the Gene's auditorium.'

'Can we pack everybody in?'

'I guesstimate there are five hundred people here, so I'd say, nope, they won't all get a seat. Folks have to take a number from our assistants wandering through the crowd. Then we'll draw numbers out of this here bass drum to see who gets in.'

'Oh, what fun!'

'Now, Tom, don't be disrespectful. This is a murder trial, after all. It's serious business. It's not a play. It's not *The Teahouse of the August Moon*.'

'What about official witnesses and victims, Tim? Do they need a lottery number?'

'Don't be silly, Tom. Of course not. They have the best seats in the house. Front row, center. To avoid the crowd, witnesses and victims should enter the Gene by the side door.'

Peter Peter says he will go fetch a number. He wishes me luck and pats himself on the shoulder.

As Thelma, Esther, and I weave through the crowd, I notice that the jail looks even more dismal than usual, as though another layer of soot settled on it overnight. And the lawn we cross is so infested with weeds that we decapitate dandelions with almost every step we take. I must invent a natural pesticide (maybe using cayenne pepper) to keep the dandelion population at bay.

A long-haired boy with an acoustic guitar

strapped to his back ambles up. 'Hey, aren't you Boo?'

I nod uneasily.

The hippie's face lights up. 'How about an autograph?'

'Bug off,' Esther spits.

'I'm writing a song about you and Johnny, Boo. It's called 'The Gun and the Damage Done.' '

'We're in a hurry,' Thelma tells the hippie.

'Break a leg, my man,' the hippie says.

An albino girl, with normal eyesight restored by Zig, points at me. 'I love you, Boo!' she squeals.

My bodyguards, Thelma and Esther, walk on either side of me. Thelma tells me my story has managed to travel from dorm to dorm across Town.

'But like all stories that spread around heaven,' Esther says, 'it's been perverted in the telling.'

When we reach the side door of the prison, a girl jailer in a purple armband is there to greet us. She checks our names off her list of witnesses and then leads us down a hallway to a waiting room where another jailer, the big-nosed Ringo again, stands watch over peanut girl Sandy Goldberg and portal seeker Benny Baggarly.

Benny barely looks up, but Sandy waves and says, 'Hello, Thelma. Hello, Boo.' She is still wearing tight braids, which stick straight out from both sides of her head as though she uses pipe cleaners as a support system. 'Gosh, I never knew my afterlife would be so busy,' she says.

'With badminton finals and this trial, I'm, like, super booked. If you can believe it, I'm even more popular here than I was back home!'

We take our seats. Picture a dentist's waiting room, Mother and Father, and you will imagine this space. It is even painted the mint green of toothpaste found in America.

Esther whispers to me, 'I have another peanut butter sandwich in my purse. Should I slip it to the nutter?'

'Food allergies do not exist in heaven,' I say. 'Nobody dies here of anaphylactic shock.'

Unlike Esther and me, Thelma is good at small talk, so she asks Sandy about her badminton tournaments. While Sandy talks about vertical jump smashes and sliced drop shots, another witness is brought to the room. It is Albert Schmidt, the Deborah's baby-faced manager, whom we met on the day Willa Blake threw herself off the roof of the asylum. Because he is tiny and wears a red bow tie and a straw hat, he reminds me of the little monkeys that played cymbals on street corners in the olden days.

Thelma interrupts Sandy's description of her trademark shot, a round-the-head forehand overhead. 'What are *you* doing here?' she asks Albert.

'To tell you the truth, I'm not sure,' Albert tells us. 'The warden sent word she wanted me to come.'

'Maybe to talk about sadness and confusion,' I suggest.

Just then, Charles 'Czar' Lindblom shows up,

his hair oiled back and his jeans ironed with a crease.

'Try not to beat me into a coma, okay?' he says to Thelma and me.

'I should feel sorry for that fella,' Thelma whispers to me. 'But instead I want to slap him upside his head.'

Czar sits down beside Benny Baggarly. I wonder if Benny harbors ill will toward Czar with the hauntings exposed as the hoax of a hypnotist. I guess not, since Benny offers him a comic book he has brought along.

For the most part, we sit in silence. I fret about Johnny. Is he waiting in the auditorium where the trial will take place? Is he nervous about the outcome? Will he be happy to see the girls and me?

'When will this Punch and Judy show get started?' Esther asks Ringo, who stands in the doorway shifting his weight from leg to leg.

'Hold your horses, love,' he replies.

Esther says, '*Love?!* Who are you calling love? I'm not your love, mister!'

Ringo gives her an amused look. 'Don't be such a twat,' he says.

'*Twat?!*' Esther says. 'How'd you like a kick in the nuts?'

'Oh, sod off,' Ringo replies.

'Settle down now,' Thelma tells Esther.

We end up waiting another hour, all of us growing more and more fidgety. Finally, another jailer tells Ringo to escort us to the trial. We march down several corridors and then enter the auditorium, which looks disturbingly like all the other theaters in heaven, theaters where we are entertained by plays, concerts, and dances put on by townies. This trial, I understand, is another kind of entertainment for the audience that has come today. Townies with winning raffle tickets — all two hundred of them — are already seated when the other witnesses and I are led to the front row.

Thelma spots Peter Peter and waves.

'Rest in peace, Boo!' somebody calls out, and Ringo cries, 'No shouting! Shouters will be thrown out!'

When we move to our seats, Czar turns to look at the audience. He spreads his arms wide and smiles broadly. I would not be surprised if he took a bow. Esther kicks him in the shin. 'Sorry,' she mutters, though I suspect she is anything but.

There are seven empty flip-up seats in the front row. I sit in the middle, with Esther and Thelma on either side. Beside Esther are Czar and Benny. Beside Thelma are Sandy and Albert. Once we are all seated, the audience claps as though we are members of an orchestra tuning up to perform a concert.

In the center of the stage is a heavy padded armchair that looks less threadbare than most of the furniture in heaven. A spotlight is trained on the chair, which is covered in red fabric, a poor color choice because it evokes blood.

Desk chairs are set in a row on both sides of the stage. They will accommodate the warden and the thirteen jurors (one townie chosen randomly from each of the zones). Once we witnesses are seated, they march out from the wings and take their seats behind the desks. The warden is wearing her cashmerelike sweater and her badge (a good sign). As the house lights dim, she nods into the wings, and council president Reginald Washington and jailer Ringo lead Johnny Henzel onto the stage. Members of the audience gasp, though there is nothing unusual about Johnny. He is not dressed in the regular prison garb of orange shorts and an orange T-shirt, but instead in clean jeans and a plain white T-shirt. He looks healthier than the last time I saw him. Indeed, his appearance is heartening, apart from the handcuffs around his wrists.

A few people in the audience hiss as Ringo escorts my friend to the hot seat, sits him down, and then unlocks his handcuffs. I am sitting right in front of Johnny, though several yards away. His eyes blink because the spotlight is on him. With the house lights off, he may not be able to see much of the audience. I wave to him, and I think I catch his eye, but then he looks away. He stares straight up at the spotlight like a boy blinding himself during an eclipse by looking into the sun.

Reginald stands at the front left side of the stage. He sets his notes on a podium and introduces himself by speaking into the podium microphone. 'Reginald Washington, president of the do-good council of Eleven for eight years running,' he says. 'I hope to win a third term, so if any of you good people are from Eleven, remember this face in next spring's election.' He gives the audience a smile that looks misleadingly sweet.

Reginald says we are here today for a first in the history of our heaven, a trial at which an accused will be judged for crimes committed not only in the afterlife but also down in America. When he says 'down in America,' he glances at me, but I look away. I look at Johnny, who is still staring upward at the humming spotlights.

I feel almost jet-lagged from lack of sleep. Esther and Thelma pat their own knees, which means they are patting mine. Esther takes my CO_2 bag from her sunflower purse. 'Just in case,' she says, handing it over.

I fold and unfold the bag as Reginald explains the details of the accusations against Johnny. He starts with Johnny's rebirth and quotes Thelma as saying the newborn was bewildered and in tears. 'The accused told the rebirthing nurse he'd been shot in the head at his junior high and endured five weeks in a coma before succumbing to his injuries.'

Reginald adds that Thelma paired him with another newbie killed in the same shooting. 'That boy, Oliver Dalrymple, was unaware of the real cause of his death.'

Somebody in the audience shouts, 'Boo!'

'No bloody shouting!' Ringo yells into a bullhorn from where he is stationed at the side of the stage.

I watch Johnny, but he does not appear to be listening to Reginald. He looks innocent, as he did on the day during the tornado drill in Hoffman Estates — when everyone else was scared and excited and he sat quietly under his desk and calmly asked to draw me.

Reginald continues presenting what he calls 'the facts.' He says he mulled over whether it was wise and safe to send our little group on a journey to track down 'the mysterious Gunboy.' 'Though I had misgivings, former council member Thelma Rudd pleaded with me to assist this boy in distress who was not adapting well to his new habitat.'

'Baloney,' mutters Thelma. She brought along a Japanese hand fan and is waving it in front of her face. 'Reginald suggested the road trip himself.'

Reginald recounts our trip, including Johnny's disappearance after we witnessed what Reginald calls 'an apparent suicide' at the Deborah Blau Infirmary. He describes the 'unprovoked and violent attack' on Charles Lindblom and the 'shocking and disturbing revelations' of Sandy Goldberg.

From her seat, Sandy pipes up: 'All I remember, everybody, is that there was just two guys killed. A crazy one and a weird one. That's basically all I got to say.'

Reginald stops his talk and smiles uneasily at Sandy. 'Thank you, Ms. Goldberg,' he says. 'But no further interruptions, please.' He goes on to mention that the do-good council from Eleven ordered our recapture. 'There was an urgent need not only to protect townies from this dangerous boy but also to separate the victim, Oliver Dalrymple, from the killer who cut short his first life.'

'Boo!' a girl calls out.

'Put a sock in it!' Ringo shouts.

Reginald continues: 'I interviewed John Henzel several times in his jail cell about the wicked crimes of which he stands accused. It is time I share with you what I learned, particularly in recent days. Mr. Henzel, are you ready to tell us your story?'

Johnny stops gazing at the rafters. He lowers his eyes till they are level with the audience. Ringo crosses the stage and hands him a microphone. Johnny turns it on. A squeal rips through the hall, and I jump in my seat. It takes me a moment to realize the noise is from the microphone, not from Johnny.

When the squeal dies, Johnny holds the microphone to his mouth. 'I am Gunboy,' he says.

From behind me, somebody whispers, 'Kill him, kill him.'

'You're confessing to your crimes?' Reginald asks.

I can barely breathe.

'Yeah,' Johnny says with conviction.

'When did you discover you were the so-called Gunboy?'

'I've always known. Even back in America I knew.'

'You knew down below.'

'Yeah.'

'How?'

'Somebody told me every day of my life.'

'Who was that somebody?'

'Zig.'

A sharp intake of breath from the audience.

'You mean you talk to Zig?' Reginald feigns surprise, though I can tell this exchange was planned. It almost seems as if we are watching a play in which the lines have been memorized.

'I've always talked to him. He tells me to do things.'

'What kind of things?'

'Bad things. Real bad things.'

Esther whispers to me, 'A crock of sh*t.' However, there is a tinge of doubt in her voice.

'Does he tell you to kill people?'

'He orders me to. He talks to me through dogs and roaches.'

Grumblings in the audience. A boy hollers, 'Throw the b*stard off the roof!'

Ringo yells back, 'You're banished!'

There is a pause as the house lights go up. I turn in my seat and see two jailers shuffle through the audience toward one of the boys from the gommer meeting I attended. It is the boy whose killer threw him off a bridge. The jailers pull him from his seat and drag him from the hall. '*Kill him! Kill him!*' the gommer yells, fist-punching the air.

Through his bullhorn, Ringo says, 'Any of you other twats want out?'

I glance at Johnny. He is staring at me. He does not speak into the microphone, but I am close enough to read his lips when he mouths the words 'I want out.'

The lights dim again. Reginald says, 'Did Zig tell you to murder Mr. Dalrymple at your school in America?'

My holey heart twinges in my chest.

Johnny swallows loudly. His gulp sounds in the mike.

'Yes,' he whispers.

'Why target Mr. Dalrymple?'

Johnny is barely audible now. 'Boo was in the wrong place,' he mutters. 'He was an angel on Earth. He didn't belong there.'

'An angel on Earth? What do you mean?'

Johnny speaks almost tenderly now. 'Boo was strong and smart and pure,' he says. 'Too perfect for America. He belonged *here*. Zig said so.'

I am feeling weak, stupid, tainted. Why is he making up these ludicrous claims? My breathing is shallow, but I cannot even raise my CO_2 bag to my face. I narrow my eyes at Johnny, but he avoids my gaze.

Thelma tut-tuts. Esther whispers, 'I'll be d*mned.'

'Zig spoke through your dog, a basset hound?'

'Yeah.'

Giggles and hoots from the audience as people picture a talking basset hound with floppy ears and stringy drool.

'So you stole your father's gun. You brought it to school and you killed Mr. Dalrymple and terrorized your classmates.'

'I did,' Johnny says.

'And you shot yourself in the head because you were also an angel on Earth.'

'No, I was a monster!' His voice is suddenly angry. He slaps the arm of his chair. 'I'm still a monster. I was supposed to go to hell. That was the deal. Zig said I'd be sent to hell.'

'So why did you end up here?'

'Zig's a f*cking fraud!' he shouts into the rafters. 'A two-faced liar who sent me to heaven instead!'

Nobody is laughing or hooting anymore. Nobody makes a peep. The audience is awestruck.

'Why do you think Zig lied to you?'

'Zig wants me to kill people here too. I'm his assassin, man. I'm his Gunboy. He talked to me through a roach.'

Reginald explains to us that Johnny found a roach at a dormitory in Ten and that the insect has since gone missing.

'What did Zig the roach tell you to do in heaven?'

'To weed out kids who don't belong here.'

Hogwash, I think to myself.

Thelma whispers, 'What's going on in that boy's head?'

'And whom did Zig tell you to murder here?' Reginald asks Johnny, who glances down at us witnesses before him. His eyes home in on Czar.

'Zig said the hypnotist was a f*cking fraud and didn't deserve an afterlife.'

I glance at Czar, who looks dumbfounded and scared, as though he believes Zig did in fact order his death.

'Luckily, Mr. Lindblom survived your beastly attack. But another poor soul wasn't as fortunate, isn't that right?'

Johnny nods.

'You managed to end a townie's afterlife, didn't you, Mr. Henzel?'

246

'Yeah, I did,' Johnny mutters.

'Who?'

I am thoroughly confused at this point.

'Some loony girl named Willa who didn't belong here either. I pushed her off the roof of the Deborah.'

A roar goes up from the audience, a roar so loud it drowns out Ringo's shouts into his bullhorn. Somebody behind me shrills, 'Stop him before he kills again!' A girl runs down the center aisle grasping what looks like a penknife, but a jailer tackles her to the floor. Beside me, Thelma lets out a yelp. Something has just glanced off her head and is rolling across the stage. It is a rotten apple! A volley of apples follows, thumping and splattering against the stage. Reginald darts into the wings, and many of the jurors scramble out of their seats and follow.

Throughout the mayhem, Johnny sits in his red velvet seat and stares up at the lights above. He is mumbling to himself. He is pretending, I believe, to converse with Zig.

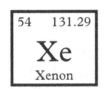

54 131.29

Xe

Xenon

We witnesses have been escorted back to our waiting room because a time-out was called in the trial. Thelma, though, is off in the restroom with Sandy, who offered to scrub the apple gook out of her cornrows with a handkerchief.

Esther is arguing with Ringo, who wants us to sit and wait in silence. Esther wants to question Albert Schmidt, the asylum manager, who is waving Thelma's hand fan in front of his face and muttering, 'Dear me.'

'No way did Johnny push Willa,' Esther shouts at Ringo. 'I saw that chick jump. She was bonkers, wasn't she, Albert? She was always threatening to kill herself. She was completely out of her mind!'

'Dear me,' Albert repeats.

'For a little person, you sure got a big f*cking mouth,' Ringo says to Esther, his arms crossed over his chest.

Esther goes almost as purple as a do-good armband. 'I'm reporting you, assh*le. I'll get you fired.'

'Yeah, get me sacked. You'll be doing me a favor. I'm tired of this bloody job anyway. I should be a tailor rather than a jailer. Much less headache.'

I tell Esther to come sit with me. 'It's not

worth getting riled,' I say, even though I am riled myself and feel sick to my stomach.

'Oh, Esther,' I whisper, my voice cracking as though I am finally going through puberty. 'Johnny wants to redie.'

'What are you talking about?' she says, but by her anxious look, I can tell she knows exactly what I am talking about.

'He wants the redeath penalty.'

Redeath, I realize, may be the portal he thinks he has found.

Esther shakes her head. 'What kind of game is that imbecile playing? He's so calm and collected even though he's saying the craziest things. It's like he wants to appear sane so that he seems even more dangerous.'

'Sane?' Czar scoffs. 'As sane as Jack the Ripper.'

Esther shoots back, 'Too bad you aren't still in a coma.'

'For shame!' Benny Baggarly says. 'Czar almost redied.'

'Dear me!' Albert Schmidt repeats, waving his fan frantically. 'A patient was murdered on my watch. How will I ever forgive myself?'

Ringo cries, *I'll* murder somebody if you all don't shut the f*ck up!'

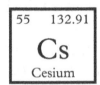

55	132.91
Cs	
Cesium	

I believe that Johnny, despite his claims, has no clear recollection of the broken boy he used to be. Zig edited Johnny's memories, which is why he has trouble recalling the last months of his time in America. The Gunboy he sees in his nightmares is his madness, yes, but this insanity no longer swallows him whole as it eventually did in his former life. Perhaps, though, it still nips at his heels from time to time here in heaven and makes him claim, for instance, that he pushed a sadcon from a rooftop.

We are all back in the auditorium, and Reginald is wrapping up his interrogation. 'I have one final question for you, Mr. Henzel,' he says, putting down his notes and resting his hands on the podium. He does not look at Johnny when he asks this question. He looks instead at the audience.

'What do you consider a just punishment for the crimes you're pleading guilty to?'

I expect members of the audience, gommers especially, to cry out the penalty they deem fitting, but nobody says a word. We all hold our breath. Even the humming from the spotlights overhead seems to cease.

Johnny lifts his microphone to his lips. He looks my way. He touches a finger to his eyelid and then reaches out his hand as if to touch me too.

'An eye for an eye,' he says.

'Which means?' Reginald asks.

His eyes still on me, Johnny says, 'A tooth for a tooth.'

I shake my head and mouth the word 'No.'

'Damn it,' says Esther.

'Heaven help us,' says Thelma.

'*Justice!*' cry the gommers. '*Justice! Justice!*'

'You're requesting the redeath penalty?' Reginald asks.

'I am,' says Johnny.

'Yes, *yes!*' cry the gommers.

'Well, the jurors will certainly take your request into consideration,' Reginald says.

Thelma turns to me, her face stricken. 'They'll never agree to it. Nobody here has ever been put to redeath.'

'Insanity,' Esther whispers. 'Pure insanity.'

Reginald says he has heard enough. 'I have no need to hear from any of the witnesses because the accused admits his guilt.' He shuffles his notes and then takes a seat.

The warden comes to the podium to address the jurors. 'There is still one person,' she says, 'whom I believe you need to hear from.' She looks over at me.

'Boo! Boo!' the audience chants. 'Boo! Boo!'

Ringo has given up scolding the crowd. He actually puts his bullhorn to his lips and says, 'Boo! Boo!'

'Mr. Dalrymple, would you come to the stage?'

For a second, I am frozen in my seat.

'Go, honey,' Thelma says. 'Go save your friend from himself.'

I rise and shuffle past the other witnesses. Czar looks peeved that he will not be addressing the crowd.

On the side of the stage, I climb the few steps to where the podium is positioned. Meanwhile, two jailers carry out another armchair, a baby-blue one, and set it down about a yard from Johnny's chair.

The warden smiles at me, but her forehead has worry lines that look bizarre on a thirteen-year-old who never ages. She motions to the baby-blue chair.

When I draw close, Johnny says, 'Hey, Boo,' nonchalantly, as though I just ran into him at the school cafeteria.

'Hello, Johnny,' I say.

As I sit down in the witness's armchair, a jailer passes me a microphone.

At the podium, Lydia says, 'Mr. Dalrymple, I realize you feel sympathy for the accused. Why show him mercy when he showed none to you?'

I look toward the audience. Because of the spotlights, I cannot see terribly well, but I can make out Thelma and Esther. Thelma's cheeks puff out as though she is holding her breath. Esther clutches her sunflower purse. She nods at me.

I turn to Johnny, who stares at me expectantly. His lips utter three words so softly that only I can hear. 'Let me go,' he says.

I look away. Out in the dark theater, townies

await my answer. 'Is this horrid boy worth saving?' these people seem to ask. I want to explain that the boy sitting beside me is not a monster. His madness is the monster. I try to speak, but again Johnny mutters under his breath: 'Let me go, Boo. You promised.'

I shiver. It is as though heaven's usual temperature has just dropped twenty degrees. I try to speak but find I cannot. I open the CO_2 bag in my lap. It is ripped along its creases from my incessant folding and unfolding.

'Mr. Dalrymple, are you okay?' says Lydia Finkle in her fake cashmere.

I nod. I close my eyes. I am bone-weary.

Let me go. Let me go. Let me go.

I picture you, Father and Mother, in your living room. You are building a shelf on the wall. It will be the stage on which my urn will stand. You do not want to let me go. In any case, do we ever really let anyone go? Even those who are no longer with us are still with us.

I must have muttered something aloud because Lydia Finkle says, 'Excuse me, Mr. Dalrymple, but we can't hear you. Could you speak into the mike?'

I blink open my eyes. I lift the microphone to my lips and whisper, 'Oh, my goodness.'

Then it starts. For a second, when I feel the wetness on my cheeks, I think I am bleeding. My hand drops the microphone, and I swat at my cheeks.

Tears.

I am shocked. I emit a groan.

The groan gives way to a sob.

I shut my eyes again. I see Johnny and me, not as we are now, sitting in judgment in front of two hundred people, but as we were then, lying on the floor of Helen Keller. One boy with a hole in his torso, one boy with a hole in his head. Two blood brothers with their blood leaking from their bodies, the rivulets coming together like fingers interlacing.

I see the ghastly wounds, the pooling blood, the terrible sorrow.

I start weeping so violently that I choke on my tears. I lean forward, drop my CO_2 bag. My head spins. I keel over onto the floor.

Blackness. A few missing frames in a film reel.

I come to. I turn over and look up into the rafters and spotlights. My vision is fuzzy. I blink away tears. Johnny is kneeling beside me, his hands resting lightly on my neck. 'I'd never hurt you,' he whispers.

'Stop him! Stop that monster!' one of the girl jurors screams. I glance sideways. Ringo is running toward us. He hooks an arm around Johnny's neck and jerks him away from me. More jailers emerge from the wings. They descend on Johnny and carry him off, one jailer with his hands under Johnny's armpits, one jailer grasping his feet.

Into her microphone, Lydia Finkle says, 'Mr. Dalrymple, are you all right?'

I sit up as Thelma and Esther rush up the steps to the stage. They hurry over to me. Peter Peter also appears.

Esther kneels beside me. She is wide-eyed, both astonished and vexed. 'That idiot!' she cries. 'What the hell's he doing? He had his hands around your neck! Was he pretending to strangle you?'

I reach up and touch my neck. It feels fine.

Johnny starts yelling from the wings. '*Booooo! Booooo!*' he shouts in the same critical tone an audience uses when a performance is not to its liking. When he is dragged far enough away that I can no longer hear his voice, I pick up the microphone off the stage floor and hold it to my lips. 'Everything Johnny said,' I say, 'is true.'

56	137.33
Ba	
Barium	

57	138.91
La	
Lanthanum	

58	140.12

Ce
Cerium

I cry all the time now. I order a stir-fry in the cafeteria and tears dribble down my face ('I'm very sensitive to onions,' I lie to the waitress). At Curios, tears fall on my typewriter keys as I type up a notice about our sea monkeys, which are repassing one by one. When I read the novel *Tarzan of the Apes*, I weep when Lord and Lady Greystoke are killed. At this point, I would blubber if, during a trying investigation, Nancy Drew broke a fingernail.

My nickname may soon be Boo Hoo (ha-ha).

I used to pride myself on my independence. In America, I could spend days speaking to no one but you, Mother and Father. I had my morning constitutionals. I had my documentaries on PBS television. I had my books. I had my visits to the library, a place where spending time in one's head is highly valued.

I am still independent, but also lonely — a new feeling for me. I spend plenty of time by myself in my office, where I play the Wobblin' Goblin music box, which is working again. I identify with that poor creature up in the sky, almost falling but somehow managing to stay afloat.

Thelma, Esther, and Peter Peter believe that my mind was muddled after I fainted onstage.

That is why, they reason, I corroborated Johnny's version of events. 'You didn't know what you were saying, did you, Boo?' Esther asks. 'I was confused,' I tell her. 'Sad and confused.' She seems to believe me — or perhaps only pretends and actually wonders whether I am seeking some sort of revenge.

Thelma and Peter Peter worry about me. Peter Peter invites me on father-son outings. Last week, he taught me to catch a football. Thelma came along because her throwing arm is even better than his. The two of them have been seeing a lot of each other. They often exchange gifts. Yesterday, Thelma made him a loaf of zucchini bread, and Peter Peter gave her a half-ounce sample from our bottle of Tigress perfume.

As for Johnny, I have not seen him. Until the do-good council decides on his sentence, I am not allowed to visit. Nonetheless, I go to the jail every day in case a decision is reached.

Tim Lu: 'The Grade F is still awaiting his sentence.'

Tom Lu: 'So no visitors today.'

Tim Lu: 'When will the pathetic victim get on with his afterlife?'

The gommers still demonstrate outside the Gene, clamoring for the redeath penalty. The method they favor is especially barbaric: a stoning.

I was subject to a kind of stoning, Mother and Father. On the first day of eighth grade, three days before my passing, I arrived home with a bloody nose because Kevin Stein, Nelson Bliss, and Henry Axworthy had whipped rocks at me in the field behind our school. 'I was away all summer,' Kevin cried, 'and boy oh boy did I miss torturing you, Boo,' a remark that drew much guffawing from his friends.

Father, you wet a washcloth with warm water and gently wiped away my blood. You said, 'Age thirteen was the most dangerous year of my life, son.'

My dear gentle father, you, too, had attracted the wrath of bullies.

'But you'll grow up, Oliver,' you said. 'You'll leave eighth grade far behind.'

'Father,' I say aloud now, alone in my room, 'I'm stuck at age thirteen. I'm stuck here for a frigging lifetime.'

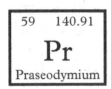

59	140.91

Pr

Praseodymium

One morning two weeks after the trial, I rise at dawn, slip on my cutoff jeans and my peace T-shirt (a decal of a hand making the peace sign), and bicycle all the way to the Gene. As I ride up to the jail, Tim and Tom Lu are on the front steps unrolling a scroll. They tack it to the door and then scurry inside when they see me coming up the driveway.

The notice on the door reads as follows:

IN THE MATTER OF JOHN HENZEL

After due consideration, the thirteen members of the jury assigned to hear the trial of John Henzel, reborn on October 12, 1979, and formerly residing in the GUT district of Eleven, have reached a unanimous decision in the sentencing of the prisoner found guilty of murder and attempted murder. In a manner and on a date to be revealed in the coming days, Mr. Henzel will hereby be put to

REDEATH.

I rip down the notice and tear it up. As I fling the bits of paper onto the stairs of the Gene, the front door opens and Tim and Tom Lu step back out.

'Despite that T-shirt of his, the victim sure doesn't look very peaceful,' Tim says. He has a second scroll in his hands.

'No, I'd say he looks unhinged,' Tom replies.

'I'd go so far as to say 'demented,' ' Tim adds.

They stare at me as unblinking as cats. I scowl back.

'Luckily, we made several copies of our communiqué,' Tim says, and tacks a second notice to the door.

A few days later, it is also announced that the jury has given its consent to the stoning, which will be held within a week. Technically, however, the stoning will be a 'bricking' because, in Town, bricks are easier to come by than large stones. Townies remove loose ones from the exterior walls of schools and dorms, and the holes grow over with new bricks in the same manner that a broken window remakes itself. The bricking being organized is a horrific game of murderball. It will occur on the basketball court of the Marcy, the gymnasium where Johnny and I holed up while on the lam. The brickers will stand on the overhead running track while Johnny kneels handcuffed and ankle-cuffed in the center circle of the basketball court. When the clock strikes midnight, they will all launch their bricks at Johnny. They will keep bashing him with bricks till he is crushed, till he is redead.

The execution is set up in such a way that no one person is the executioner and no one person shoulders the blame. Spread the responsibility among enough people and no one person need feel too guilty. 'If I hadn't thrown a brick, he'd have redied anyway,' each bricker can claim.

In a murder mystery, the most important piece of evidence is the dead body. Yet, in this killing, there will be no body. Traces of the crime will vanish as Johnny's corpse repasses. Even his spilled blood will disappear into thin air. All that will remain will be a vile quarry of thrown bricks. The pockmarks caused by these bricks will even fade from the gymnasium floor within a few days.

Townies need to apply to the Gene to serve as brickers. They can leave their applications with the Lu brothers in the jail's lobby. Jail authorities expect a large turnout, Thelma tells me. Gommer groups urge all their members across Town to take part. The loathsome slogan they came up with is this: 'Give as good as you got.'

I am trying to relate these events to you coolly, Mother and Father. I am trying to stay calm. Yet I am sickened; I am revolted. My heart twinges nonstop, but my tears have all but dried up. I want to speak to Johnny. He must recant what he said at the trial — and so must I. Yet Johnny is refusing to see me, even though he has been granted permission.

I can no longer sleep. At night, I lie in Johnny's bed and have crazy, illogical thoughts. For instance, in my insomniac stupor, I wonder whether Zig might reincarnate Johnny as a new son for you to raise, Mother and Father. It brings me peace of mind to think of you caring for a reincarnated Johnny. He could have my room, my models of Saturn and its moons, my periodic table, my dictionaries of etymology.

On the day before the bricking, there is a knock on my door at seven thirty in the morning. Probably Thelma with some news. But when I open the door, I find Reginald Washington in the hallway.

'Good morning, Boo,' Reginald says with a tight smile. 'May I call you Boo?'

Even though he said, 'may I,' I shake my head.

'Oh, sorry, it's just that John calls you Boo all the time.'

'You can call me Mr. Dalrymple, Mr. Washington.'

I feel oddly jealous that he is in touch with Johnny even though they certainly do not have the blendship that Johnny and I have.

'May I come in for a minute? I have a message from John.'

I do not want this weasel here in our private space, but if he has word from Johnny, I must consent. I wave the council president in and sit on Johnny's unmade bed while Reginald sits on mine.

'I could have sent Tim and Tom Lu, but I thought it best that I deliver this message myself,' he says.

I look down. There is a stain of orange pekoe tea on the sleeve of my robe. I am becoming unkempt.

'Mr. Dalrymple, I know you wish to speak to

John. Well, he has agreed to see you.'

I clap my hands. 'Thank Zig,' I say.

'There's one condition of John's, however. He wants to speak to you, but, well . . . not right away.'

'What do you mean? The bricking is tomorrow night!'

'He wants to speak to you on the basketball court before the . . . beforehand.'

The council president cannot muster the courage to say the word 'execution.'

'He wants to say good-bye, Boo.'

I glare at him. The pink starfish-like blotch on his forehead seems larger than before, but this cannot be.

'Mr. Dalrymple' — he corrects himself — 'he wants you to be the last person he speaks to.'

I cover my face with my hands.

'The situation has been hard on us all,' he says. 'But let's not forget we're respecting John's wishes. We should take heart in that.'

I uncover my face. 'You think your intelligence quotient is high and enviable, don't you, Mr. Washington? You are proud of your brains.'

He throws me a puzzled look.

'Let me tell you something,' I add. 'If I had a brick, I'd gladly beat those dear brains of yours out.'

He stares, looking scared, as though I might pull a rock-filled flashlight from under Johnny's pillow. There is no flashlight, but there is a little revolver hidden under the mattress of Johnny's bed.

'I accept your anger,' he says, one hand up to

264

his heart. 'I understand your pain.'

'Vamoose!' I say, a word I adore but have little occasion to use. (Etymology: a bastardized pronunciation of the Spanish *vamos*, which means 'let us go.')

Reginald pats his knees. He stands. 'Please do come,' he says. Then he lets himself out and closes the door behind him.

I remain sitting on Johnny's bed. Unlike the princess with the pea under her mattress, I cannot feel the lump. I get up and lift the corner of the mattress. 'Hello, my little pretty,' I say. I take the revolver out of its hiding place and cup it in my hands. It nestles there like a giant death's head cockroach.

The revolver is loaded. The bullets, of course, fit perfectly.

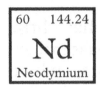

60 144.24

Nd

Neodymium

'Throw rice, not bricks' is the slogan of a pacifist group that sprang up to oppose Johnny's redeath penalty. Group members encourage couples across Town to tie the knot, to offset hatred with love. I have never discussed love before because it is not a topic as fascinating as, say, electricity and garbage chutes. But, yes, two townies can fall in love and even wed here. They hold their wedding at a house of good with a member of the do-good council as their priest. Pledges of 'I do' are exchanged, confetti is thrown, and tin cans are tied to the backs of bicycles.

Esther considers the wedding campaign lame. Nonetheless, she sits beside me with a plastic Baggie filled with rice dyed pink. I have a Baggie of blue rice. We are in the chapel of the Jonathan Livingston House of Good, where Liz McDougall, the vice president of the do-good council from Eleven, stands on a little stage in a shiny robe that looks to be made out of a theater curtain. 'We are gathered here today,' she says, 'to celebrate the love between Thelma Rudd and Peter Peterman.'

When their names are spoken, the bride and groom swing open the doors at the back of the chapel. They march down the center aisle wearing matching macramé vests, which Esther calls hideous — but the party pooper has tears in her eyes. As do I.

When the bride and groom reach the foot of the little stage, Liz McDougall says, 'Thelma Rudd, do you take Peter Peterman as your husband and equal and promise to help him remain an honest and upstanding townie in the eyes of Zig?'

Thelma nods her beaded head. 'Do I ever!' she exclaims.

'Peter Peterman, do you take Thelma Rudd as your wife and equal and promise to help her remain an honest and upstanding townie in the eyes of Zig?'

'I certainly do.'

I always wished I had attended your wedding, Father and Mother, so this day is special to me.

'I now pronounce you husband and wife,' Liz McDougall says. 'You may kiss!'

Thelma and Peter Peter turn to face the two dozen guests and then peck each other on the lips. People cheer and clap. Esther and I stand and throw fistfuls of rice into the air. It rains down hard on our heads.

The newlyweds lead us all out of the chapel and into the garden at the back of the house of good. Set up under an awning is a table with a bowl of punch and plates of sandwiches. Liz McDougall also serves as the hostess. While Esther is off fetching us food, I sit on the grass beside a bed of daisies and try to think of what to say to Johnny when I see him tonight.

Czar wanders over and sits beside me. He is wearing a T-shirt printed with a tuxedo jacket.

His hair is shorter, so now his ears seem to stick out even more. Despite how big they are, they are also thin and delicate. They look as though they might break if I tweaked them.

'Have you found me a portal yet?' he asks.

'Death might be the ultimate portal, Czar.'

'Yeah, but once you walk through that door, there's no turning back.'

'Some of us don't want to come back.'

'You're doing okay here.'

'I'm not talking about me. I'm talking about Johnny.'

'Listen,' he says, 'Petey says we're too old to bear grudges. As usual, he's right. So I want you to know I won't throw bricks tonight. For cripes' sake, I live in a glass house.'

How odd that the hypnotist and I have forgiven Johnny, but the gommers have not. I hear they are the only ones who applied to be brickers. They want payback no matter what the cost.

In the middle of the garden is a little gazebo with a shingled roof. Thelma climbs its steps and asks for our attention. 'Me and Peter Peter are going to have a bigger party one day to celebrate our wedding. But today's event ain't about us. It's about a boy I met months back. I have a song I want to sing for that boy, Johnny Henzel. May he rest in peace.'

Thelma starts singing a song about a new kid in town called Johnny-come-lately, whom everybody loves. While she sings, Czar fishes his blue bauble necklace out from under his tuxedo T-shirt. He takes the necklace off and slips it over my head. The bauble, which is the size of a Susan B. Anthony coin, rests against my heart.

'Wear it tonight, kid,' he says. 'It'll bring you luck.'

61	[144.91]

Pm

Promethium

Tonight Zig conjures up holy mackerel clouds so thick they hide the honey moon that should rightly be Thelma's and Peter Peter's on the eve of their marriage. Yet perhaps a dark, menacing sky is more fitting under the circumstances. After all, no one in our little group (the newlyweds, Esther, and me) is in the mood to celebrate as we bike to the Marcy, guided only by the light of the streetlamps.

Despite the darkness, Thelma insists I wear a hooded sweatshirt with the hood up so that I am less recognizable. She does not want townies badgering me tonight with nosy questions or tactless comments. I also wear overalls, which I chose because they have big pockets to conceal a little revolver.

As the four of us near the Marcy, my holey heart twinges, my intestines knot, and my stomach somersaults. In spite of the late hour, dozens of townies are zooming down the road in the direction of the gymnasium. Those opposed to the redeath penalty are holding a redie-in during which participants will writhe on the ground and scream in feigned agony to protest the bricking. Meanwhile, those foes of Johnny's who cannot stomach the idea of actually wielding bricks will demonstrate outside the

Marcy with their usual slogans and placards. As we approach, I spot a gommer carrying a placard that reads, THIS TOWN AIN'T BIG ENOUGH FOR THE BOTH OF US.

The two groups are gathering at opposite ends of the Marcy's lit softball field. It would be thoughtful of me to go thank the hundreds of opponents of the bricking, but Thelma disagrees. She fears my presence on the field might trigger a scuffle between the opposing camps, so we ride past both groups and park our bicycles in the Marcy's circular driveway next to a hedge of evergreens — each bush trimmed, regrettably, in the shape of a bullet.

Johnny Henzel is already inside. This morning, he was transferred here, tied again to a stretcher. I wonder if his jailers are detaining him in the janitor's office in the bowels of the building. If so, has he thought fondly of the time he spent in that room with me?

The three hundred brickers are also already inside the Marcy. At the door to the sports center stands a line of jailers, burly pubescent boys in purple armbands who will allow inside only those townies whose names appear on official lists. Those lists are in the possession of Tim and Tom Lu. The twins have donned T-shirts decorated with the zodiac symbol for Gemini.

Tom says, 'Overalls and a hooded sweatshirt. That's not a very attractive look, is it, Tim?'

I lower my hood.

'It's the murder victim, Tom. And now he's also a fashion victim.'

'Poor, poor boy,' Tom replies. 'He'll never recover from the strain he's been under.'

'Mark my words,' Tim says. 'He'll end up at the Deborah.'

'Shut your traps!' Thelma cries, a hand raised in the air. 'Or I'll smack your faces so hard you'll be looking backward.'

'My, that sounds like a threat,' says Tom.

'Oh, what a violent world we live in,' says Tim.

'In the end, we are all truly victims,' says Tom.

Thelma narrows her eyes at the boys, and they finally pipe down. Since the names of my traveling companions are not on the official lists, Esther, Thelma, and Peter Peter must now bid me good-bye and go join the bricking opponents on the softball field, where they, too, will squirm on the ground in mock death throes as part of the redie-in.

Thelma cups my cheeks in her palms the way you used to, Mother. She says, 'Mama has faith in you, child.'

Old boy Peter Peter says, 'Whatever you do, son, you'll do us proud.' He ruffles my hair the way you used to, Father.

Esther pulls me aside and gives me an almost embarrassed look. Her cheeks are flushed. Finally, she says, 'Give Johnny my love, okay?' Then, because I am still averse to hugs, she gives me a light kick in the shins, what she calls a 'love tap.' I return the kick. Then Peter Peter and Thelma join in, and under the puzzled gaze of the evil twins and the jailers, my friends and I stand at the entrance to the gymnasium kicking one another.

When I finally pull myself away from my makeshift family and walk into the Marcy, I have the curious feeling — call it a sixth sense — that I am off to meet my maker.

62	150.36
Sm	
Samarium	

The brickers wear pillowcases over their heads with eyeholes cut out. Their droopy hoods make them look like a slovenly offshoot of the Ku Klux Klan. They stand immobile, hand in hand, on the overhead track, all three hundred of them. They wear gym shorts, T-shirts, and ringed knee socks as if a bricking in a gymnasium were a real sporting event. Under their hoods, are they sweating? Are they queasy and woozy? Are they already regretting the part they will play tonight? Or are they so bloodthirsty they can hardly wait for my part to end and for theirs to begin?

I stand alone in the center circle of the basketball court where Reginald leaves me. The lights overhead are bright and cheery, as though the Trojan basketball team from Helen Keller will soon burst from the locker room and Cynthia Orwell and her cheerleading squad will shake their pompoms and do the splits. Shall I attempt cartwheels and backflips to entertain the brickers as they wait? From where I stand, I cannot see the bricks stacked on the overhead track, but I know they are there somewhere. Six hundred bricks. Two bricks apiece. Enough bricks to bash in the brain of the only Trojan who will emerge from the locker room.

Casper the Friendly Ghost reads eleven forty.

274

In a few minutes, Johnny Henzel will be led out. He and I will have fifteen minutes together before the clock strikes midnight and the bricks fly.

Why has Zig himself not put a stop to this folly? Has he no shame? No wisdom? No superpowers? What is the use of a god without superpowers? Zig's only response so far has been to put the ball in my court. Or the bullets, I should say. Two bullets are inside the little revolver that lies in the left pocket of my overalls. I feared that the jailers might search me, but they did not. Ringo, in fact, even wished me luck earlier. While Reginald was preoccupied, the British jailer leaned in close and gave me a fixed look. 'I will miss Johnny boy,' he whispered. 'I sometimes played my guitar outside his cell door so he'd feel less lonesome. I'd even take his special requests.'

Now, as I wait, I stick my hand in my pocket and stroke the little revolver with the tip of a finger, just as Johnny would stroke his roach's back. Around my neck I wear Czar's blue bauble. It lies against my heart under my sweatshirt.

Up on the running track, one of the brickers breaks from the ranks and hurries down the track toward the exit sign. A moment later, three more brickers do likewise. The brickers on either side of the gaps move together and clasp each other's hands again to close the circle. Reginald told me some brickers might drop out at the last minute. Consequently, jail authorities signed up alternates to step in as needed. Soon the four

275

hooded alternates appear along the track and squeeze into the ring.

Casper the Friendly Ghost reads eleven forty-five.

'Red Rover, Red Rover,' I mutter, stroking the revolver, 'send Johnny right over.'

As you know, Mother and Father, I do not usually perspire, but I am sweating now, so much so I must smell as oniony as my old roommate.

The doors to the boys' locker room open, and Johnny and Reginald appear. Johnny is barefoot and bare-chested. He wears only gym shorts, plus cuffs around his ankles and wrists. Reginald, in gym clothes, wears a pillowcase over his head and a whistle around his neck. He grasps Johnny by the arm and leads him toward me in a slow shuffle. The expression 'dead man's walk' comes to mind.

When the two boys reach the center circle, Johnny nods at me. Reginald helps Johnny kneel, a clumsy movement given the two pairs of cuffs. Johnny almost keels over, but Reginald pulls him up. I kneel, too, just in front of Johnny. Reginald blinks at me through his eyeholes and then he gives Johnny a pat on the head as a master would do to his basset hound. Without a word, the do-good president retreats back to the doorway of the locker room, where he will stand watch.

I stare at Johnny, who glances up at the three hundred brickers on the overhead track above us. They are not allowed to talk, but a few emit coughs. One hacks so violently I should lend him my new CO_2 bag, which is in the right pocket of my overalls.

Johnny's cheeks are pimply, and his lips are chapped. He leans toward me and, in a near whisper, says, 'At my trial, I said one thing that was really true.'

'What?'

'You're strong and smart and pure. Don't forget that, even when I'm not around anymore to remind you. Promise me.'

My heart twinges. 'Promise.'

'A lot of what I said was bullsh*t. Talking to Zig, killing Willa, all bullsh*t. But you knew that already 'cause you're smart.'

'I know Gunboy is not you. Not the real you.'

He smirks and says, 'There's a little Gunboy in all of us.'

'Johnny, I have a gun with me *now*. The one from Curios.' I pat the lump in my left pocket. 'I found bullets. Two bullets.'

His eyebrows raise. 'Really?'

I nod.

'Well, that's perfect.' Looking up, he calls out, 'Thank Zig!'

I am startled by *Blaberus craniifer*, which suddenly climbs out of the pocket of Johnny's shorts, scurries up his chest and neck, and then burrows into his tangled hair. I glance up at the brickers and over at Reginald, but nobody seems to have noticed.

Johnny seems unfazed that a roach is crawling across his scalp. 'Zig never talks to me,' he says. 'I wish he would, but the b*stard has never said two words to me. Though I think those bullets of yours count as two words.'

I am afraid he may be right.

277

'But Zig gave me Rover, and the roach talks. Remember I thought the voice was Willa's? Well, in jail the whispering got louder and clearer, and I realized who it is.'

'Who?'

He leans closer and bores his eyes into mine. 'The people in my hospital room. My sister mostly. My folks too. Sometimes a nurse or doctor. I can hear *them*, but they can't hear me.'

He has been hallucinating, just like Thelma when she stopped eating and saw toucans in the trees. 'Oh, Johnny, you are not in a hospital anymore,' I insist. 'Your mind is playing tricks.'

'I'm alive down in America!' he says, eyes flashing. 'I died, you see. But only for a few minutes. My heart stopped beating, but the doctors got it pumping again. I came back to life and I'm getting stronger, but I'm still comatose. I just gotta wake up now. And to wake up there, I can't be alive here, you understand?'

The cockroach emerges from his hairline and perches above his left eyebrow.

'I can hear Brenda right now,' he says, glancing up to Rover. 'She's saying, 'Come on, Johnny. Open your eyes!' '

I do not know what to say. My heart shudders. My breathing goes shallow. My eyes water. The tears drip, and I wipe them away with my thumbs.

'Oh, don't be sad for me, Boo,' he says in a kind voice. 'I'm going home. I'm going back to our old hometown. Everything will be hunky-dory.'

He is as mad as Willa with her suicide leap to

278

America. And, what is worse, I want to share in this madness. 'Can I go with you?' I say, my voice breaking.

'No, man, you gotta stay in Town.'

'Do not leave me alone!' I beg.

'You aren't alone. You got Thelma and Esther and you'll make new friends.'

'I do not make friends easily. I am an oddball.'

'You gotta stay, 'cause you're dead. Sorry, man, but you're really truly doorknob dead.'

He squirms, trying to get comfortable despite the cuffs restraining his wrists and ankles. When he settles down, he says, 'I'll get another chance at life, Boo. A real life.'

Rover beetles across his forehead and burrows back into his hair. It is eerie how calm Johnny looks, whereas my hair must be standing straight up and my skin must be albino white. 'I am really scared,' I say. 'Aren't you?'

'I don't think it'll hurt much,' he says. 'I was expecting hundreds of bricks. A bullet will sure as hell hurt a lot less.'

A deep sigh from me. 'I can't. I . . . '

'Well, *I* can't. Not in cuffs. So you got to.'

I start crying again. I glance over at Reginald Washington in the doorway to the locker room, but given the pillowcase, I cannot gauge his reaction.

'There are two bullets left,' I say pleadingly. 'Two. One for you, one for me.'

'Don't be an idiot!' he cries. Lowering his voice, he says, 'You're dead, man. There's no bullet for you! You must've got two in case the first don't work. Understand? Shoot me in the heart, and if I don't disappear right away, shoot me in the head.'

I take out the CO_2 bag and hold it to my mouth. I inhale and exhale, and the bag puffs up and crinkles back down with my breath.

'Listen,' he says, his voice gentler now. 'We never got a chance to know each other too good down in America. But up in Town, we got to be best friends. Aren't we best friends?'

I nod as I breathe into my bag.

'Well, only my best friend can do this for me.'

I stop breathing into the bag. 'Please don't make me.'

My voice is shrill, childish. I am too weak. I am far too weak.

Johnny closes his eyes. When he opens them again, a tear trickles down his cheek. I reach up and wipe it with my thumb. He flinches at my touch.

'Give me a hug. You can do it. And while we're hugging, you take out the gun and you slip it between us so nobody else sees. You point it at my heart.' He glances down at his chest, the bull's-eye. 'Then you just pull the trigger, and get out of here. Easy as peach pie.'

My tears give way to racking sobs. Snot drips from my nostrils and runs into my mouth. I wipe my lips. I wipe my face. I jab my fingertips into the corners of my eyes.

'Help me go home,' Johnny says softly. 'Help me grow up. Help me get past thirteen.'

I pinch the skin on my arm to control my sobs. There are footsteps overhead: more brickers are quitting their jobs. Perhaps if I sob loudly enough, I will drive them all away. But I will never drive them all away. If I do not shoot Johnny, he will die in any case, but in a much ghastlier manner.

Johnny smiles at me, and a dimple pocks his cheek. His eyes are not smiling, though. The whites of his eyes are red.

'Please,' Johnny whispers.

And so I lean toward my mad blood brother. I hug him to me. His body smells as oniony as my own. His skin feels feverish, and yet *I* shiver.

The death's head has scrambled down his neck and now perches on his shoulder, like a fairy in a children's book.

I slip my hand into the pocket of my overalls.

'Thank you, Oliver,' Johnny whispers.

I pull out the revolver. 'Close your eyes, dear Johnny,' I say into his ear.

His eyelids clamp shut. His face grimaces. His whole body tenses. I pull back a little. I point the gun at his skinny chest. My hand does not even shake.

'Zig have mercy,' I mutter.

I pull the trigger.

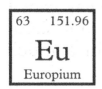

63	151.96
Eu	
Europium	

Johnny Henzel does not vanish. Instead, his body falls backward in the center circle. His head smacks against the floor. The brickers, seemingly all three hundred of them, gasp together in the echo of the bang. Some yell, '*No! No!*' as I lift the revolver to shoot again, this time pointing at Johnny's head. A bricker flings a brick and hits me in the thigh just as the gun goes off. The bullet misses Johnny and ricochets off the floor. Reginald is running toward me. He stumbles, falls, and rolls, the pillowcase slipping off his head. 'I've been shot!' he yells, even though he has not been. Another brick hits the court, breaks in two, and tumbles toward Reginald. He sits up and grabs the whistle from around his neck. His cheeks puff cartoonishly as he blows. The shrillness needles through my brain.

On the overhead track, there is movement and noise and cursing, but I do not glance up. I stare at Johnny. At the red bull's-eye in the center of his chest.

I want to unlock the cuffs from around his ankles and wrists. It must hurt him to lie in such an awkward position. 'Do you have the keys to the cuffs?' I call to Reginald, who grasps his ankle, which he twisted in his fall.

'What did you do!?' Reginald whines, his face distorted.

'I killed Johnny,' I reply.

'You didn't, you idiot! He's still alive! He's still here!'

I put down the revolver, crawl to Johnny, and lean over him. His eyes are closed. His face is relaxed. There is no tension left. He is as peaceful as an angel. The wound in his chest is the size of a nickel, and the blood looks oddly fake, like the zombie ketchup we townies squirt on ourselves on Halloween.

I place my ear to his chest as dozens of brickers descend into the gymnasium, pulling their pillowcases from their heads. They surround Johnny and me, a few with bricks in their hands as though they may still beat Johnny's brains out, or maybe even mine. Benny Baggarly is here. He picks up the revolver and points it at the ceiling. He pulls the trigger again and again, but of course the gun does not shoot.

The brickers jabber. Reginald groans. Johnny stays silent.

'Please quiet down,' I say to the brickers. A few kneel beside Johnny and me as I listen to Johnny's chest.

I sit back up. 'There is no heartbeat,' I say. 'He is redead.'

'He's not redead!' Reginald cries out, exasperated. He drags himself toward me through the crowd of brickers. He thinks me mad. I see it in his mean, angry, splotchy face.

At that moment, the death's head scurries out from underneath Johnny and climbs atop his shoulder. A few brickers gasp. Rover sits for a second or two, the death mask on its pronotum seeming to pulsate. And then — *poof!* — the roach disappears into thin air.

64	157.25
Gd	
Gadolinium	

65	158.93
Tb	
Terbium	

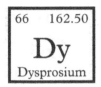

Dy

66   162.50

Dysprosium

I am sent to the Deborah to recover. A six-month stay imposed on me for my own good by Reginald Washington and his do-good council. Yes, Mother and Father, I have become a sadcon — a third-floor sadcon to be precise, the category of unstable patients forbidden from leaving the asylum grounds. Because I stay calm and collected in the days after I kill Johnny, people assume I am in shock. They tiptoe around me, literally (the ballerina-looking nurse who earlier brought me my breakfast of gruel and English muffin with jam walked as if she were afraid to make the floorboards squeak).

Albert Schmidt, the baby-faced asylum manager, often drops by my room (thankfully, not Willa Blake's old one) to check on me.

'How are you getting on?' he always asks.

'Hunkily-dorily,' I reply, coining an adverb.

He does not believe me, of course. Nobody does. I do not even know if I believe myself. I lie on my bed and gaze at the creeping ceiling cracks and twirling ceiling fan, just as I used to do in my room in our apartment, and I miss you both dearly, Mother and Father, and I miss the models of the planets that hung from my ceiling, and I even miss the cobwebs that gathered there because, on my insistence, you gave the spiders the freedom to spin their webs.

Most of all, I miss Johnny.

At least once a day, I go down to the courtyard. I like the courtyard. The sad and confused seem less so here. Bushes blossom with red, yellow, and orange roses. A pergola has trellises overrun with thick vines like those you described in *Jack and the Beanstalk*, Mother. How I regret not having listened raptly when you read me fairy tales in my childhood. Remember how I used to scoff at *The Little Engine That Could* and ask for encyclopedia entries on train combustion? For my limited interest in fictional worlds, I am sorry.

Today when I enter the courtyard, some sadcons are sitting on benches and reading about fictional worlds in novels (*Flowers in the Attic* and *We Have Always Lived in the Castle*). Others are playing gentle games like four square, hopscotch, and jacks. As I stroll by, a few sadcons nod at me or tip their balloon hats. I have become rather famous here. Yet they are too shy to approach and so keep at a safe distance. They think me dodgy and erratic because, despite appearing docile, I did kill a boy.

I sit on my favorite bench. It is my favorite for two reasons. First, it has wise graffiti carved into it: ETERNAL HAPPINESS IS JUST PLAIN CRAZY. Second, it is beside a yellow rosebush whose thorns are sharp. I like to prick a finger and time, with Casper the Friendly Ghost's help, how fast the tiny wound heals. Today my nick takes a mere twenty-two minutes to vanish (a record).

After the nick heals, I look up from my hand

and see Esther Haglund coming into the courtyard for a visit. Luckily, she is a full-fledged do-gooder now (third-floor sadcons are allowed visits from do-gooders only). Esther comes weekly to update me on the world outside the Deborah. Today all the sadcons eye her because to match her purple armband, she has on a purple velvet gown — her most flamboyant outfit to date. Zig only knows how she managed to bicycle here. I should ask her to make me a purple velvet suit: if I am to be an oddball, I should look the part.

Esther sits down on my bench, and her feet do not touch the ground. On her feet are slippers with gold sparkles glued to them. She picks a yellow rose and tucks it into her fluffy hair. An artist might capture the beauty of this scene in paint.

'Johnny's still redead, I presume,' I say.

Esther nods. Two weeks ago, she told me his body had been taken on a stretcher from the Marcy Lewis Gymnasium to the Sal Paradise Infirmary in Five.

'The nurses still think he'll heal and wake up.'

'But his heart isn't beating,' I point out.

'They think it'll start up again.'

'It never will.'

'You don't know that!' she snaps. She rubs her eyes. She looks dumbfounded and frustrated. 'Well, if he's redead for good,' she asks, 'why's this happening? Why's Johnny sticking around?' Her bulbous brow knits. She wants me to solve the puzzle of the first redead townie who does not vanish in the blink of an eye.

'It is a true mystery,' I say. 'One of my theories is that perhaps Zig believes I need Johnny around, so he left him, or at least part of him, here in Town.'

Esther taps my knee, and I wince because I have relapsed into my hands-off policy. 'You don't need Johnny anymore, Boo,' she says. 'We all have to get on with our afterlives without him.'

'Oh dear, I can't imagine that,' I say.

She stares at me a moment and then shakes her head. 'You should start imagining it. Maybe then Zig will let Johnny go.'

'No,' I simply say, with a shake of my head.

It starts to rain, a light sprinkling at first that nonetheless chases the sadcons and the nurses out of the courtyard and back into the Deborah. Esther stays put even when the rain comes down in cats and dogs and soaks her puffy hair, velvet dress, and sparkly shoes.

We sit and watch the fat raindrops pound the roses. They lose several petals. Yet they are hardy boys (like Frank and Joe, ha-ha), so they will bounce back, I am sure. And so will we, I suppose. I want to share this thought with Esther, but when I turn to her, she looks so wilted that I have my doubts.

She slips off the bench. She pushes her wet hair out of her eyes and gives me a weary look.

'What is it, Esther Haglund?'

'I don't think I'll come back to see you,' she says.

I wait in the rain for her to go on, but she just stands there eyeing me as if she has guessed something vital about me that I have not yet figured out myself.

'I know it is not as easy as peach pie to be my friend,' I finally say.

She does not reply. She just sighs. Then she turns on her sparkly heels and walks in her bowlegged gait out of my afterlife.

67   164.93
Ho
Holmium

During my time at the Deborah, I take a still-life drawing class and, through much practice, learn to sketch vases, bicycles, desk lamps, pinwheels, typewriters, throw pillows, and the like. I hone my artistic skills to become a more balanced individual. I will never be a gifted artist like Johnny, but I am now at least above average. Next I will graduate to portraits. The first person I will draw will be Johnny, once I complete my six-month stay.

Sadcons have the option of speaking to a counselor here, but I opt not to. I do not interact much with the other sadcons either. In any case, they are wary of me. They conclude that I am an unlucky friend to have, the same decision Esther has come to. When I feel lonely, I ask Albert Schmidt to play a game of chess. Dr. Schmidt, as he is called here, is good at his job as asylum manager because he does not push anyone to get better. His policy is to live and let live. He likes having all us sadcons around. He calls us his children. He is usually kind, but occasionally grows testy if he does not win at chess, so sometimes I lose on purpose.

I gain roof privileges from Dr. Schmidt after letting him win several games in a row. At first, I was denied them lest I throw myself off à la Willa

Blake. Once on the roof, I sketch stars in my notepad and undertake the grueling task of mapping the night sky. My favorite constellation to date is shaped like an ankylosaur.

To keep busy, I also volunteer in the kitchen. I like doing dishes: it is calming to scrape away the remains of our meals and then soap up our chipped dishes and get them gleaming again. For some reason, Zig has not sent us a dishwasher yet. Perhaps we are not ready for that test.

I also enjoy peeling potatoes. I have even become adept at making sweet potato pie, like the one mentioned in Mother's favorite song, Sarah Vaughan's 'It's Crazy.' My secret ingredient is the Indian spice garam masala, which I found at the back of the Deborah's pantry. I wish I could make my pie for the both of you. It is much healthier than the pizza pies you scarf down.

To keep fit, I do calisthenics in the courtyard with a Bicentennial sweatband wrapped around my forehead. Dr. Schmidt recommends exercise to combat sadness and confusion. When he spots us exercising, he pretends to be a drill sergeant and cries, 'Hup, two, three, four! Hup, two, three, four!' Thankfully, he never attempts to touch us. No pats on the shoulder. No hugs. I think he, too, dislikes being touched. A nurse named Francine, who used to be hard of hearing in America and now still talks too loudly, once laid a hand on his back and he cringed.

Dr. Schmidt died in a school-bus accident. He and three other townies killed in the accident keep in touch and sometimes get together to play

Mille Bornes in the games room. He is the grandson of a silent-screen star whose name eludes me since I do not even know the names of current movie stars. I believe, though, that the actress once played Jane in a Tarzan movie.

Even though I respect Dr. Schmidt, he will never become a best friend, not like the blendship I had with Johnny. After all, blendships are rare, as I am sure you two will agree, being in a blendship yourselves.

Johnny is still here in Town, resting in peace at the Sal Paradise Infirmary. His heart is still quiet. The do-good council is unsure what to do with Johnny's body.

Townies sometimes slip into the infirmary to steal peeks at the famous 'half-deader,' as they call him. Despite the nurses' watch, some townies manage to touch his skin to feel how dry and cool it is. They run a fingertip around the circumference of his chest wound, which has dried but not healed.

I know all this because Czar told me so in a letter. He said he snuck into the Sal himself, and when he saw Johnny's lifeless body and touched his chest wound, he decided to place a blue bauble necklace around my friend's neck. 'The poor bugger deserves some magic,' he wrote. 'Maybe the topaz will kick-start his heart.' A noble position, I feel.

Other than Czar and Esther, I have had little contact with the outside world. I refuse other visitors, and now I say no even to Thelma and Peter Peter because I believe they, too, need a break from me. I write them to apologize. They write back, but I do not open that letter, or the later ones they send.

Many strangers also write me. I presume they are gommers. Dr. Schmidt tells me some gommers see me as a hero, while others see me as a nuisance for spoiling their bricking fun. I throw all these letters down the garbage chute unopened.

Esther Haglund does not write and, as she promised, does not visit. I do not write her either. I respect her decision. I miss her, though.

A month before my six-month stay ends, I move to the second floor of the Deborah. Several of my fellow patients and I apply for day passes to work as sorters at a nearby supply warehouse. Zig made an overnight delivery, and I have high hopes of stumbling on another clue from him or instructions — something like the bullets he sent me. I want to know how I should proceed from here because, honestly, I feel adrift. I need some direction to decide what I will do with the rest of my afterlife.

At the warehouse, I drag mattresses and box springs around, load lamps into grocery carts, stack desks on dollies, sort dozens of T-shirts according to size, and fill boxes with art supplies. While I work, I daydream that the warehouse is a portal that will teleport me back to Hoffman Estates, where I can visit you, Mother and Father. Silly, I know.

Some of the sorters pilfer belongings — I see a surly sadcon named Clementine stick a donkey marionette into her knapsack — but I do not steal a thing. In any case, nothing out of the ordinary comes my way that day or the other days I volunteer. Nothing curious. Perhaps I have lost my ability to discern.

Or perhaps Zig is telling me to find my own way, fly on my own angel wings, as it were (ha-ha).

One evening, while I sit on my bed at the Deborah and draw a still life of a scruffy one-eared teddy bear that once shared its life with Willa Blake, an idea pops into my head. I mull it over and decide it is indeed splendid. I know what I ought to do with my afterlife, and with the still life that is Johnny Henzel.

I immediately write Peter Peter in care of Curios. I apologize for my long silence. I ask for my old job back provided he can forgive me for stealing one of his curious objects (the revolver). I arrange to see him and Thelma on the Friday before the Monday of my release from the Deborah.

We meet in the art room, a neutral ground that Dr. Schmidt favors for get-togethers between sadcons and non-sadcons. On the walls of the room, I hang many of my still-life drawings because there is a link between them and the favor I will ask Peter Peter and Thelma.

They show up wearing matching straw hats tied with red ribbons, like those worn by gondoliers. Thelma goes teary-eyed and says, 'My baby's lost weight.' I tell her she knows as well as I that weight loss is impossible in Town unless a townie lops off, say, his own hand or foot. I tell her she has lost not a single pound since last I saw her, and she hugs her fat stomach tightly, which means she is hugging me.

Peter Peter has a gift for me in an oblong box that looks like the type that fountain pens come in. Inside is not a pen, however. Instead, the gift is a one-of-a-kind newly arrived curious object, a mercury thermometer that shows that the Deborah's art room is seventy-seven degrees Fahrenheit and twenty-five degrees Celsius. Mercury, also known as quicksilver, is element No. 80, abbreviated as Hg.

'I want you to keep the thermometer till you return to work at Curios,' Peter Peter says.

'I am touched,' I tell them. 'Touched in the sense of emotionally moved, not in the sense of slightly mad.'

Thelma shows me her gap-toothed smile. Peter Peter chuckles. These people do care about me. It is hard to imagine why at this point in my afterlife.

I tell them my splendid idea.

68	167.26
Er	
Erbium	

69	168.93
Tm	
Thulium	

70	173.05
Yb	
Ytterbium	

Three months later, a new exhibition is set to begin its run at Curios. It is simply called *Zoo*, like the name of the pet shop Johnny had planned to open one day.

My posters for the exhibition mention that *Zoo* will pay tribute to the late animals that once called Town their home: the gerbil Lars, the budgie Gloria, the kitten Crappy, the roach Rover, and the sea monkeys, which we never bothered to name.

Over the past week, townies have written their names on our sign-up sheet for a guided visit of *Zoo* to be held on Sunday evening. For the event, places are limited to thirteen and reserved on a first-come, first-served basis.

When Sunday evening arrives, I gather my audience in front of the door leading into the exhibition hall that houses *Zoo*. Above the door is a sign painted with a big red *Z*, a big white *O*, and a big blue *O* (the colors are Thelma's idea; she is patriotic). An ornate old bureau is set in front of the door so nobody can slip into *Zoo* before I am ready. When a boy in an NBC peacock T-shirt tries sliding the bureau away, Czar, who now serves as the security guard at Curios, yells, 'Get your dirty paws off that, you motherf*cking, assl*cking ignoramus!'

I feel bad for the peacock boy because he and all my visitors tonight are the kind of avid pupils, bookworms, and loners who would spend their lunch hours studying in the library at Helen Keller. In other words, they are versions of yours truly.

When Casper the Friendly Ghost reads eight o'clock, I emerge from a table in the corner, where I have been quietly polishing Susan B. Anthony coins with a toothbrush dipped in white vinegar. I introduce myself as Oliver Dalrymple, their *Zoo* guide this evening.

'Hey, you're that kid!' says a girl who — oddly enough — has the end of her arm shoved inside a sock puppet of a tabby kitten, possibly a likeness of Crappy. When she talks, she makes the kitten's mouth move. 'You're Gunboy, aren't you?' she asks.

Townies have begun to call me Gunboy.

'There's a little Gunboy in all of us,' I reply.

I nod toward Czar. He begins dragging the bureau away from the door with help from Peter Peter, who has come out of his office to assist.

My guests eye me warily, now that they know who I am. They seem to fear I may draw a revolver and shoot them down.

I open the doors to the exhibition hall and lead them inside. Around the rectangular room are displays commemorating Town's animal life. The gerbil display, for instance, is Lars's former terrarium with its little exercise wheel and water bottle and even a few of his half-chewed toilet rolls, all of which Peter Peter saved because he is a pack rat (or perhaps a pack gerbil, ha-ha).

Now that I, too, am an artist of sorts, I made a faux gerbil using scraps from a leatherette handbag and the brown bristles of old hairbrushes. Posted on a bristol board beside the gerbil display is the story of Lars, mentioning such details as his Latin name (*Meriones unguiculatus*), the zone he was discovered in (Three), the date of his discovery in a crate of tennis balls (September 25, 1974), his favorite food (parsnips), and his life span in heaven years (two years, one month, four days).

Around the room are similar displays for the other creatures. I made a tabby out of felt and fabric, and a budgie out of yellow and green feather boas.

As for *Blaberus craniifer*, we have plenty of Johnny's drawings, from thumb sketches in India ink to full-page sketches in colored pencil. I made a life-size figurine of the cockroach out of clay and painted a detailed black blotch on its head to replicate the death mask that gives the insect its name.

I still do not understand why Rover vanished instead of Johnny, but perhaps it had simply reached the end of its natural life in heaven. Or perhaps it died of a broken heart (a cockroach's heart, by the way, has thirteen chambers).

My guests listen politely as I give my talk about *Zoo* and the creatures in it. I try to pique their curiosity by telling amusing anecdotes: for example, that Crappy was so named because she was separated from her mother too young and thus took a long time to learn how to use the litter box containing playground sand as her kitty

300

litter (an example of which is on display).

A gloomy-looking fellow, whom somebody called an old boy, says, 'We were *all* separated from our mothers too young.'

After I finish my talk, I lead my visitors to the end of the exhibition hall, where, hanging from the ceiling, is a red velvet curtain.

'What's behind it? The Wizard of Oz?' says a smart aleck.

I shake my head and draw the curtain to reveal a door leading into a smaller exhibition hall (formerly a storage room). I open the door and guide my visitors inside. It is dark in this second room, and so nobody sees at first what is on display. With the light from Casper the Friendly Ghost, I find the floor lamp and click it on.

'Behold the star attraction,' I say.

At the back of the windowless room, lying on a single bed, is a boy. We all approach his bed.

'It's just a kid sleeping,' the smart aleck says. 'Big whoop!'

'Rise and shine!' says puppet girl, and snaps her free fingers in his face.

'He won't wake up,' I tell her.

We all continue staring at the boy in the bed. Nobody makes a sound.

Finally, a fat girl exclaims, 'Jeez, it's the half-deader!'

The other twelve visitors also arrive at the same conclusion: before them lies the body of Johnny Henzel.

Johnny Henzel is my splendid idea.

Let me tell you, Mother and Father, that nobody was initially receptive to my plan. I first had to persuade Peter Peter and Thelma, who found the idea a little ghoulish. As for Reginald Washington, well, he wanted me confined to the Deborah for an extra six months simply for *suggesting* my idea. I explained, however, that tucking Johnny away in an infirmary and forgetting about him would do no one any good. We need to remember him. We need to talk about his life here and in America to better understand his story. As a result, we can be better prepared should Zig one day send us another boy like Johnny Henzel.

My aim, you see, is to honor my friend, but also to avoid another bricking of another sadcon.

In the end, Reginald and the do-good council gave my *Zoo* the green light, at least on a trial basis, thanks partly to support the project obtained from warden Lydia Finkle. When I asked Reginald what he meant by 'trial basis,' he replied, 'We'll shut you down, Mr. Dalrymple, if you go mental again.'

For opening night, Johnny is wearing cutoff jeans and a tank top printed with Tony the Tiger of Frosted Flakes fame. The blue bauble sits atop the bullet wound. On his feet, he wears gym socks whose bumblebee stripes (yellow and black) are the Helen Keller colors.

His eyes are closed. He does not look peaceful, nor does he look in pain. He looks absorbed, as if he is figuring out a tricky arithmetic problem in his head.

Czar comes into the hall and warns visitors not to get too close to Johnny. 'Don't smother the guy, folks,' he orders. 'Give him some air.'

'We can't smother somebody who isn't alive,' say the girl and Crappy 2.

'Hello there, Johnny,' I say, leaning over the bed. 'How are you doing this fine evening?' I do not expect an answer. If he did blink open his eyes and say, 'Hunky-dory,' thirteen townies might develop their own holey hearts (ha-ha).

Around the room, I posted all of Johnny's drawings and paintings that I could gather together. He had done portraits and caricatures of Esther, Thelma, and me, as well as his parents and Brenda, his jailer Ringo, his basset hound — and of course Gunboy. He drew dorms (the Frank and Joe), trees, bicycles, warehouses, jungle gyms, basketball nets, dandelions, even a row of urinals.

I give my thirteen visitors the facts that I recall from Johnny's life in Hoffman Estates and from his afterlife in Town. I do not hide embarrassing details. I tell them I now suspect that the camp (the infamous Squeaky Fromme) he attended in the summer before our passing was actually a kind of mental asylum like the Deborah.

Since it is too late for mercy, I try to elicit sympathy for my friend. I tell my audience that a troubled mind can cause a boy to do strange things. 'He had an illness as serious as the cancer that felled certain thirteen-year-olds before they came to Town,' I say.

I allow the visitors to touch Johnny's arms and legs. 'Gross!' the fat girl cries, but the others take turns running a hand along his limbs. They tell me his skin is cool.

'Does he have rigor mortis?' the old boy asks.

'Good question,' I say. 'But no, he does not.' To prove this, I lift one of his arms and bend it back and forth at the elbow.

'Is he in a coma?' asks a boy with a walleye (strabismus).

'No, the comatose still have functioning hearts, whereas Johnny's is as quiet as a piece of lapis lazuli.' I refer to lapis lazuli in particular because its name translates as 'stone of heaven.'

'Is the bullet still in him?' the same boy asks.

I move the fake topaz away from his dented wound. The dried blood is almost black.

'The bullet hasn't resurfaced,' I tell my guests.

The hand-puppet girl suggests that Johnny's bullet may have dissolved, and I admit she may be right. 'Can we see the gun?' she asks.

There are drawers that slide out from beneath the bed. Two are used to store extra clothes because I change Johnny's tank top, shorts, socks, and boxers weekly, with Czar's help. Even though Johnny no longer sweats, he retains an oniony odor, but it is so faint I have to put my nose almost against his scalp to detect it.

Another drawer contains the revolver. I open it and pull out the gun. Several of the visitors gasp. The fat girl clasps her hands over her mouth.

The smart aleck says, 'It ain't loaded, I hope,' but he has an excited look that says otherwise.

I pass the revolver around. Some of my guests take it as though it were a hot potato or a grenade set to go off.

The puppet girl holds Crappy 2 close to my face. One of its button eyes is coming loose, the black thread hanging like an optic nerve. 'When you pointed that gun at your friend's chest,' Crappy 2 says, 'what was going through your mind?'

'It may sound strange for me to say so,' I answer, 'but I thought I was saving Johnny.'

'Maybe when he shot you,' Crappy 2 replies, 'Johnny thought he was saving you too.'

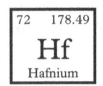

72	178.49

Hf
Hafnium

Later that evening, after everyone has left Curios, I am sweeping the floor in Johnny's room when I hear footsteps in *Zoo*. The red velvet curtain is pushed aside, and there stands Esther Haglund in the doorway. She is wearing a shiny white dress, and her hair is piled atop her head in ringlets.

'Wow, you look just like an angel, Esther,' I say. I have not seen her since my early days at the Deborah.

'I want to show Johnny I made an effort,' she says, smoothing out the front of her dress. 'It's taffeta, but not real silk. Unfortunately, that b*stard Zig is stingy with his silk.'

I heard from Thelma that Esther moved to Three, where she now makes clothes for other townies, with help — believe it or not — from former jailer Ringo, who finally quit his job at the Gene to become a tailor.

Thelma must have told Esther about *Zoo* and its main attraction. My old friend goes over and sits on the side of Johnny's bed and, with a deep sigh, touches a finger to the bridge of his nose, just as I once did to dearly departed Uncle Seymour.

I wonder if Esther was in love with Johnny Henzel. Perhaps that is why she needed time away from him and me. I picture the broken plastic heart from the Operation game in her chest, and my eyes tear up, something they have not done in some time. I turn away so Esther does not see me.

'Excuse me a minute, Esther. I need to fetch something from my office,' I say, to give her time alone with Johnny.

In my office, I sit at my desk. A blank sheet of paper is in my typewriter. I have been working again on the story of my afterlife. I have finally reached the present day and am not sure where the story goes next.

No one has read my story yet. I wanted you to be the first, Mother and Father. The pages of my manuscript are in a three-ringed binder kept in a locked drawer of my desk. I fetch the drawer key from inside the base of the Wobblin' Goblin music box, open the drawer, and take out the binder. On my way out of my office, I also grab the box of Lucky Charms from a crowded shelf. Peter Peter will be cross if we eat the cereal, but so be it. Given all we have been through, Esther and I deserve this gift from Zig.

She and I sit on threadbare armchairs we drag into Johnny's *Zoo* room. We share the box of cereal, our hands digging in search of the marshmallows in the shapes of hearts, moons, stars, clovers, and diamonds. Esther finds the prize at the bottom of the box: an elf figurine. She gives it to me. 'Elves are my f*cking bête noire,' she says. 'Back in Utah, I was always asked to play one in the Christmas pageant.'

As we snack, I read the story of my afterlife

aloud. To Esther, but also to Johnny. My blood brother still has a concentrated look on his face as though he is trying to figure out what our story means.

Sometimes during my reading Esther stops me to make a correction or clarify some aspect of our adventures. She nods her head a lot and even says 'Amen,' the way I imagine Christians do in church when ministers read from their Bible.

I read up to the part where Esther arrives at Zoo. It is three fifteen by this time. My voice is going hoarse. Esther's eyes are blinking shut, and her ringlets have come undone. 'It's time you put this baby to bed,' she says.

I assume she means she is the baby who is ready for bed (we will have to sleep on sofas at Curios tonight), but then she clarifies: 'Go finish this chapter and then come read it to me.'

So that is what I do.

Here is one more chapter, dear Mother and Father. It is dedicated to you, as is every page herein. I have gradually lost faith that I will ever find a way to deliver to you the story of my afterlife, and so I will stop for now and say good-bye. I want to stop while I still remember what the two of you look like. In time, your faces will grow dimmer and dimmer. It will be as though you died instead of me. But even when I cannot see your faces anymore, please know this: your son still loves you. How curious that I never told you so before.

74 183.84
W
Tungsten

75 186.21
Re
Rhenium

76 190.23
Os
Osmium

77 192.22
Ir
Iridium

78 195.08
Pt
Platinum

79 196.97
Au
Gold

80 200.59
Hg
Mercury

81 204.38
Tl
Thallium

82 207.2
Pb
Lead

83 208.98
Bi
Bismuth

84 [208.98]
Po
Polonium

85 [209.99]
At
Astatine

86 [222.02]
Rn
Radon

87 [223.02]
Fr
Francium

88 [228.03]
Ra
Radon

89 [227.03]
Ac
Actinium

90 232.04	
Th	
Thorium	

91 231.04	
Pa	
Protactinium	

92 238.03	
U	
Uranium	

93 [237.05]	
Np	
Neptunium	

94 [244.06]	
Pu	
Plutonium	

Dear Father and Mother, I have now lived in town as long as I lived in America: thirteen years. I am no longer a newbie. It is hard to believe I ever was. Yet I have changed little in the intervening years. After all, we townies idle. Thelma Rudd claims I am now more mature. Perhaps, but I do not feel so.

Over the years, I have continued to live at the Frank and Joe and to do the same work at Curios. I am now the museum's curator, a position I inherited when dear Peter Peter repassed more than eight years ago.

Thelma held a wake as Peter Peter approached fifty years old. A wake in Town, however, is different from a wake in America. In our wakes, we five-decade-old townies are not yet dead (or redead). Each night as we near fifty, our friends gather in our room. Zig does not necessarily steal us away on the exact date of our fiftieth rebirthday; we may disappear a week or two before or after this date (in the same way that a pregnant lady in America does not necessarily deliver *exactly* nine months after conception). During his wake, Peter Peter's friends sat cramped together around his bed and talked. Peter Peter lay under the covers listening. One night he closed his eyes . . . and *poof.* No fade-out. No fifty-year aging all at once. Thelma screamed (though she had promised Peter Peter she would stay calm).

The other old boy, Peter Peter's friend Czar, refused to have a wake. He said it was embarrassing to have people watch you redie. He said it was akin to having people watch you 'take a crap.' As a result, he forbade anyone from being present in his room when he repassed, two months after Peter Peter.

Over the years, I have kept myself busy with various projects. I teach a constellation class at the Franny Glass School in Thirteen. After my first five years in Town, Zig changed the night sky backdrop, and thus I needed to start mapping anew. As time passes in heaven, the stars do not change places, not till the day when Zig changes the complete backdrop. I tell my students this is a metaphor for life: we go along thinking nothing will be different, till the day everything suddenly changes at once.

One morning about six years ago, a kite sailed in over the South Wall in Seven. Because the kite is red with one big yellow star and four smaller yellow stars, the design of the Chinese flag, certain townies believed it came from Chinese thirteen-year-olds in a nearby terrarium. Sadly, no note was tied to its tail, so we are unsure of its origin, but at least it gave us proof we are not alone. The 'Chinese' kite is now on display in Hall 3 at Curios.

Four years ago, a large upper section of the Southwest Corner in Six crumbled, severely injuring several townies gathered at the bottom of the wall for a folk festival dedicated to the music of Bob Dylan. Was this incident intentional on Zig's part (perhaps not a fan of Mr. Dylan's work) or simple neglect? Some think the former; I presume the latter. The damaged wall grew back within sixteen days, by which time all of the injured had been released from the Paul Atreides Infirmary in Seven.

Some changes have been on a smaller scale. Guess what! We have a dog, a French poodle that arrived only two months ago in a warehouse located just down the street from Curios. Pierre (named by Thelma in honor of Peter Peter) has a woolly chocolate coat, which we do not clip, and a little pink tongue, the tip of which often sticks out of his mouth. His favorite foods are black-eyed peas, carrot greens, and butternut squash, and, thank Zig, this carnivore thrives on a vegetarian diet, though of course he will grow no bigger. He will idle like the rest of us.

I could continue citing other interesting developments in Town in the intervening years, but let us move on to the reason I am writing to you again after such a long pause.

Something magical is happening in Town, and it has renewed my faith that I may eventually manage to deliver my story to you.

The magic involves Johnny Henzel.

For many years, Johnny played a much smaller role in my afterlife. Yes, I continued to check on him and change his clothes as needed, but for a long time he did not occupy my thoughts the way he had during my first year or two here.

There is an old wives' tale in America that hair

and fingernails keep growing after a person's death. In the case of townies, ours do, but in the case of Johnny, this was false. In the years he lay in bed at *Zoo*, his hair stayed the same length it was on the day I shot him: four inches at its longest. Yet last week, while changing his clothes, I noticed his hair seemed longer. I fetched my ruler and measured: five and a third inches. Then I spotted his fingernails. Before his redeath, he had chewed them down to the quick, so imagine my shock when I saw crescent moons appearing where no nails had been before.

My old friend is growing.

Johnny Henzel goes from five feet three to five feet four, then five five, then five six. The peach fuzz above his lip and on his chin turns into dark whiskers. Dark hair also sprouts along his arms and legs, in his armpits, and in his pubic region.

For a few days, I shave his face with the electric razor displayed in Hall 2, but then I abandon this ploy. Instead, I close off his room at *Zoo* with a heavy armoire and lie that I am redesigning the space to boost attendance. People believe me because over the years Johnny has drawn fewer and fewer visitors. Most townies have seen him. They know his story; he is old news. Johnny would, however, attract hordes of bedazzled townies if they knew he was the first among us to grow past age thirteen.

'What is this magic?' I ask Johnny as I dab acne cream on a pimple on his cheek. I slip a thermometer into his mouth to see whether there is a change in his normal body temperature of ninety-six degrees. He has never grown cold.

316

He has always felt as though he died only five minutes before, but now his temperature has risen a degree.

I close down Curios altogether, with the excuse that I am planning a major revamp, and do not allow others on the premises at all. I stay here practically around the clock, zipping out only to pick up takeout meals at a cafeteria.

I claim I need my solitude. Only Pierre stays behind to keep me company. When townies ask about my design plans, I remain vague. I speak of flowing creative juices, a visiting muse. The artistic townies eat up such talk, including Thelma, who pats my head encouragingly. Esther, though, looks doubtful. 'What are you scheming?' she asks, narrowing her eyes. Yet even she leaves me alone since she is busy planning her wedding. She will marry her tailor partner, Ringo (whose real name, by the way, is Nigel Bell).

Once Curios is closed down, I move sofa cushions into Johnny's room to sleep on. We are roommates again. Given Johnny's steady growth, I change his clothes often. I have to wrestle with his big lanky body. His arms and legs are gangly, his feet long, his toes pointy. I clip his fingernails and toenails daily but no longer trim his hair. His hair and beard grow as long as a flower-power hippie's. His chest fills out, making his bull's-eye wound look smaller.

I watch him age about a year every two days, and soon he is Town's first real man. His body grows to six feet one inch and stops. He keeps aging, though. I see the changes mostly in his face; all the baby fat in his cheeks melts away, and his cheekbones stand out. I estimate he is nearing twenty-six years old, the same age he would be if he were still in America.

I think he may be handsome, but I am not sure: I have always had trouble seeing beauty in human beings. What I find beautiful — a crop of pimples in the pattern of an ankylosaur constellation, for example — others find repugnant.

Every day, I lift his eyelids to check his pupils, but they remain dilated and motionless. I put my ear to his chest. His heart offers not one chug.

One evening, as I am examining him, I see something frightening: a red pool spreading out beneath his left palm. I grab his hand, turn it over. His left wrist has been slashed several times. Blood seeps from the gashes and runs down his arm.

Then I notice his right wrist. It, too, is oozing blood.

I yank open the drawer beneath his bed, pull out an old T-shirt, dab at the blood. Within minutes, the gashes on both wrists have scabbed over.

'What in hell's name is going on?' I say aloud.

At five in the morning on September 7 (my rebirthday), I slink out to a supply warehouse to filch some clothing for Johnny. It has been about five weeks since he began to grow. I hope to find him some extra-large gym shorts and tank tops, the kind made for the biggest boys among us. As a precaution, I fill my flashlight with rocks. Zig knows what type of enemy I may encounter in these strange and uncertain times. I still do not understand how Johnny's wrists bled. His scabs have healed, but deep zigzag scars linger.

I head off to the warehouse, one hand on my flashlight, the other holding Pierre's leash. The dog scurries down the sidewalk, tugging surprisingly hard for such a small creature.

As I approach the warehouse on Carrie White Street, the two quarter-pie windows above the warehouse doors go from dark to bright. Whenever a delivery comes in, Zig automatically turns on the lights as a kind of beacon to us townies. *Perfect*, I think. *I will have first dibs before the sorters arrive at eight thirty.*

Outside the warehouse are two security guards sitting on overturned buckets and playing crazy eights on a wobbly card table. They are used to my visits. As curator at Curios, I have a special pass to visit warehouses in search of curious objects. The guards barely glance up from their game, despite the presence of Pierre, who usually elicits so much cooing and fussing from passersby that I tend to walk him only early in the morning or late at night.

I grasp the metal door handle, heave the door open, and slip inside the warehouse. I unhook Pierre from his leash so he can scramble over the hoard of goods Zig has bestowed on us. As usual, the delivery looks like a yard sale of unwanted, unloved items: used desks, mattresses, and stoves; piles of secondhand T-shirts; a jumble of compact discs; boxes of paperback books, their corners curled with age; even a half dozen scratched, tarnished tubas, their mouths all facing one another as though they are conversing.

I am on my knees riffling through a box of secondhand gym shorts when I hear Pierre's sharp yaps coming from the other side of the warehouse.

Pierre can do a trick whereby he throws back his head and imitates the *wee-ooo-wee-ooo* sound of a European police siren. We tell ourselves he learned this in the streets of Paris. Everybody loves it when he does his trick. I myself find his howl grating, and so when he starts up in the warehouse now, I put down my armful of gym shorts and go to shut him up.

I spot him in front of an old school locker that stands upright between a refrigerator and a photocopier. He is pawing the locker between howls. Pierre arrived in a cardboard box of throw cushions himself, and perhaps this locker contains another dog or a cat or even Town's first raccoon. As I approach the locker, however, I realize there is something familiar about it: a dent halfway up its army-green surface, as though a student's head was once butted against its door.

It is then I notice the number on the metal plate near the top. It is 106. 'Holy smokes,' I say to Pierre, who finally stops his barking.

'What kind of tomfoolery are you up to, Zig?' I say aloud as I touch a palm against the locker's cool surface. What will I find inside? The periodic table? Photographs of Richard Dawkins and Jane Goodall? My old gym clothes? My protractor?

As I inch the locker door open, its rusty hinges let out a series of squeaks that, considering my nerves, could also be coming from me.

Inside the locker is a face I have not seen in thirteen years.

The locker itself is empty, but its rear panel is missing, and, instead of revealing the back of the warehouse, the space opens onto a hallway where there hangs a black-and-white portrait of a blind and deaf high-school graduate wearing a mortarboard on her head.

In the years since I last saw Helen Keller, she has not changed one iota. She has been locked in time like me. She gives me an encouraging look, as encouraging a look as a blind lady can. 'Come along now, child,' she seems to say. 'Don't be afraid.'

Helen faced many ordeals in her life boldly and bravely, and so must I. I look down at Pierre. He looks up, wet-eyed, tongue tip sticking out. He emits a low squeal.

'Stay,' I say to him. 'I'll be back.'

Will I, though?

I wedge myself into the portal before me. I know I will fit: Jermaine Tucker once shut me inside this very locker. I close the door behind me so that Pierre cannot climb through. Just as I slip out of the locker and into the hallway of my old school, the bell rings. Hordes of students spill from the classrooms up and down the corridor. For a moment, I am frozen. My heartbeat quickens because I fear seeing Jermaine Tucker, Kevin

Stein, Henry Axworthy, and their ilk — but of course I do not. I do not recognize any of the seventh graders and eighth graders jabbering and cursing and giggling and roughhousing. Thirteen years have passed.

Am I invisible? I hold my hands to my face. They look pale but solid. The ghost around my wrist, Casper, now reads three thirty. The bell that rang is the last bell of the day.

'Do you mind?' says an Asian girl with butterfly clips in her hair and a shell necklace around her neck. 'You're, like, totally blocking my way.'

I am not invisible.

I step aside so the new owner of my old locker can fetch her belongings. Since I stepped out of it, the locker has closed behind me. The girl fiddles with her lock, and I almost ask if the combination is still 7–25–34. But she does not give me a second glance, nor do the other students. Yet the blind Helen seems to. 'Get a move on,' I imagine her saying. 'You have a haunting to do.'

I swerve through the crowd as the students jostle one another. Unfurled on a wall is a team banner reading, TROJAN, SLAY THY ENEMY! The walls have been repainted: they were once pale yellow but are now spearmint green.

I pass an empty classroom, the room where I used to study science. On the teacher's desk is a plastic model of the human heart with its chambers, valves, and arteries exposed. I am drawn toward it, but before I can examine the heart, another item attracts my attention.

Thumbtacked to a corkboard is, lo and behold, a periodic table. An updated periodic table!

'May I help you?'

I turn around and face a man whose head is bald but whose chest must be furry because a tuft of black hair pokes out of the top of his shirt. I have not seen an adult — other than the grown-up Johnny Henzel — in thirteen years, so I am startled, as though I just stumbled on a bear in the woods.

'Your periodic table,' I say to this man whom I do not recognize, 'it has one hundred and nine elements now.'

The science teacher glances at the periodic table and then looks back at me. 'That's right. One hundred and nine, yes.'

'I thought there were only one hundred and six. I imagine that' — here I read from the table — 'bohrium, hassium, and meitnerium were discovered in the last dozen years.'

Speared behind the teacher's ear is a long pencil indented with teeth marks. The man gives me a quizzical look. 'Oh, we're making new discoveries all the time,' he says. 'You never know what'll turn up next.'

Peter Peter used to say more or less the same thing about objects destined for Curios.

'Good day to you, sir,' I say to the science teacher.

'Good day to you too,' the man says, scratching a patch of psoriasis on his elbow.

I turn and walk from the room into the crowded corridor. I am pushed along, past bulletin boards filled with students' reproductions of album art (*Little Earthquakes, Lucky Town, Nevermind,*

99.9F°), a poster for auditions for a play (*Death of a Salesman*), and a perplexing campaign flyer for student council (PHIL PRATT IS PHAT!).

Out of the corner of my eye, I glimpse Mr. Miller, my English teacher to whom I taught the difference between 'who' and 'whom.' He now has a potbelly, and his salt-and-pepper hair is now just salt. Another actual adult. I avert my gaze lest he think he has seen a ghost. Down the hall and across the lobby I hurry. As I push through Helen Keller's front doors, I realize that the last time I left this school, I was lying on a stretcher, a blanket thrown over my corpse.

Outside I see so many things I have not seen in a dog's age. Speaking of dogs, at the edge of the school driveway, I see a German shepherd, which runs by me leash-less. I see a dozen sparrows flutter into a tree. Around me are bungalows, automobiles, school buses, mailboxes, stop signs, traffic lights, and convenience stores. How liberating and peculiar to be free of the towering Great Walls that imprison us townies.

My eyes go watery from joy!

As I admire my surroundings, a gray squirrel bounds toward me and stands with its tail twitching and paws limp-wristed. 'Thank you, Zig,' I say to the squirrel, as though *Sciurus carolinensis* were my god. The animal snatches a maple key and then scrabbles up a tree. I wish it were fall so I could see orange and red maple leaves! I wish it were winter so I could see snow, and perhaps grasp a bumper and skitch down the street!

On the edge of the sidewalk is an anthill teeming with ants. I drop to my knees. I am awed by my little friends' strength and purposefulness. An ant can carry fifty times its body weight. Were I an ant, I could carry an ice-cream truck on my back. I mention such a truck because one passes by, ringing its bell and attracting a Pied Piper line of students. Townies would be envious, since ice cream is not among the foods Zig sends. For a frozen treat, we townies make do with putting peeled bananas in the freezer and then running them through a food processor.

Compared with Town, Hoffman Estates has such a variety of humans! After thirteen years of nothing but thirteen-year-olds, it is heavenly (ha-ha) to see, for example, an old man walking with a cane. How old is he? Sadly, I can no longer tell age. Sixty-two? Eighty-nine? Running beneath the translucent skin on his forearms are whole tributaries of snaky blue veins, so he must be very old.

'It's beautiful out, *n'est-ce pas?*' I say to the man, whose nose has the same texture as cauliflower.

He looks up. An airplane is passing, creating contrails across the wild blue yonder. 'The sky used to be bluer in my day,' he says.

'But it *is* your day,' I reply. 'You aren't dead yet.'

The next person I pass is a man in a tank top with ballooning muscles like a cartoon superhero's. Then I see a shawled lady pushing an actual toddler in a stroller. In the child's hair is

326

clamped a swarm of bumblebee barrettes. As you know, I was never fond of young children because conversing with them is dull, yet I actually babble 'Gitchy gitchy goo!' at the child.

I must stop all this staring at my surroundings and make haste. Who knows how long this haunting will last? I once thought a haunting would be unfair to you, cruel even. I have changed my mind. Perhaps I am being selfish, but I want to see your faces again. Zig willing, I will.

I start running. I am a speed demon. I intend to head straight for Clippers, since at this time of the day that is where you should be, but since Sandpits is on the way, I cut through our apartment complex. I take Hill Drive, and I am huffing and puffing by the time I reach 222. I stop and glance at the second-floor balcony. Through the balcony door, I glimpse movement, a person walking past. You may be home early! Or perhaps you have taken the day off because it is the anniversary of my death.

I hurry up the walkway and into our low-rise. When I reach Apartment 6 on the second floor, I see on our door a wreath made of sticks twisted together with little plastic cardinals nesting within. Mother, you must have made it in one of your arts and crafts workshops. I bang the door knocker without thinking what I will say if you answer and find your late son standing before you. I do not have time to think because I fear that Zig will reel me back any second — perhaps even the very second I glimpse your faces and you glimpse mine. Perhaps when the door swings open, I will vanish and you will have the ghost of your son burned on your retinas as your only proof I was ever there.

But when the door swings open, you are not whom I see. Whom I see is an older teenager with a nest of messy black hair. He wears a black T-shirt with the name ROBERT SMITH written across the chest in white letters designed to look like dripping paint.

'Are you the paperboy?' Robert Smith asks.

His lips are orangey red. His skin is as white as mine, but I believe he has applied powder, because I can see that it is caked in his nostril folds. He looks almost like the zombies that townies dress as on Halloween.

I stare at him. I am sure I am wide-eyed, as though he were the ghost, not I.

Is he your foster son, Mother and Father?

From the apartment comes music, a slow song featuring a sad violin and sung by a gloomy man who keeps repeating that he is always wishing for 'impossible things.'

Robert Smith repeats his question: 'Is it collection day? You deliver the *Tribune*?'

I slowly shake my head. Then I say, 'May I speak to Mr. and Mrs. Dalrymple?'

'Who?'

'The Dalrymples.'

'Never heard of them.'

He is not your foster son.

'They're barbers,' I say. 'They run Clippers out by the highway.'

'You got the wrong building. All the buildings look alike in this sh*thole.'

328

'The Dalrymples used to live in Apartment 6 at 222 Hill Drive. I am certain of that.'

'Well, they don't no more. Me and my mom have been here three years now.'

Oh dear! It never occurred to me you may have moved. I am unsure what to do. I hesitate. Robert Smith stares at me with his mascaraed eyes. Finally, I take a step forward. 'May I come in and look around?' I ask.

On his middle finger, Robert Smith is wearing a silver ring with a skull engraving, a kind of death's head ring. I notice it because he reaches across the doorway to block my entry. He frowns his black eyebrows. 'No, you little freak,' he says. 'You can't come in.'

A boy in pancake makeup with bouffant hair is calling me a freak.

'Pretty please,' I say.

Robert Smith slams the door.

Automobiles, trucks, and buses zoom along the highway. They seem to move faster than they did thirteen years ago, but perhaps my memory is faulty, since the fastest thing in Town is a ten-speed bicycle. The vehicles zipping by also seem louder and dirtier than before. The exhaust they belch is stomach-turning; the honks they emit are earsplitting. Town may have its flaws, but at least the air is clean and the worst noise is a tone-deaf townie lying to himself that he can master the saxophone.

I stand at a crosswalk with two girls, both wearing striped wool sweaters unraveling at the waist, pink tutus(!), and thick-soled oxblood boots. One of the girls, the one with big eyeglasses, says to the other, 'You're so bogus!'

Seeing the girl's glasses, I realize I still have my twenty-twenty vision. I wonder if you will recognize me without eyeglasses. What am I thinking? Of course you will. Will I recognize *you* is the question I should ask. You have aged thirteen years. Perhaps your hair is salt. Perhaps you are flabby, jowly, and wrinkly.

The light turns green, and I cross the highway. More fast-food joints have sprung up. Despite how garish the jumble of fluorescent signs is, I am awed. After all, heaven has no giant yellow sombreros advertising tacos and no giant dancing lobsters promoting seafood. The lobsters, I must say, seem overly happy for crustaceans that will be torn asunder and have their flesh sucked out of their claws.

The sidewalk here is no safer than before. The strip of lawn between it and the oncoming traffic is so thin a car could easily jump the curb and strike a person. I hope you always remain alert as you walk to work.

I spot a baseball cap lying in the grass. It is all blue except for a red letter *C* (the Chicago Cubs). I adjust the back strap and don the cap, pulling the visor down low. I should be an incognito ghost, just in case I bump into somebody who knows me.

Should I just walk into Clippers and say, 'Hello there, Mother and Father'? You may accidentally jab your customers in the eyes with your scissors. Or faint and strike your heads so hard you get a concussion. Casper says it is now ten after four. Should I wait outside your shop till your customers leave? Will Zig give me enough haunting time?

An eighteen-wheeler roars past, beeping its horn. The noise is like an electric prod, and I start to run. I run at top speed till I reach the strip mall and then slow to a jog. I pass the druggist's, the pizza parlor, the pet shop, and the dry cleaner's, and I cannot believe my eyes. I stop dead in my tracks. Your barber pole is no longer there! The red and white stripes are gone. The blood and the bandages are a thing of the past.

Like a fifty-year-old townie, Clippers has vanished. *Poof!*

In its place stands a plant shop called Back to the Garden. I hurry to the window. Baskets of flowers have replaced your bottles of shampoos and hair tonics. Hung on the window is a poster of Adam and Eve, their bodies covered in vines. The sign reads, PLANTS: A GIFT THAT GROWS ON YOU. I press my nose against the glass and see an Asian man dressed in an apron who is selling a bouquet of gerberas to an old lady with lavender hair.

Where are you, dear Father and Mother?

There is a phone booth outside the pet shop. I trot back and leaf through the white pages. I find all the Dalrymples living in Cook County. Eight listings, but none of the names are yours or even Aunt Rose's. I flick through the yellow pages so wildly that I rip a page in half. There is no Clippers among the barbershop listings.

I rest my forehead against the glass of the booth. 'Help me, Zig,' I whisper, my hope fading. 'You brought me here. Tell me what to do.'

I see a cat sleeping in the pet-shop window. A Siamese. Then I notice the shop's name on its front door.

In 1979, the pet shop was called Animal Lovers.

Today its name is Zoo.

Lordy! Lordy!

I hurry out of the phone booth and push open the shop's front door. A bell jingles, and the cat in the window lifts its sleepy head and throws me a look of ennui. Behind the cash register stands a young woman in a purple velour tracksuit. She is affixing discount stickers to boxes of birdseed and barely gives me a glance.

The name cannot be a coincidence, can it? I wander the aisles pondering what to do. The only customer in the store is an older teenager whose kneecaps stick out of big holes in his pale blue jeans. He is grimacing as he drags a hefty bag of dog kibble to the checkout counter.

I end up at the back of the shop in the rodent department, which smells strongly of wood chips. Shelves are stacked with terrariums of gerbils, hamsters, guinea pigs, rats, and mice. I drum my fingers against the glass of the mouse terrarium and eight pairs of nostrils sniff the air. The mice stare at me, beady-eyed and alarmed. As a ghost, I am only scary enough to give the willies to a litter of mice.

There are also tanks here containing tarantulas and lizards, and I notice a pair of beautiful geckos whose yellow bodies are covered with dark spots like a banana going mushy. Their little pink tongues dart in and out, reminding me of Pierre.

Another tank catches my eye. It is filled with insects crawling all over one another. Holy moly! They are death's head cockroaches! Dozens and dozens of *Blaberus craniifer*! I remember that this roach species is often used as lizard food.

Behind the wall of terrariums is a small area where employees tend the animals. Someone is there now. I see the person between the tanks. He is standing at a sink. His back is to me, but I see his dark ponytail, which extends to his shoulder blades. He is wearing khaki shorts and a sweatshirt.

The little hairs on the back of my neck go stiff. I know this man.

He turns around and approaches the wall of tanks, lifts the wire-mesh lid of a terrarium, and drops in an empty paper-towel roll for the gerbils to chew apart.

Petrified, frozen in place, I watch the man. From somewhere in the shop, a parrot emits a loud squawk, and the cashier calls out, 'Shut up, Aristotle!'

Johnny Henzel looks exactly the same as he does in Town. His hair is the same length, as is his beard. His cheekbones are just as sharp, his eyelashes just as dark. He even has the same pimple on his cheek.

He tried telling me the truth years ago. He was still in a coma here in America, he said. Rover was a bug, he claimed, but in the sense of a listening device that transmitted the voices of those around his hospital bed. Only *he* could hear those voices.

I did not believe him. He was a half-deader, but I thought him half-mad.

Patients in long comas often wake forgetting their past. Has Johnny forgotten his? Has he forgotten all about Town? All about me?

I step closer to the terrariums, my face between the gecko tank and the lizard tank. I remove my Cubs cap and drop it on the floor.

Johnny has turned away from me. He takes a bag of rabbit pellets from a shelf and cuts it open with a pair of scissors.

I begin to hum a song, quietly at first and then louder.

The song is by Cole Porter, its lyrics a portmanteau.

Johnny puts down the pellets and turns slowly around. He knits his brow, creating the approximately-equal-to symbol ($\approx$) in the middle of his forehead.

He takes a few steps forward and stares at my face between the terrariums. His mouth falls open. His eyes go wide.

I stop humming. In a loud whisper, I say, 'Boo!'

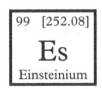

99 [252.08]

Es

Einsteinium

'I thought I was f*cking crazy, man. Like maybe I dreamt it all up while I was comatose for all those months. Town, the Great Walls, Thelma and Esther, Zig, the death's head, the bricking.'

Though still recognizable, Johnny's voice is much deeper than before. He and I are in the back room of Zoo, the door pushed half-closed. Beside us is a stack of cardboard boxes, and the bored-looking Siamese is now curled up atop them. Inside the boxes are tins of a cat food with an apt name: 9 Lives.

Johnny looks me up and down. 'Man oh man, I can't believe you're here,' he says. 'It's so awesome, but also real f*cking freaky.'

It is strange seeing him too. He is no longer the boy I knew. He is over six feet tall. He has a beard, which he keeps stroking. He is standing close and smells oniony, perhaps because he has no one here to remind him to shower.

'Where are my parents, Johnny?' I say, my voice squeaky. 'I can find neither hide nor hair of them. I just stopped by 222 Hill Drive, but they are no longer there. A fellow with a powdered face lives in their apartment.'

'Oh, jeez, your folks left years and years ago, back when I was in ninth grade. I heard they went to Alaska, but I'm not a hundred percent sure.'

'Alaska!?' I cry. 'I have serious doubts Zig will grant me enough haunting time for a trip to the largest state in the union.'

The back room is furnished with a scratched desk that looks much like Johnny's old desk at the Frank and Joe. Scattered across the top are rubber chew toys for dogs: colorful bones, a plucked rooster, a great white shark. Beside the desk is a door to the outside propped open with, of all things, a brick.

'So you found a damn portal!' Johnny says.

'On my rebirthday, no less,' I say. 'Zig has granted me permission to visit you after all these years. But why now? I do not have the foggiest idea.'

'I think I know.' He pushes up the sleeves of his sweatshirt and holds his hands out palms up. Around both his wrists are flesh-colored bandages.

There is shame in his voice when he says, 'I did a real stupid thing.'

'Oh, Johnny, why would you do that?'

He smirks at me. 'Once a sadcon, always a sadcon.'

I touch one of the bandages with the tip of my finger. I know what lies beneath: the same ugly scars are on his wrists back in Town. It dawns on me that his doppelgänger at Curios probably started aging on the day Johnny sliced through his veins here in America.

'My shrink has me on anti-sadcon pills, but the f*cking things don't always work.'

He gives me a searching look. 'You'll think I'm nuts, but sometimes I miss Town. Sometimes I put my ear against my tank of roaches, hoping I'll hear voices from Town. Maybe even you talking to me again, correcting my grammar.'

I do not mention his twin at Curios lest I frighten him. 'You can never go back, Johnny,' I say with finality.

He nods his head, looking a little morose, but then he brightens. 'Man, you're so young!' he exclaims. 'Or I'm so old. I don't know which. You're just a little kid. In my mind, I remembered you older.'

'I am older than I used to be in the mental sense, but of course not in the physical.'

'Whereas I'm old and I'm mental,' he says, and lets out a guffaw.

Though his joke is macabre, I do crack a smile.

'I've missed you, man.' He reaches out and gently ruffles my staticky hair the way you used to, Father. 'You saved me, Boo. You saved my life. And now here you are again when I need you most.'

The Siamese meows as if agreeing with Johnny. Its eyes are the same sky blue as mine.

'You're a sign,' Johnny says.

'Of what?'

'Of life,' he says. 'The life I'm supposed to hang on to.'

Should I finally ask why he shot me?

Perhaps it is best that I not know.

We are standing near a bulletin board, and a photo thumb-tacked to it catches my eye: Johnny with Zoo's cashier. They wear matching T-shirts, the word NIRVANA written across the chest. Below the word is a kind of smiley face, but the eyes are X's and the mouth is squiggly. Above their heads Johnny and the girl hold large signs. His reads GRAND; hers reads OPENING.

'Is that your sister?' I ask.

'Yeah, Brenda's the only one I told about Town. I said the place was probably just some weird, psychedelic dream, but she was like, 'No, no, Johnny. You died and that's where you went.' She believed even when I had trouble believing.'

'There is a family resemblance,' I say. 'You have the same coppery eyes. Also the same dimple in your left cheek.'

'Oh, I have to introduce you two. She'll frigging flip out. Stay put, okay? I'll be right back.'

Johnny pushes the door open and heads into Zoo. I can hear a customer talking loudly to Brenda about Zig knows what. 'Are you sure it clumps?' the lady says. 'I need it to clump. And it's gotta flush. It's gotta flush *and* clump.'

Taped to the opposite wall of the back room are dozens of photographs of Johnny and Brenda. I cross the floor for a better look. My eyes dart here and there, seeing Johnny throughout his life. A prom-goer in a baby-blue tuxedo with his arm around an older Cynthia Orwell. A seventh-grade track star with a gold medal around his neck. A young driver sitting at the wheel of a convertible, a basset hound beside him in the passenger's seat. A squinting bearded artist standing beside a swirling abstract mural painted on a brick wall.

Then I see this photo: a hollow-eyed eighth grader sitting up in bed, his head in bandages. Johnny is clutching a heart-shaped throw cushion. Stitched across the heart is a single word: HERO.

An odd gift for a boy who shot another.

'I have customers, Johnny,' Brenda says out in Zoo. 'Your surprise can't wait?'

I turn around as Johnny and his sister walk into the back room. They stop in the doorway.

Johnny grins wildly.

Brenda frowns. 'Customers aren't allowed back here,' she says. Then her frown vanishes, and she gapes at me.

'No, no,' she whispers. 'No freaking way.'

'Yes freaking way,' Johnny replies.

Brenda takes a few steps forward, one arm outstretched. She wants to touch me, I think. She wants to see whether her hand passes right through.

'He's solid,' Johnny says.

'Hello, Brenda Henzel,' I say, backing against the wall. 'You have certainly matured since last we met.'

A strangled whimper escapes her mouth. Her arm drops to her side. Her eyes roll backward. Her knees buckle, and she falls hard, slapping against the concrete floor.

'Dear me,' I say to the heap of purple velour.

Johnny hurries over. 'Sh*t, sh*t, sh*t,' he mutters as he goes down on his knees to help his sister.

'She experienced a drop in the amount of blood flow to her brain,' I say to explain why a person faints.

Johnny turns Brenda faceup and gently pats her cheek. She is as white as a sliced potato, except for a red mark at her hairline where her head must have bounced off the concrete.

'Have any smelling salts?' I ask, standing over them.

'Smelling salts?' Johnny says. 'What the f*ck's that?'

'Ammonia carbonate.'

The chemical formula is $(NH_4)_2CO_3$, but I do not say so because now is not the time.

'The only ammonia I got here is Windex,' Johnny says, his voice shriller.

Brenda flutters her eyelids and emits a groan. The Siamese jumps down from its 9 Lives and sniffs her scalp.

'Perhaps I should skedaddle,' I say. 'She may black out again if she comes to and sees a ghost hovering.'

Johnny gives me a look of regret. 'But where'll you go?'

'Back home. Back to Town.'

'How'll you get there, Boo?'

Like a religious fanatic, I say, 'Zig will show me the way.'

I undo my Casper the Friendly Ghost wristwatch and hand it over as a souvenir. 'So you will always remember the time,' I say.

I mean not only this moment in time, but also our time together in Town.

Johnny's mouth is smiling, but his eyes still

look somewhat doleful. 'As if I would've forgot,' he says.

' 'Forgotten,' ' I correct.

Then Brenda opens her eyes, focuses on my face, and screams blue murder.

After I bolt away from Zoo, I drift through the vast stretches of bungalows that populate Hoffman Estates. On one street, a little girl about seven years old asks if I would like a before-dinner mint. She is standing at the end of her driveway with a fake tiara on her head. In her hand, she has a hard candy wrapped in green cellophane. I am touched by her kindness, particularly since Zig does not give us townies candy.

A little later, as I am sucking on the mint, I step into the road without looking both ways and nearly get clipped by a station wagon. 'Watch it, goofball!' the driver yells. I realize I am now on Meadow Lane, the street where Johnny and I once lay in the snow to watch the heavens.

I meander around Sandpits for a while. Have you gone to Anchorage, dear Mother and Father? When we sailed to Alaska, we all expressed a wish to move there one day. Are you in the land of the moose? Without your presence here, Sandpits no longer holds much appeal, so I vamoose and head toward Helen Keller.

As I cross the long field that stretches out behind the school, I feel a queasiness in my gut. I do not understand my reaction until, in the yellowing grass, I spot an empty can of cola lying on its side. I stop in my tracks. I recall that this is the field where Kevin Stein, Nelson Bliss, and Henry Axworthy attacked me with stones on the first day of eighth grade.

I also remember something I had forgotten.

After my attackers threw their rocks and I fell to the ground stunned and bleeding, they stood over me and made a pact. Pig-nosed Kevin held his hand to his heart and put on a solemn voice. 'I pledge to make every day of this school year a living hell for Oliver 'Boo' Dalrymple,' he said. Nelson repeated the line, and so did Henry. Then, the three of them together cried, 'One nation under God, amen!'

There was an empty can of pop lying nearby. Lemon soda. Kevin picked up the can. Then he unzipped the fly of his jeans and fished around for his penis. He did not turn away. He dared me to watch. I closed my eyes, but I could hear him. He was urinating into the pop can. The sound was like liquid being poured into a beaker.

'Hold him down,' he told Nelson and Henry, who then sat on my arms.

I told myself it did not matter: after all, it was mostly water with traces of inorganic salts and organic compounds. *Relax and just swallow*, I told myself. Yet I did not surrender quietly this time. I fought. I screamed. I tried hooking my legs around my assailants to knock them off. I did not manage, though. Nelson's grimy fingers wrenched my mouth open, and Kevin poured the warm urine down my throat. I sputtered and choked. It went up my bloody nose, all over my face, in my hair, and even in my ears.

They won. They would always win.

How strange that I am recalling this now.

It is a memory that Zig found fit to erase.

For thirteen years, this memory lay in a kind of vault. Also in there was the despair I felt. It comes back to me now. Even after they left me, I remained lying in this field for an hour or two. Drained. Forlorn. Beaten.

Now, in the distance, a half dozen kids run screaming across the same field. Whether they are terrorizing one another or just playing I cannot tell. A robin lands a yard away. It stares at me, head tilted one way and then the other, as though I am a tricky puzzle it is trying to solve.

'Hello, angel,' I say to the bird.

It flies away, and then I walk over to the empty can of pop. I jump up and down on the thing till it is good and flat. Then I pick it up and wing it across the field like a Frisbee.

I head back to the long brick school that is Helen Keller. I worry its doors may be locked because it is now suppertime. Will I need to break in? But no, the doors are open, and a few boys mill around in the lobby. They are dressed in what look like pajamas but are actually judo uniforms tied with orange belts. They pay me no mind. I walk down the hall past showcases with sports trophies locked behind glass.

Johnny won track-and-field trophies for Helen Keller in seventh grade. I expect, however, that he was not allowed to complete eighth grade here. Which school did he attend instead? A kind of reform school, I imagine.

Zig permitted this haunting, I suppose, to

show me that Johnny has managed to carry on with his life, even though certain ghosts haunt him still. I am one of those ghosts. Perhaps I helped him today. I dearly hope so.

When I reach my old locker, I see that No. 106 is padlocked. I assume I know the combination: I turn the dial to 7, to 25, and then to 34. I yank the lock and it opens.

I check behind me, but no one is around. Only Helen Keller's eyes watch from across the hall.

I squeak the door open, expecting the rear panel to be missing and the locker to be empty. But the panel is in place and the locker full. The objects in it, though, do not belong to the Asian girl I met earlier in the hallway. Holy moly, they belong to me!

My periodic table is taped to the back of the door. Above it are my photos of Jane Goodall and Richard Dawkins. Jane with her sleek blond ponytail and her pursed lips. Richard with his impish grin and his unruly eyebrows. 'Hello there, hello,' I say. 'You two look good. You have not aged a single day.'

My compass and protractor set is in my locker, as are my chemistry and mathematics textbooks. My school copy of *Lord of the Flies*, its spine still unbroken. My forest green cardigan sweater that Grandmother gave me for my thirteenth birthday. My French-English dictionary. My cracked-vinyl gym bag with my gym clothes still inside: yellow shorts, Trojan T-shirt, even a jockstrap.

I riffle through my belongings. At the back of the top shelf is a paper bag. I assume it is the lunch you made me thirteen years ago, Mother and Father. I pull it toward me. It is heavy. Heavier than a peanut butter sandwich, a granola bar, and a box of raisins should be.

I open the paper bag.

Inside is a revolver.

Not the one from Curios.

Uncle Seymour's gun.

I glance up. Helen Keller stares at me from her wall. She nods her mortarboard head. At least in my mind she does.

Then I remember.

Me aiming this gun at my own chest. Johnny yelling, 'No!' Throwing himself at me. The panic in his eyes. The scars on his wrists. The wrenching and the wrestling. The loud bang.

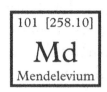

101 [258.10]

Md

Mendelevium

Hydrogen, helium, lithium, beryllium, boron, carbon, nitrogen, oxygen, fluorine, neon, sodium, magnesium, aluminum, silicon, phosphorus, sulfur, chlorine, argon, potassium, calcium, scandium, titanium, vanadium, chromium, manganese, iron, cobalt, nickel, copper, zinc, gallium, germanium, arsenic, selenium, bromine, krypton, rubidium, strontium, yttrium, zirconium, niobium, molybdenum, technetium, ruthenium, rhodium, palladium, silver, cadmium, indium, tin, antimony, tellurium, iodine, xenon, cesium, barium, lanthanum, cerium, praseodymium, neodymium, promethium, samarium, europium, gadolinium, terbium, dysprosium, holmium, erbium, thulium, ytterbium, lutetium, hafnium, tantalum, tungsten, rhenium, osmium, iridium, platinum, gold, mercury, thallium, lead, bismuth, polonium, astatine, radon, francium, radium, actinium, thorium, protactinium, uranium, neptunium, plutonium, americium, curium, berkelium, californium, einsteinium, fermium, mendelevium, nobelium, lawrencium, rutherfordium, dubnium, seaborgium, bohrium, hassium, meitnerium.

I curl myself into no. 106 and slam the door. I am swallowed by darkness. I am cramped, sweaty, shaky. I gasp for breath. There is a paper bag in my hand, but I cannot use it for CO_2. I let it go, and the gun clunks at my feet. I start weeping quietly, and the sleeves of my cardigan sweater hang around me like an embrace. This locker is my coffin. May I never leave it.

Time creeps along. I cannot tell how much time. Twenty minutes? Two hours? But eventually the locker's back panel is tugged open, and before me stands a boy with a Mohawk stiffened with white glue (polyvinyl acetate). 'Jesus!' he cries. 'You almost gave me a heart attack!'

When I unfold myself and slip out of the locker, I feel lifeless. I am a zombie. The walking dead. The warehouse is now filled with dozens of sorters rummaging through the delivered goods and piling items into buggies and onto dollies. They are as diligent as worker ants.

'What were you doing in there?' the punk rocker asks.

'Looking for unusual finds,' I mutter.

'There's nothing unusual about this beat-up locker.'

'Au contraire,' I reply.

I glance back inside the locker. It is empty

once again. All my belongings are gone, including the paper bag. I close the locker door.

I arrange for the punk rocker to deliver No. 106 to Curios later in the week. I ask him the time now, and he says five to eleven. I was away for several hours.

I pick up my rock-filled flashlight and shuffle back to the Guy Montag Library. Coming up the library's walkway, I hear a yapping, and Pierre clambers out of the bushes that grow alongside the building. Heavens, I had forgotten all about the dog. He leaps up and down to welcome me back. I carry him inside. When we reach Curios on the third floor, I am hesitant to enter, but I force myself to undo the chain lock. My footsteps echo and Pierre's nails clickety-clack as we walk through the exhibit halls. Despite the dozens of displays, the space feels empty, as though not a soul is around. I say to Pierre, 'Let's see if his soul is still here.'

We head to Johnny's room, and I drag the armoire away from his door. When I go inside, I am not shocked to find the bed empty. Lying atop it are red gym shorts, a white tank top, and a blue bauble. I slip the items into the drawer underneath the bed where the revolver still resides.

Just in case, I check to see whether Zig filled the gun with bullets during my absence, but there are none inside. Well, I guess I cannot shoot myself in my stupid brain or defective heart.

I doff my T-shirt and jeans and climb under the covers in only my shorts. A slight whiff of onions lingers. Pierre hops onto the bed and curls up at my feet. I am very, very tired, yet I wonder whether I will ever fall asleep again, and if I do, will I ever wake?

My voice trembles slightly when, to the ceiling fan, I say, 'Tell me a bedtime story, Zig. But please, no more fairy tales. No more fiction.'

The ceiling fan whirls and twirls.

'I want the truth.'

As usual, Zig says nothing. But he does not need to reply. I now know the truth. I know in my holey heart what you, dear Mother and Father, have long known: your son was Gunboy.

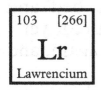

103	[266]
Lr	
Lawrencium	

PLEASE.

104 [267.12]
Rf
Rutherfdium

PLEASE.

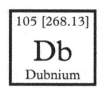

FORGIVE ME.

Seven weeks have passed, Mother and Father, and during this time, I have told not a soul but you about my haunting and the mysteries it unraveled. To keep my sanity, I have kept busy. I have revamped Curios. Let me share with you an exhibition I have designed called *Curiouser and Curiouser*. Esther suggested the title, which comes from *Alice's Adventures in Wonderland*, a fictional book I intend to read one day.

Tonight is the grand reopening of Curios. In the past weeks, I moved every object in the museum's collection into basement storage at the library. Down went our dollar coins, Chinese kite, batteries, out-of-order phones, personal computer (a new arrival), condoms, diapers, *Encyclopaedia Britannica* Volume Ma to Mi, roll-on deodorant, pet terrariums, animal replicas, corned beef, boxes of Hamburger Helper, lucky rabbit's foot, ceramic statue of Jesus's supposedly virgin mother, wallaby postal stamps from Australia, and on and on.

As for the little revolver, I threw it down the garbage chute. It is gone forever. Or perhaps not forever, because for all I know Zig may boomerang it back one day.

After I moved all the curiosities downstairs, I began traveling to Town's infirmaries, which, over the years, have all received photocopiers from Zig's warehouse deliveries. I spent day after day photocopying the documents I planned to display as part of *Curiouser and Curiouser*.

Tonight is October 31. As on every Halloween, I simply throw a white sheet over my head. Through its eyeholes, I can gauge the reactions of my visitors, who come as zombies, witches, mummies, monsters, archangels, goblins, and the like. They come with their fake blood and gore. They come with fake arrows through their heads. They come with fake knives sticking out of their backs. These dead children walk around the halls of my museum in wonder. I cannot always see their wonder under their masks and makeup, but I can sense it.

There are no displays tonight as such. Instead, the actual walls are the exhibits. I have divided the museum into thirteen areas, each identified by a large number painted its own distinct color on bristol board. Using simple glue sticks, I wallpapered the walls with photocopies of every page of the surviving rebirthing books from the thirteen infirmaries. On these pages are listed newborns' names, the city they came from, the date of their rebirth, the cause of their passing, and the zip code of their assigned address. Most of the pages are typewritten, but the oldest books (I found one dating back to 1938) are handwritten, the ink so faded it is often illegible. The pages run chronologically in a horizontal fashion across the walls, the oldest in the top left corner, the newest in the bottom right corner.

Curiouser and Curiouser is a memorial to

356

everyone who has ever come to Town. My aim is for each of my fellow townies to feel he or she is a beautiful, curious object.

I did not know how people would react. Would they be impressed? Bored? It appears the former is the case. They are reading the documents as though they are pages from a fascinating novel. Council president Reginald Washington (a pirate) is here, as are jail warden Lydia Finkle (a witch), asylum manager Dr. Albert Schmidt (a ghoul), and former Schaumburg resident Sandy Goldberg (a giant felt peanut).

The irksome twins Tim and Tom Lu come as well, wearing fake mustaches and carrying canes. They are dressed as Thompson and Thomson from *Tintin*.

Tim says to Tom, 'I wonder if after all these years Oliver Dalrymple is still the victim.'

'Would it were true,' I reply.

Like many other visitors, Tim and Tom climb the stepladders placed in the halls to search for their own names on the rebirthing lists. Meanwhile, Pierre weaves in and out of people's legs and yaps like a mad dog and, when egged on, does his *wee-ooo-wee-ooo*.

My friends are here too. Thelma is dressed as Sherlock Holmes in a tweed deerstalker, Esther as a gypsy medium in a headscarf decorated with signs of the zodiac, and Ringo as a mummy wrapped in white bandages stained with fake blood.

Ringo's costume reminds me of your old red-and-white barber's pole, Father and Mother. Did you take it with you to Alaska? I do not know for sure you went there, but I do like thinking of you mingling with bears and moose in downtown Anchorage and admiring the aurora borealis at night.

I tell my friends to meet me in Johnny's room. I have a toast to make. I go to my office and, from my bottom desk drawer, fetch a bottle of a French red wine called Château Bel-Air, which came to Town in 1977. I conceal it, with plastic glasses and a corkscrew, in a wicker picnic basket.

When I arrive in Johnny's room, the section of the exhibition I reserved for the reborn children of Eleven, my three friends are waiting with Pierre, who, if he *is* from Paris, is perhaps familiar with Château Bel-Air (ha-ha). I tell any other visitors to clear out for a moment because I have vital business to attend to. Once the others are gone, I close the door and press its push lock.

I show my friends what is in the picnic basket. Ringo, who claims to have been a virtual wino back in Detroit, says, 'That's bloody fantastic, mate!' Esther, Thelma, and I have never tasted wine before. I ask Ringo to do the honors, and he clenches the bottle between his bandaged thighs and deftly threads the screw into the cork. He yanks out the cork with a sound like the pop of a pistol. We all sit in the middle of the floor as though in a powwow. I fill the glasses halfway and pass them around.

Thelma gets giggly even before taking a sip. 'Reginald better not find out. We'll get detention for a year.'

I raise my glass and say, 'A toast to Johnny Henzel.'

My friends raise their glasses. The girls both give me nervous grins. We rarely speak about Johnny nowadays. Maybe Esther and Thelma made a pact long ago to avoid mentioning him in front of me. Or perhaps they just stopped thinking about him years ago and are embarrassed they have forgotten all about their old friend.

'He was born in America on Halloween,' I add.

'To Johnny Henzel,' they all say, clinking glasses.

I like to think that Johnny's stay in Town was no mistake. Zig *wanted* him in Town, at least for a little while, so we could become friends, the fast friends we should have been in our earthly lives. Had we been best friends back then, Johnny might not have slashed his wrists and I might not have stolen Uncle Seymour's gun. We could have helped each other in America the way we helped each other in the sweet hereafter.

My friends sip their wine. I lack a mouth hole in my costume, so I must raise my glass beneath the sheet to drink. The wine is warm and syrupy.

Esther says, 'This stuff tastes better than I expected.'

Thelma says, 'It tastes like adulthood.'

'It tastes nutmeggy,' Ringo says. He inspects the label on the bottle. 'Seventy-seven was an ace year.'

'Nutmeggy?' Esther rolls her eyes.

Ringo gulps from his glass. Then he says, 'So

where the hell's Johnny boy?'

'Is he cooped up in the basement?' Esther asks.

I shake my head. 'He flew the coop.'

Esther and Thelma lift their eyebrows. Thelma then holds up her Sherlock Holmes magnifying glass as though to examine the ghost before her more closely.

'He re-redied,' I clarify.

'I'll be damned!' Ringo cries.

Thelma puts down her magnifying glass. 'He vanished?'

'*Poof!*' I say.

'When?' Esther asks.

'On the seventh of September,' I say. I do not mention Johnny turning into Town's first man. I am not ready for full disclosure at the moment. One day, perhaps.

'Cripes, Boo!' Esther says. 'You should have told us!'

'We could have held a funeral,' Thelma says. 'We could have honored him.'

'I honored him for thirteen years,' I say from beneath my sheet. 'Maybe that was enough.'

Thelma pats my ghost head. 'You hunky-dory?'

'Not really.' I take a big gulp from my wine, which warms my belly.

Ringo asks if I organized *Curiouser and Curiouser* as a distraction from my mourning. 'Keep your mind off things?' he says.

I nod, even though I am not sure this is true. I do not know if I have been mourning Johnny Henzel. Maybe I have been. He was, after all, a kind of hero to me. But the person I have really been mourning is Oliver Dalrymple.

The boy I thought I was but was not.

My friends and I drink the rest of the bottle of wine. Ringo keeps saying, 'Feel anything? Feel anything?' as though we are on the verge of becoming whole different people.

But I am already a whole different person.

My friends giggle when they notice that their teeth are stained purple. I swallow my last gulp of wine and stand. I am dizzy and queasy but a bit hunkier-dorier. I go to the wall where Johnny's bed once was. I wave my friends over to see a page from the infirmary in Eleven. It is pasted in the middle of the wall. Esther must stand on tippytoe.

'I typed that up,' Thelma says about the page.

'Your spelling is atrocious,' Ringo says.

These are the first entries on the page:

Kendra Phillips	Murray, UT	5 July 79	lukemia	TIP
Nick Easterling	Tewksbury, MA	17 July 79	fell out of tree fort	BAG
Haley Pierson-Cox	Louisville, CO	28 July 79	pnamonia	LOT
Jane Brunk	Vienna, VA	31 July 79	hit by bus	HAM
Lisa Antonopoulos	Sherwood, OR	22 Aug. 79	smoke inalation	PAT

A dozen entries down, this is how the page ends:

| Oliver Dalrymple | Hoffman Estates, IL | 7 Sept. 79 | holy heart | GUT |
| John Henzel | Hoffman Estates, IL | 12 Oct. 79 | bullet in brain | GUT |

I point to my cause of death. I tell my friends that I think the hole in my heart has finally closed over. 'I can't feel it twinging anymore,' I say. 'I don't know if this is good news.'

Esther's zodiac scarf has slipped down, and the scorpion seems about to pinch her nose with its claws. She says, 'It's good news, Boo.'

Thelma agrees: 'It means you've healed.'

'Thirteen years is a long time to heal,' I reply. 'In my healing ledger, it is record-breaking.'

'Too bad that people down in America don't heal fast,' Thelma says. 'Like our moms and dads and sisters and brothers after we passed. If only their hearts healed lickety-split.'

We all think of our families and get a little blue, perhaps because we are blotto — a word you liked to use to describe yourselves whenever you drank dry martinis after work.

Mother and Father, I now keep locker No. 106 in my office and occasionally check inside to see if it opens onto another world. So far, no, but perhaps one day there will appear an Alaskan barbershop. Inside the locker, I store the book I have written, which is ready and waiting for delivery. I will hand it to you and then retreat back to my world, and you will read my story and finally understand the nitty-gritty of my life and afterlife. Afterward, you will close my book and lay me to rest, and my ghost will no longer haunt you.

Esther interrupts everybody's reveries. 'Let's not be sad and confused tonight,' she says.

I tell my friends there is a second bottle of wine in my office. A bottle of white wine from the Napa Valley.

'Oh, go get it!' Ringo cries. 'We can get sh*tfaced and then go to that big Halloween do in the Northeast Corner.' He is sparkly-eyed beneath his bandages. 'Let's go wild and crazy tonight!' He does a cartwheel across the room, a miracle given his costume and his bellyful of wine. Pierre barks and bounces up and down on his woolly legs. Ringo scoops the dog up and does a pogo dance with Pierre in his arms.

'Can you go wild and crazy, Estie?' Ringo shouts to Esther.

'You better believe it.' Esther bounces on her toes.

'What about you, Thelma?'

'Lordy, yes.'

'And you, Boo? Can you go wild and crazy?'

I mull the question over.

'There is a distinct possibility,' I say.

Acknowledgments

Many thanks to Paul Taunton at Knopf Canada and Lexy Bloom at Vintage Books in New York, and to Dean Cooke, Ron Eckel, and Suzanne Brandreth at the Cooke Agency. Additional thanks to Jessica Grant, Ross Rogers, David Posel, Lois Carson, and Frank Smith. *Un gros merci à Christian Dorais.*

Other titles published by Ulverscroft:

GATES OF PARADISE

Virginia Andrews

The car crash that kills Heaven and Logan leaves Annie Casteel Stonewall orphaned and crippled. Whisked off to Farthinggale Manor by the possessive Tony Tatterton, Annie pines for her lost family, but especially for Luke, her half-brother — friend of her childhood, her fantasy prince, her loving confidante. Without the warm glow of his love, Annie is lost in the shadows of despair. And when she discovers Troy's cottage hidden in Farthinggale's woods, the mystery of her past deepens. But even as she yearns to see Luke again, her hopes and dreams are darkened by the sinister Casteel spell ... treacherous, powerful and evil!